Come Again!

The Second Greatest Story

Come Again!

The Second Greatest Story Ever Told

Ed Jones

Ringpull

First published by Ringpull Press in 1993

Ringpull Press Ltd
86A Church Street
Littleborough
OL15 8AU

A CIP catalogue record for this book
is available from the British Library
ISBN 1 898051 02 X

Typeset in 12/12.5 pt Melior
Filmset by Datix International Ltd, Bungay Suffolk
Printed in England by Clays Ltd, St Ives plc

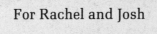

For Rachel and Josh

A Good Man

Father Vernon was a good man, a devout Catholic and a conscientious worker, a man full of the kind of self-doubt that inclines a person to profound spirituality.

That his Church career should come to ultimate ruin was, therefore, more surprising to the people who knew and loved him than it was to the priest himself.

His modest parish was located on a battered estate, on the outskirts of Bolton, on the hill behind Safeways, just off the busy road to Bury.

It was a forlorn development for a forlorn people.

The church itself reflected the mood of the area, having its windows boarded up and its doors bolted shut. This was a matter of some regret to Father Vernon who, despite all the evidence to the contrary, believed in the basic innocence of humanity. A notion which, oddly enough, he never applied to himself.

The priest had utmost faith in youth. They were his greatest love and he would hear no word against them. Even though local teenagers had broken every pane of glass in the church and burned the vestry to the ground twice, Father Vernon's faith stood, like a rock, unshaken. Having been brought up in Belfast where youths are apt to express their anger with a rocket launcher, the young priest had seen worse. Much worse.

'What they need is a youth club,' had been his response to the arsonists.

'What they need is a bloody good hiding!' replied his housekeeper. 'Like I used to get.' The poor woman was so drunk she could hardly get her words out. 'Never did me any harm!'

There was no point in arguing with Mary when

1

she was drunk, and that was most of the time. But Father Vernon loved her in the way he loved all of God's children. Unconditionally.

'I come from a very devout family,' she would slur.

Although she was the energetic priest's house-keeper, in truth it was he who looked after her. And for her sins Mary Magdalen Maloney was besotted with the man she knew she could never have. And on the nights that she didn't just pass out, she cried herself to sleep for unrequited love.

Of the spiritual kind, Father Vernon had a lot of love to give and as a consequence was held in high regard by his flock. He had time for everyone but himself and this suited him down to the ground as he couldn't bear his own company.

There were no end of visits to be made to the aged and infirm and there were circulars to be typed that no one ever read. And when the youth club was finally established in a scruffy building that used to be a post office, the handsome young clergyman would busy himself behind the coffee bar, or spend time chatting to the youths who loved and respected him because he loved and respected them.

At the end of an evening he would return to the Presbytery and if Mary had already passed out he would go straight to his desk. His typewriter would click often into the small hours. Only then would the exhausted man tidy his old bureau, return each item carefully to its place, make a Horlicks and resign himself to the torments of the night.

Like all Catholic priests Father Vernon had taken a vow of chastity. But unlike some he had kept faithfully to his word. The poor man had never, in all his days sought relief of any kind, not even through masturbation. Which was, of course, good for his soul and some might argue his body too, but it was a terrible burden on his mind.

Images of nudity, male and female, plagued his consciousness. He would marvel at the beauty of an ancient painting only to catch himself ogling some puffy little cherub. He was disturbed by billboards advertising underwear. And, worst of all, he found himself strangely drawn to certain young women from the youth club and parts of their anatomy would momentarily distract his attention.

At night buried thoughts from the day would crop up in the afflicted man's meditations and the effort required to suppress them was enormous, often enough to send him off to sleep. Whereupon the battle was lost.

What had been fairly tame day-dreams now became the most monstrous hallucinations. Scenes of buggery, rape and sodomy – huge orgies of bestiality and indulgence, reminiscent of the paintings of Hieronymus Bosch played themselves out before his helpless gaze.

People he knew – young people from the youth club whom he loved piously – were now unashamedly flaunting their bodies and performing feats of obscenity that poor Father Vernon suspected weren't even possible.

And on top of all this, God had lately seen fit to torment him with blasphemous visions. Episodes of breath-taking indecency were interrupted by short religious sequences, rather like the stations of the cross, in which God, represented by a naked man of great physical beauty would talk to him on matters of theology and current affairs.

On occasion his suffering would reach such excruciating intensity that his body gave way to convulsions. At such times the frenzied priest would cry out in his sleep, cursing the Almighty aloud and wake up in terror, feeling abandoned by God. And wet. And lonely.

3

In the Closet.

'Dear boy. Hello! Let's go straight into the closet,' was Canon Drinkwater's regular friendly greeting.

The ancient priest greatly admired Father Vernon and was touched that the enthusiastic young man would drive all the way to Manchester three times a week to make his confession. It's even possible that the Canon rather enjoyed some of the saucy details of his young friend's conscience, too.

The old man's voice echoed in the darkness of the confessional: 'We are all God's children, and especially you, my son.'

This morning Father Vernon was particularly upset about his dream of the night before. 'But He appears naked, the most vile blasphemy,' stammered the priest.

'There are many ways of interpreting dreams,' assured the inappropriately named Drinkwater, who never touched a drop of the stuff. 'Why don't you start at the beginning, as usual.'

Although he didn't appreciate it, Father Vernon was very healthy spiritually. There wasn't a single thought or deed that the young priest was afraid to confess, which meant that there were no murky depths to his being — nowhere for a germ of evil to grow. Each wicked thought was meticulously confessed — every amoral, base, blasphemous, corrupt, depraved, diabolical, fiendish, foul, heinous, irreligious, malevolent, malicious, nefarious, pernicious, perverted, reprobate, satanic, sinful, unprincipled, ungodly, or vile conception, conscious or unconscious was systematically admitted, out loud in the confessional.

This was not simply a matter of religious duty,

4

either. It was a question of survival. Father Vernon simply could not live with sin.

When he had related the main part of his dream of the night before, the dejected young priest said: 'Surely I am the most iniquitous of God's children.'

To which his old friend replied: 'My son, you are the least sinful man I have ever known and I have been on God's earth for a long time.' Cannon Drinkwater's age was a matter of conjecture. It was rumoured in the diocese that he was as old as the century, but no one knew for sure. The old man was as tough as nails and showed no signs of decline.

'But yesterday, at the youth club. One of the young women. She's as sweet as an angel. Fifteen years old. I found myself entranced by her bosom. And later, in my dream, she was the one cavorting in the olive grove.'

'And is she buxom for her years?' inquired the wise old Canon.

'Well, yes.'

Father Vernon heard a sigh from the other side of the confessional.

'And did you place your hand on the young woman's breast?'

'Of course not!' Father Vernon recoiled from the very idea.

'And did you change your attitude to the girl. Did you let your gaze linger on her chest?'

'No Father, not for a moment longer than – I mean as soon as I realised I looked away.'

There was another sigh in the darkness.

'And did you talk to the little angel longer than was necessary?'

'No Father, she spoke to me about a problem she has at home. She's experimenting with drugs.'

'And was the advice you offered coloured in any way by your carnal feelings?'

'No Father.'

'Then you have not sinned.'

'But my dream . . .'

'Dreams are acts of God in themselves.' The tone of the old man's voice signalled that there was to be no further argument. 'My son, these thoughts and feelings are not sins. Think of them as trials sent by God. Each ungodly sentiment is like a test of your merit. There are no sinful thoughts – or feelings. The question is does one act on them?'

These thrice weekly interviews were a joy to both men. Father Vernon had heard this argument a thousand times and even though he didn't believe a word of it, he still derived some comfort from their meetings.

Probably, he supposed, the fact of confession itself did him some good. And indeed it did. For a whole morning following his act of contrition – sometimes longer, he would live like a free man, breathe easily and feel some of the joys of life.

And Canon Drinkwater had a genuine and deep respect for his young friend, most especially his honesty. The two men had been great friends since the time when Father Vernon was a student priest and the older man his mentor.

When Canon Drinkwater said: 'Dear boy, you are an example to us all,' the modest young man didn't know how true it was.

For poor Canon Drinkwater was a sinner indeed and, what's more, he was incapable of admitting it.

Not only did the old man admire the young priest's honesty in the confessional, he envied it, which was a sin in itself. But compared to other of his transgressions envy was among the least significant.

And whereas in the confessional Father Vernon was specific and exhaustive, Canon Drinkwater tended to be general and selective, never really getting

6

to the point. And whereas the younger man's conscience was burdened for a day or two at most, in the older man seeds of wickedness had germinated over time and flourished until his ancient soul was overgrown with thistles and thorn.

Twice a week the aged priest drove his carefully-maintained old car to a certain address near the city centre, whereupon he was received by a handsome woman not quite one third of his age.

And never once had the old man breathed a word of this to anyone. Not even to God.

And there were other unspoken sins, too. A lifetime of them.

Only once in his entire career had Canon Drinkwater ever bared his soul. This had been during a pilgrimage to Rome when as a younger priest he met the Pope. He opened his heart in the confessional to a Vatican bishop who spoke only Latin and Polish. And although the foreigner didn't understand a word of his highly specific, positively frank confession, he felt like a new man.

And later that day, as he stalked the streets of the city of Rome he felt able to turn down the professional services of quite the prettiest young woman he'd ever set eyes on. And he was so uplifted by this exceptional experience that he decided to test out his resolve the next day, only to fail gloriously and relapse into a life-long isolation of the spirit.

And so, today, Canon Drinkwater too profited from Father Vernon's confessions. Because a man who can't confess his own sins, can sometimes understand and forgive the sins of another with great generosity and through his involvement in the soul of another, come to relieve his own.

The old man's love for his young friend was, therefore, essentially self seeking, but it was nonetheless profound and his admiration for the young priest was sincere.

7

Theirs was a deep and cherished friendship.

Father Vernon ventured one more question: 'What do you make of my insane vision, Father?' He was referring to the bit of his dream in which God – or at least an obscene representation of Him – had spoken of sending an agent to earth, specifically Bolton, in the form of a young woman.

'It's probably more a question you should put to a psychologist than a theologian,' was the old priest's reply. 'Now come along. You can tell me the finer details of last night's dream over a glass of sherry.'

Betty's Labour.

The Sunnymeadow estate appears to be entirely devoid of adults.

Even the parents seem to be youths. There are youths and elderly people in copious quantities, but no adults to be seen anywhere.

Almost all the families on the estate have split up and nearly all the fathers are stepfathers. And of course all the children are God's children. In fact, most of the children on the estate are born to teenagers, and to Father Vernon it sometimes seemed that the children were all children of children.

Betty was seventeen, the proud owner of two *Reebok* shell suits and a little red-haired baby girl, aged one. Little Lisa had already been walking for two months and it was difficult to buy the right footwear for the little mite, because shoes for one-years-olds aren't designed for ardent explorers.

Like all the children on the estate the infant would have to grow up fast and walking would only be the start of her troubles. Turn your back for a second and she was gone. One day she was returned from an expedition by the police. Betty was hanging round on a corner near her flat with a group of youngsters.

'Where the bloody 'ell have you been?' she asked the astonished-looking child, expecting a reply. The embarrassed young mother had only just realised her daughter had gone missing.

'She was entertaining shoppers at Safeways,' reported the constable, who was actually an adult. 'An old lady put her in a trolley and wheeled her to the station. We knew who she was straight away — regular little gaol bird, aren't we, Tiny?'

Tiny, as she was known to the police, just stood there gazing at the beaming giant who was bent over her, making stupid faces.

'You should keep her on a lead, Betty,' was the giant's parting shot. Betty wasn't her real name and she objected to it when it was used by the wrong person.

'It's not fucking Betty,' snarled Betty just as the copper was out of earshot. 'Cheeky git!'

Her friends laughed at her insolence and made a fuss of Lisa.

The poor little babe would stand and stare at whatever was going on with such intensity that the young people she spent her time with took it for granted that the toddler understood exactly what was going on around her. And from the look on her face it seemed for all the world as if she did.

Giving birth was seen as a form of escape for the young women on the estate. By doing so it was possible to acquire priority housing and approximately double the social security, which meant that for a short time at least a young mother could achieve a degree of independence.

In many cases of course this path led to ruin, with mother and toddler trapped in unsuitable accommodation in bad company. Even in the best cases the self sufficiency is short lived, as debts accumulate and costs mount up. Especially as new men come and go leaving more children behind.

But for now Betty was doing alright. To be honest she wasn't really interested in men and had only gone with Lisa's father for social reassurance. She wasn't the most attractive girl in the world, being rather manly in appearance – especially in her shell-suit and trainers – and she'd known, even at the tender age of fifteen, that if she got pregnant, the young man would leave her to it.

And this suited her fine as she wanted someone to give her love to who wouldn't demand sex in return.

But the first six months of motherhood had been a terrible blow. The teenager's natural love for the child, boundless while the stripling nestled cosily in her womb, was used up in the first thirty-six hours of the infant's life.

After that Betty had to draw on her youthfulness to survive and in those first months she suffered terribly, hardly venturing beyond the post office and the corner shop, toiling painfully away in near isolation.

And then, when exactly six months had passed, the beautiful little baby began to sleep through the night and Betty's life returned almost to normal.

With an incredible burst of energy she returned to the youth club and, with babe tucked gracelessly under her arm, she resumed her life where she'd left it just hours before going into labour. She took part in projects organised by Father Vernon, served behind the coffee bar and again took to hanging around on street corners with the other youths.

And so did little Lisa.

A Good-Looking Corpse.

Sick again.

There was another great, belching retch and now it was even coming down her nose.

'Shit,' she coughed, though no one was there to hear.

'This is the last time,' she thought.

She thought that every time.

Theresa Green was sitting on someone's wall a little way down the road from her house, her head in her hands and a pool of puke between her feet. Well, mainly bile actually. The cider and chips were further down the hill.

'I didn't have that much!' she thought and let out an involuntary 'uurrgh' as she vomited again.

Poor girl. She was only sixteen and she'd done it all. Or at least she thought she had. And that's what counts.

She'd had sex. Didn't think much of it. Got pregnant and had an abortion. Didn't think much of that. But did it again anyway. Took acid. Liked it at first. Then after twenty minutes quickly changed her mind. And spent the next eight hours in acute panic. But at least she'd done it. Then she left school, got a job. Didn't think much of that. Packed her job in, went on the dole. Didn't think much of that.

Didn't think much of herself, really. Though everyone else did. She made sure of that. It was the only thing she thought a lot of, what people thought of her.

Good job they couldn't see her now. Though if they had she would have played the whole thing up and made a joke of it. Like: 'Anyone want a chip?' or, 'Cup of hot soup, anyone?'

She hadn't been feeling that witty, lately. She'd been spending time on her own. Getting drunk on her own. Sometimes she'd drink half a bottle of sherry before she went out. Which is why she always seemed more drunk than anyone else, more quickly.

But she was still popular. She got drunk and made a fool of herself, but she didn't show up anyone else. She needed to be liked too much for that.

She was very glamorous and wore bright red, *Collection 2000* lipstick and make-up in copious quantities. But she never flirted with the other girl's boyfriends and only let the best-looking boys sleep with her. And afterwards she joked with her girlfriends about the size of their willies.

But not lately. Lately she was depressed. And everyone knew it.

'I'm going to die soon,' she told her friends. She meant it too. And they believed her. Well, some did.

Betty didn't.

'Don't be bloody daft!' she scoffed.

Theresa loved Betty. She was the only girl who didn't look up to her and the only one who wouldn't stand any of her bullshit.

'Course you ain't gunna die.'

'Live fast, die young, leave a good-looking corpse,' declared Theresa.

Betty was impressed. 'That's a good one.'

'I made it up,' she lied.

'Bollocks you did,' said Betty.

And that was why she liked her.

She wished Betty was there now and thought about going round to see her. But Betty didn't like her getting paralytic, so she staggered homeward.

She was sick and tired, she really was. It was about time something happened.

That night it did.

She walked out in front of a car.

And the car never stopped.

And she saw God in heaven.

And He had very serious words with her.

In the morning she woke up in the gutter.

She limped home, looking bedraggled and went straight to bed.

When she woke up she had a banging head-ache. So she turned over, aching and moaning.

And a few moments later she felt violently sick.

She ran into the bathroom and puked into the toilet.

The vomit was bright green.

Theresa blinked at it in disbelief. It wasn't just bright green, it was brilliant green. Like paint.

'Oh fuck,' she thought. And when she looked in the mirror she said, 'So much for the good-lookin' corpse!'

She wished she hadn't drunk anything the night before. Then she put her head in her hands and really wished it.

Then suddenly she felt fine. Her head-ache had vanished. So she sighed, flushed the chain and went back to her room.

When she got back to her room she sat on the bed and wished it was neat and tidy. Then she sighed, put her head in her hands and really wished it was tidy. And when she looked up it was.

She gasped and gazed about the room in amazement.

Then her legs made her stand up.

She thought about what had happened the night before and gasped again. The car. She remembered about the car.

She checked herself for bruises.

Nothing.

She suddenly wanted to get out of the house.

'Where the bloody 'ell are you going?' asked her mother as she stomped down the stairs. 'I want a bloody word with you!'

Theresa really wished her mother could be nice to her for once. She really wished she could. Just once.

She walked past without saying a word.

'I've got a tenner for you here,' her mum said suddenly.

Theresa stopped dead in her tracks and looked at her mum, who was standing there, smiling stupidly at her.

The woman said: 'I love you darling,' and Theresa ran down the path, terrified.

Something was badly wrong.

Nicola's Dad.

'Your mother arranged for you to go horse riding this afternoon, so you'll bloody well go!'

Nicola Carson stood facing her father over a gulf far wider than the generation gap.

'I've already arranged to meet my friends.'

'Well they'll have to *hang around* all afternoon without you, won't they?' The words "hang around" hung around in the air for a moment.

'I don't like horse riding. I can't stand it.'

In as many ways as possible they were opposites. She had made sure of it, having systematically expelled every likeness to him from her being.

If he was rock, then she was thin air.

'Most of the little urchins you choose for friends would kill to own a pony like yours.'

The truth of her father's statement stung her. The girls on Sunnymeadow worshipped the handsome dapple-grey mare, but Nicola had rejected the beloved animal because it had been a gift from her father.

'Well why don't I give it to one of them, if they'd love it so much?' she spat.

He was old and ugly. She was young and almost impossibly beautiful. And this, for some reason, stung the older man.

She was putting on her fashionably tatty town coat.

'Well, if you are going to hang around the streets you could at least make yourself presentable,' he croaked. 'Even those little sluts you brought home last week were a darn sight smarter than you . . . ' He had to go to the door and shout the remainder of his speech down the path after her. 'And make sure you're back at a reasonable hour, young lady!'

In many ways Bill Carson had given up trying to control his rebellious daughter. Now he confined his efforts to a kind of guerrilla war. If he couldn't stop her doing whatever she pleased, he could make it as miserable as possible for her. He would ambush her with irritating arguments and snipe at her with crotchety remarks.

He was death and she was raging, thundering life.

But what really annoyed Nicola was that some of her friends, who he invariably referred to as 'little sluts', actually found him attractive and flirted with him in a girlish sort of way. And in his own way the flattered, young-looking forty-five year old encouraged them. He was never so charming and polite – or 'slimy' as his daughter called it.

It was too vile for words. And so Nicola responded in deeds. She avoided introducing him to anyone unless it was impossible to avoid and only returned home when she absolutely had to.

15

And to make matters worse, lately Bill Carson had become a local celebrity.

Bolton's first radio evangelist.

Years ago when the family still lived in Scotland, Bill had been a minister in an obscure Presbyterian sect that was connected in some way to the Orange Order. He had suffered no divine calling to the Church. Rather he had followed in his father's footsteps.

The denomination was shrouded in mystery. Devotees saw themselves as agents of God's Law – Nicola called them agents of Sod's Law – and women were strictly excluded from all but the most frilly of duties. (Bill's own wife was nearly invisible to the eye and floated around their beautifully furnished home, flinching at raised voices and flicking a duster at highly polished surfaces)

In the early nineteen eighties, during a particularly baffling political episode in Ireland, rumoured to involve the sect in some way, Bill Carson suddenly and mysteriously resigned from the church organisation altogether. Then, miraculously, found himself appointed managing director of a medium sized road haulage company in Bolton. He had no previous experience in the field, but within two years the firm had doubled in size. Competitors hinted at some shady dealing, but nothing was ever proved.

After those two hectic years Bill was never at work. And neither was he at home. Nor at the golf club. In fact no one ever knew where he was. And, what's more, no one cared either.

The only time he was ever there was when Nicola wanted him not to be.

Then, suddenly, after years of neglect and some of recession the firm was in the hands of receivers. The creditors were appalled and Bill Carson was thrown back on his wits. This was when he thought of the

16

idea: a local radio, religious agony uncle. 'Air your religious problems live on radio and have them answered by "Father" Bill Carson'. (Of course a Presbyterian would not normally be called 'Father', but most of the callers were Catholics, so the name stuck)

Bill phoned round some of his old associates and within three weeks he was on the air. His poor daughter, who he thought would be impressed, was mortified.

'The bastard! Crafty, slimy bastard!' was how she put it to Father Vernon at the youth club, when she found out.

Father Vernon came out of the trance he had accidentally fallen into and was horrified to find that he had been staring at Nicola's breasts. He made a mental note to confess the sin to Canon Drinkwater first thing in the morning.

'I beg your pardon?' he stammered.

'Slimy fucking bastard's got himself a slot on Radio Bolton, doing a religious programme!'

Like a true professional, the young priest ignored the foul language. 'It sounds like a good way of spreading the word to me,' he ventured.

'You've got more religion in your underpants than he has in his entire fucking . . . life!'

Father Vernon blushed. 'That's what I love about young people,' he said. 'They're so generous to their parents.'

'He's such a fucking hypocrite. You should see the way he treats my mum.'

Father Vernon could see Nicola was genuinely upset.

'Why don't you try talking to him?'

'Im-fucking-possible'.

He couldn't resist a smile. 'You can even fit profanity into a one word sentence.'

17

'Fuck off!'

'No, I'm impressed, honestly.'

Jolly words weren't getting them anywhere. Nicola's shoulders slumped even lower. Father Vernon was genuinely sorry for the girl.

'Are you still using drugs, Nicola?'

'Only mum's sleeping pills.'

'Only? Strong stuff that.'

'I'm tellin' you. Give you the best dreams. Really mad.' She looked up at the young priest. 'I dreamt about you last night. And the night before. Sexy dreams.'

The priest blushed again. And ignored her remark.

'You should talk to someone.'

'I'm talking to you!'

'No, I mean a professional. Someone who can help.'

'You are helping. Look, I'm cheerful.'

They both smiled. Feebly. And Nicola sighed.

'I wish you were my dad,' she said.

Father Vernon could only smile and think what an unsuitable candidate he was.

After Brookside.

'Jesus Christ! What happened to you? You look awful!' stammered Betty. Though she had a sensitive nature it wasn't always apparent from the way she spoke.

Theresa took it in her stride: 'Can I come in, I'm freezing?'

It was always cold on Sunnymeadow. Even on a hot summer's day.

Betty's bedsit (it wasn't really a flat) was situated

in one of the newest buildings in Bolton. The council had built the block in a fit of political remorse following an incident, blown up out of all proportion by the local press, in which a police car had been stoned by youths.

'Where the fuck 'ave you been?' asked Betty swinging her astonished-looking daughter onto the sofa.

Theresa had been missing for over three weeks. Betty had been down to her house a couple of times to look for her.

Her mum didn't have a clue.

'Don't ask me, love, she's probably at her dad's, pulling the wool over his eyes. And when you see her tell her I want me video back . . . if she's taped over it I'll rip her to shreds! Oh . . . how's that little baby of yours . . . aww, look at her little filthy, dirty face.'

Little Lisa turned her nose up at the smell on the woman's breath and Betty thought better of telling her that Theresa was nowhere to be found.

'Where've you been?' Betty was getting annoyed.

'How about a brew?' suggested Theresa, avoiding Betty's pursed lower lip.

Betty's sigh was more of a gasp. 'What are you like!' she scolded, heading for the kettle and exchanging a glance with her one-year-old. The little speck tried to look more astounded than she already did, but failed. Then Betty eyed her friend more closely. 'Look at the bloody state you're in. What 'appened to your clothes?'

It really was incredible. Theresa Green was the best-dressed of all Betty's friends (not to mention her favourite). She always wore the most expensive clothes, which she was able to wangle out of her divorced dad. And here she was, dishevelled, no make up on and – well, a mess.

Theresa plonked herself on the sofa. 'What's on T.V?'

'Tell you what,' said Betty malevolently, 'why don't

you sit yourself down on the sofa an' carry on as if nothing's happened.'

'What has 'appened?'

'You bloody disappeared, that's what!'

Theresa tutted. 'Who are you, me bloody mother?'

Betty glared at her little daughter, who glared at Theresa, who stared at the T.V.

After a moment Betty said: 'Brookside's on.'

After Brookside Betty said: 'Well come on then.'

'Come on, what?'

The look on Betty's face threatened violence.

Theresa almost flinched. 'I've been away.'

'Anywhere nice?'

'Spain, Australia . . .'

'Oh yeah?'

Little Lisa looked at her mother with a stupid grin.

'Oh yeah . . . and London.'

'You 'ave been busy.'

Theresa nodded sheepishly.

'An' there's me thinkin' something terrible 'ad 'appened to you.' Betty's sarcasm was beginning to overflow.

Theresa continued to stare at the screen.

'Next time you go abroad, let me know beforehand, so I'll know you're not coming round, OK?'

No response.

'I mean I thought we were gunna watch a video on the Sunday night; if I'd known you were going on a world cruise I'd 'av made other arrangements.'

'Leave it out, Betty.'

'Oh, right. I'll just put the kettle on an' shut up.' She plonked her little daughter on Theresa's knee and went over to the little kitchen unit. In sulk mode. 'You've been gone three weeks!'

Theresa was either surprised or acting out. 'It's not three weeks, is it?'

Lisa pinched Theresa's nose, spitefully.

Theresa said 'Ouch!' too aggressively and the little tot burst into tears. Betty came over and took the child in her arms. 'Arh, what's she doin' to ya, eh?'

Theresa was suddenly overcome and took hold of her hair, as if to pull some of it out. 'I can't stand it!' she said frantically. 'You've got to help me Betty!'

The little girl stopped crying and Betty stood staring. Theresa looked scared suddenly, which scared Betty.

'Betty, I was knocked down by a car. I've been injured.'

Betty didn't know what to say.

Or believe.

'I can do things. Mad things.' Theresa's eyes were wider than Lisa's.

'I know that!' said Betty, nervously, sitting next to her friend on the sofa, trying to sound lighthearted. The infant reached out and touched her shoulder. 'What's going on? You ain't shittin' me?'

Theresa shook her head. She seemed to be holding her breath.

'Just tell me,' urged Betty and looked about in surprise. 'Theresa!'

Her friend had disappeared. Mother and daughter looked at one another, the tot's eyes wider than ever.

Then Betty screamed and jumped out of her skin as Theresa suddenly reappeared on the other side and touched her arm. Lisa beamed.

''Ow'd you do that?'

Theresa shrugged.

'Do it again.'

Theresa obliged, swapping sides.

Mother and daughter howled with laughter that sounded a bit insecure. 'You 'aven't put acid in my tea?'

Theresa shook her head. 'There's more where that came from,' said Theresa. 'D'you wanna see?'

21

Betty's head nearly came off her shoulders. 'No thanks.'

A Bad Trip.

That night as the two girls lay in Betty's small double bed, Theresa recounted the story of the previous three weeks.

Betty stared into the darkness and listened with a mixture of scepticism and awe.

'I went everywhere. All I had to do was want something to happen and it did. Fuckin' mad. I thought I 'ad gone mad for a few days.' She breathed through her nose. 'Then I got used to it. Sort of.'

She continued dreamily. 'I went to Spain. Benidorm. Stayed in a top hotel and got pissed all day. Beautiful pool.' She snorted. 'Fuckin' got kicked out didn't I?'

Betty wasn't surprised. (If it was true)

'Then I went somewhere else and met all these guys. They thought I was rich, ' Theresa laughed. 'I *was* rich. I bought 'em all drinks. All day. Shagged one of 'em. An' I 'ad 'is mate the next night. And then the other one found out and they kicked off . . . ' She laughed ironically. 'Got fuckin' kicked out again, didn't I?'

They lay in silence for a while and Betty wondered what she'd do if she had millions of pounds. 'Fuck knows,' she concluded.

Theresa turned over on her side. 'It was shit, Betty. After Spain I went to Australia. But I just got drunk with a load of people again, buyin' 'em all drinks. Bought this lad a car. Well, got 'im one.' She tutted. 'Waste of time.'

Betty didn't know what to think. Theresa was full

22

of shit sometimes. But she *had* seen her disappear with her own two eyes.

'Then I went to London. Didn't meet anyone. No one talked to me. Ended up walking round on me own. Doin' few stupid tricks to scare people. Then I got friendly with these tramps and fixed them up with a car and some clothes. A few days later they were back where I found them. Sold the car for a few quid. An' the best clothes. Drinkin' everything they could get their 'ands on.'

Betty was lost in sleepy thoughts.

'Then I came 'ere.' Theresa looked at her friend through the gloom. 'What d'you reckon, Betty?'

Betty turned over to go to sleep. 'You should have fuckin' told me where you were!'

By the morning Theresa had perked up considerably.

Betty was pottering round, feeding Lisa, changing her nappy and getting ready to go out to the shops. Theresa was sitting eating Rice Crispies and playing a few little tricks on Betty.

Betty filled the baby's bottle, put it down on the table and by the time she'd picked Lisa up onto her lap the bottle had moved so that Betty's hand grabbed comically at the air when she reached for it.

Betty either didn't notice or pretended not to.

Then little things went askew during the nappy change and when Betty sat down for her own breakfast the Rice Crispy box changed places and then she lost her spoon.

Suddenly Betty banged the table with her hand. 'For fuck's sake!'

Theresa jumped and felt stupid. She was after Betty's attention. 'Sorry.' Her hand fluttered, like an American actor's.

'It's bad enough with 'er.' Betty pointed at the little mite who looked a bit hurt.

23

'I know.' Theresa blushed and started to clear up the breakfast things to make up for it. Then she stopped, plonked herself down and sighed. Next thing the breakfast things were tidied up and the dishes were washed of their own accord.

'Lazy,' said Betty.

Then in a moment Lisa was sitting in her pram, wiped, wide-eyed and ready to go.

'Oi!' Betty sat back and rolled her eyes in exasperation. 'I wanted to do that!' she glared bad-temperedly. 'If you're gunna help, do it properly . . .'

Hurt, Theresa stared at her friend. For some reason she always craved Betty's approval.

Betty must have realised she was being a bit harsh because she smiled and changed the subject. 'I had a mad dream last night.'

Relieved, Theresa raised her eyebrows. 'Me too.'

Betty wrinkled her nose. 'Father Vernon was in it. Riding on this big purple balloon . . .'

Theresa blinked in astonishment. 'He was in mine . . .'

Betty grinned 'And there was a nude man in it.'

Theresa interjected: 'Yeah! With his arms round Father Vernon . . .'

'Yeah!'

'Both riding on a huge purple balloon . . . with jet engines?'

Betty nodded.

Theresa sat up, smiling. 'What was he like?'

'The man?'

Theresa nodded.

'Gorgeous!'

Theresa nodded again.

'The most beautiful man I've ever seen.'

'Same dream,' said Theresa.

The two teenagers looked at each other for a moment. Then Betty shrugged. 'You coming to the shops?'

They carried the pushchair down the stairs to the front door.

Then Theresa pushed the buggy down the hill.

They walked in silence for a while then Betty rested one of her hands on the pram. 'You can stay at mine, if you want.' She shrugged. 'Long as you like.'

'Thanks.' Theresa smiled. 'You're a saviour.'

Back in the Closet.

Father Vernon found himself locked in the closet at the youth club.

For some reason the door was stuck fast. Then, after a few moments of struggle the latch mysteriously gave way and the door swung open a few inches. Through the gap, the young priest caught a glimpse of Nicola Carson sitting astride the arm of a ragged old sofa.

Nicola was wearing a short skirt which rode up to the top of her legs and the young priest noticed two things that disturbed him somehow. Firstly, the exposed legs were covered in the most delicate golden down, and secondly, the young woman seemed to be showing the shapely limbs off to someone in the room, who was hidden from view. Father Vernon coughed to make known his presence, but found himself unable to come out of the closet.

His warning went unheeded.

It was as if Nicola were riding the arm of the sofa like a horse. The poor clergyman was rooted to the spot and felt a sickly sensation well up in his chest. The young woman giggled in the most unholy manner, moving herself slowly and purposefully back and forth on the imaginary saddle.

Father Vernon blinked and her skirt was gone.

This was too much and the young priest decided he would have to walk out of the closet, pretend not to notice the near nudity and head straight for the coffee bar. But something stopped him. And he rather suspected it was the devil. He felt his throat go dry and his legs turn to stone. Or was it jelly? And what in God's name was he doing spying on this juvenile erotic gymkhana?

The young woman was now down to her bra and pants and seemed to be taking instructions from the other person in the room. Father Vernon suddenly realised that there were, in fact, two other voices, one male and one female and Nicola was parading herself up and down in front of the sofa threatening to remove her only remaining garments. Surely they were scared of other youths from the club entering the room and disturbing them.

Apparently not.

The trapped priest realised the situation had gone past the point of no return. If he disturbed the youths now they would surely know he had been watching their antics and suspect the worst. If only he could close the door, or avert his gaze. But no. He was utterly transfixed.

Next thing, Nicola shrieked. She was squirming on the sofa, clinging desperately to her brilliant white pants and the young man dressed only in a pair of coloured boxer shorts, was tugging at them, trying to pull them down.

Meanwhile the other young woman, whom the stricken clergyman also recognised, was stripped to the waist of her jeans and was attacking the young man's shorts, trying to remove them too. The curious thing about the second young woman, Father Vernon couldn't help but notice, was that she didn't appear to have breasts at all, just two slightly elongated nipples.

The whole scene was now something of a commotion. The entombed priest felt a strong desire to pray, but somehow it seemed inappropriate. Then the three youths stopped fighting and engaged in a tangle of limbs. There were hands everywhere – including a cold hand on Father Vernon's heart.

He desperately replayed the scene in his head, trying to define his own role. Had he willed it to happen? Or had it been unavoidable? He should have shut the door, or at least his eyes.

Suddenly, there was an incredible fanfare and a roar of jet engines. The noise was coming from inside the closet. Surely he would be discovered now. It was very dark all of a sudden. The door must have closed.

A voice boomed.

'Dear boy – there are no sinful feelings!'

Father Vernon recognised the voice, but it was changed somehow and accompanied by the sound of angel trumpets and devil trombones. It hadn't been a closet after all. Father Vernon was floating in a giant confessional chamber on a huge purple balloon. With jet engines.

The voice echoed in the darkness.

'Dreams are acts of God in themselves.'

God was sitting right behind him in the saddle, holding on tight around his waist. They were very high.

'Listen to him,' God said. 'One theory after another.'

Although somewhat surprised, Father Vernon felt very safe. He knew God was naked, but he didn't mind. It was nice to feel so close to someone. He could see mountains and lakes stretching out before them and breathed a deep and contented sigh. The air was very clear and clean.

'The question is, does one act on one's feelings?' boomed Canon Drinkwater's voice from somewhere.

'You know that's the Archangel Gabriel?' God asked, breathing in Father Vernon's ear.

'Sounds just like an old friend of mine,' replied the priest. He was a little puzzled, but didn't press the matter. 'Do you appear like this to everyone?' he asked instead.

God gave Father Vernon a little squeeze. 'I don't usually appear at all,' He answered.

They floated among unspeakable objects for a while and all kinds of images – mostly the kind that made Father Vernon blush – flashed before them, until the dazzled priest almost forgot God was there.

Then God gave him another squeeze. 'I might not look it, but I'm really very angry indeed. I was going to abandon you altogether. But,' God pointed up ahead, 'he persuaded me to give you one more chance.'

The Archangel Gabriel was waiting at a bus stop for them.

'Dear boy, hello. You weren't expecting me here, were you?'

Father Vernon didn't get a chance to reply.

'What do you think of the new voice? Pretty awesome, eh? And what about the robe? Very Roman – don't you think?'

The Archangel really was the spitting image of his old friend Canon Drinkwater, only somehow rejuvenated.

God had dismounted. 'The Archangel here will see you back. You can expect to hear from us again soon,' He said and was gone.

Father Vernon looked at Gabriel.

'It wasn't you last time,' he managed to say.

'Oh' wasn't it?' boomed the Archangel. 'Oh well, never mind. There are many ways of interpreting dreams.'

'What's all this about?'

The oldish man threw his head back and laughed a boomy laugh. 'It's building up to something,' he resounded. 'I told you before. Don't you believe me?'

And Father Vernon felt himself falling. He was sliding down a chute like Scott from Thunderbirds on his way to launch Thunderbird One.

And then they were back at the youth club.

Father Vernon was sitting at the end of the sofa. Nicola was next to him and the young man next to her. Gabriel was kneeling on the floor behind the young woman with the strange breasts. They were all naked. And yet somehow it seemed perfectly natural.

Nicola and the young man were chatting about something and giggling. The Archangel was making love to the girl from behind. She was kneeling there on the carpet with her head propped up on her hands, smiling calmly.

Father Vernon was thinking to himself that this was surely acting on one's feelings. 'No one seems to mind, though,' he reflected.

'You see, they like to do it with an older man,' observed the old sinner, 'it gives them a sense of re-assurance.'

Father Vernon's stomach was all wet and some-one was rocking the sofa. He was thinking 'if they rock this any harder we'll all come flying off' and was hoping they wouldn't, when the thought occurred to him that someone was trying to wake him up from his dream.

Surely not just now.

Somebody was trying to wake him up.

It was Mary, Father Vernon's housekeeper.

'Wake up Father,' she was hissing. 'Father Vernon . . .'

He opened his eyes. The bedding was pulled right down.

'Mary! What is it?' stammered the priest covering

himself up. He had the uncomfortable feeling that Mary knew what he had been dreaming.

'I'm sorry to bother you, Father, But I'm afraid I've got some bad news.' The unfortunate woman smelt of drink. She must have been up all night. 'They've just phoned from St Mark's in Manchester. Cannon Drinkwater passed away in the night.'

Here's to God's Love.

'Hello, Father. I wanted to phone in last week, but I was too ashamed.'

'Don't be shy, this is your programme and God's listening to you – right now.' Bill Carson signalled to the studio engineer to get the kettle on. She showed him the back of the middle finger on her right hand. Bill pretended to be shocked and made a mock sign of the cross.

'I'd like to remain anomenus – amonemus . . . ' the woman sighed.

'Anonymous,' corrected Bill.

'Yes. I'm sorry, Father it's such a strain and it's been so long . . . I don't know what to do anymore . . .' The caller' s voice trailed off into a sob.

Bill was indicating with his head for the engineer to arrange for someone else to make the tea. She was pretending not to understand.

'That's good – let it out, God will hear you. Join me in prayer, listeners. Pray for our caller.'

More sobs.

'Can you tell me your first name? That won't do any harm, will it?' coaxed the radio evangelist, gently.

'It's Mary,' sobbed the voice. 'I come from a very

30

devout family.' The poor woman was obviously in quite bad shape and the whimper in Bill's headphones turned into a wail. He made a face to his engineer which said 'Oh dear'.

'Crying's an important part of grief, Mary,' said the man who hadn't cried since he was nine years old. 'Try to talk about it at the same time,' he added, thinking of the listeners.

'I want to talk about it Father, I can't hold it in any longer.'

'Is it someone you loved?' Bill assumed there was a bereavement.

'Yes. Oh yes. I love him today more than ever.'

'Yes yes, of course.' He made a mental note never to talk about the dead in the past tense.

'Was . . . I'm sorry . . . is he very old?'

'Thirty-three.'

'Oh dear . . . ' Bill was genuinely saddened.

'And I'm forty-seven.' There was a blubbering, slobbering sob.'

'Is he – your son?'

His engineer, who could deduct thirty-three from forty-seven without writing it down was shaking her head vigorously and grimacing. Bill was a little flustered.

'Sometimes it's very difficult to understand God's motives, especially taking someone so young away from us. You'll probably feel a lot of anger . . .'

'It's not fair, why should it happen to me? I don't deserve it!' It was said with a very slight slur which Bill missed.

'No you don't deserve it, Mary, it's right to feel cheated. Now come on, talk about it, share your grief with our listeners, let us share in your suffering. Let us pray together.'

Mary was beside herself. 'It's unbearable, Father. Terrible.'

31

'If you're listening out there, join your hands in prayer. Hear us, Lord. Listen to your daughter.'

'I'm in love with a man fourteen years my junior. And he'll never love me as long as I live,' she wailed.

Several things flashed through Bill's mind at the same time. The smirk on his engineer's face. The fact that this might be a hoax. There were sometimes impostors, often more than one in a night. If not, had the listeners understood that they had been talking at cross purposes? Could he pretend that it had been a hoax to save his face, which was flushed red.

His finger was poised over the jingle button that, once pressed signified the end of a call. With a look he appealed to his engineer for help. She shook her head and glared at the idea of stopping this one. She knew only too well that it was this kind of call that made the programme more widely popular.

'Have you any idea what it's like to live with a man who you can never have, Father?'

'Erm . . . ' He hated DJ's who say 'erm' on the air. 'You . . . live together?'

'In five whole years he's never once given me any indication that he loves me.'

All Bill could manage was: 'Very unusual circumstances,' and hope she would explain them piously.

'Every night I go to bed and I want him there with me. I want him to make love to me, Father . . .'

'Erm . . .' He said it again! 'Have you – tried talking to God about the problem?'

'That's exactly it. God is part of the problem.'

'I don't follow you. Surely God is the solution to our problems.'

'No, no.' There was a kind of slurp on the other end of the line as if the caller were taking a drink. 'He's a priest, Father. I'm in love with a Catholic priest.'

'Ah.' He almost laughed out loud. Now he understood. She must be the housekeeper to a priest. Stupid woman.

His engineer was beaming. Listeners would be rubbing their hands in glee. The cynics anyhow.

'Yes, I see the predicament.'

'Do you Father? Do you really see? Do you think there's any hope?' slurred Mary, with a note of urgency.

'There's hope for all of us, Mary,' said Bill.

'Yes, yes.'

'Pray for God's love, Mary and there will always be hope.'

'Yes. yes, I'll pray for God's love in the hope that he'll answer my prayers. Thank you Father.'

'Thank you for calling, Mary. We're praying for you.'

'Here's to God's love,' she said, apparently to herself.

During the break Bill made for the engineer's cubicle.

'Tea's on its way,' said Laura, still grinning at the last call.

'Blow the tea,' said Bill, 'I've got indigestion.' He produced a bottle of Black Label whiskey from his bag and clumsily poured a shot into a dirty coffee mug. 'Here's to God's love,' he quipped and downed it in one.

'Thirty seconds and counting,' said Laura. 'And don't breathe too hard into the mike, someone might suspect'.

'They're all bloody Catholics, anyway,' said Bill.

Fever.

It was senseless, but somewhere in his heart, Father Vernon blamed himself for Cannon Drinkwater's death. And in isolation, the poor man's life very quickly broke down.

His old bureau said something about the state of his mind. And his body. And his soul.

This usually ordered antique was covered in debris. The cubby-holes were in a state of confusion, the shelves were disorderly, anarchy ruled in the drawers and there was an unholy rebellion on the writing surface which hadn't been cleared for over a fortnight.

Like a plague, the chaos had spread outwards from his desk.

First to go was his office which was devastated. There were papers strewn all over the floor, the Tippex was nowhere to be found and the 'b' on his typewriter was sticking so that the parish circulars became bbulletins. The few parishioners who noticed it were too polite to say anything and poor Mary assumed she was experiencing double vision.

Next to go were the bedrooms and the bathroom. The beds were unmade and there was dirty washing everywhere. A faint odour emanated from the bathroom and there were little bristles and blood-stained scraps of toilet paper all round the sink where the heart-broken priest had cut himself shaving.

Downstairs, the living room was a tip and the kitchen was a sink.

And there were empty bottles hidden everywhere. Normally Father Vernon managed to keep on top of the situation but lately he had let it slide. Like the poor drunk she was, Mary assumed that empty or half empty bottles were somehow invisible for being shut up in the airing cupboard, or stored on top of a wardrobe. And now no one disposed of them they just mounted up.

The young priest himself looked ill. There were black bags under his eyes and he walked with a stoop. 'Pallid' was the word most favoured among his worried flock and there were rumours in the diocese that the young priest was dying of AIDS. Some people thought he was in love.

Finally, the social arrangements succumbed to the malady.

One night, shortly after Canon Drinkwater's death, a terrified Mary had appeared at Father Vernon's bedroom door.

'Father Vernon! Help me!'

It was about three a.m. and although he was still wide awake the young clergyman jumped out of his skin.

'Father there are slugs and snails and spiders all over the floor in my bedroom and ... ' the stricken woman shrieked. 'They're coming!' she cried, ran across the room and dived under the bedclothes.

All the flabbergasted priest could do was gasp, observe that Mary was stark naked and leap out of bed. Indeed they were both naked. He lunged for his dressing gown which was in the wardrobe.

The parish priest was just beginning to suspect that this might be another of his cruel, blasphemous nightmares, when his hopes were shattered by an empty bottle, which plunged from the top of the wardrobe and caught him painfully on the shoulder. He was definitely awake. And Mary was definitely squirming, naked, under his bedclothes.

The unfortunate woman was suffering her first serious attack of delirium tremens, but at that moment both priest and housekeeper were convinced that she'd gone stark, raving mad.

The dementia continued for days. There were hallucinations during which Mary became convinced she was possessed by demons. And there was fever during which Mary became convinced she was going to die.

However, throughout her suffering and despite a genuine concern for her own mortality, Mary refused to see a doctor, preferring instead to risk the amateur ministrations and dutiful attentions of her beloved clergyman. Even through the madness the afflicted woman could see clearly the advantage of the situation.

Her mind and body were suffering the cruel ravages of alcoholism. But deep down in the darkest caverns of her soul she was in a state of exultation and everything in her was determined to seize the opportunity that presented itself.

The first night Father Vernon sat up with Mary until morning. He hadn't slept a wink since his old friend had died and the poor grieving man didn't want ever to sleep again. So it wasn't much trouble for him to sit up with his ailing housekeeper a second night. Indeed it was a positive boon, for it enabled him to keep his intolerable thinking under control for the most of the small hours.

On the third night Mary was calmer and the fever had subsided enough for her to envisage another drink. And as she lay in the young priest's bed, feigning sleep, wondering how she might bring about circumstances favourable to her taking a swig from the bottle she had hidden under her pillow, Father Vernon slipped gently under the covers next to her.

It was a perfectly innocent move on his part. He was merely cold on top of the covers, dressed, as he was, only in his dressing gown and striped pyjamas.

He had no idea at all of the shattering effect it produced in his bed-pal.

Three's a Crowd.

'Hiya. What's the mag?' asked Michelle, sitting on the wall at the top of the hill.

'This week's *My Guy*,' replied her approaching, freckled friend.

Michelle tutted. 'That's shit.'

'No it's not!' Jo flushed. In her heart she knew that if Michelle thought it was shit, it was shit. 'It's got *Take That* photo's in it,' she explained.

'I've gone off them.' Michelle's trend-setting taste varied weekly, sometimes more. Poor Jo couldn't keep up. 'I prefer *East 17*'

'They're alright,' shrugged Jo.

'They're top,' announced Michelle. 'Did you see them on the *Chart Show*?'

'Yeah,' Jo lied and sat on the wall beside her friend.

The two fifteen-year-olds were inseparable, apart from when Michelle had a boyfriend. But even then separation never lasted long. Over half the fun for Michelle was in recounting the scenes to Jo and giggling over the details.

Sometimes Michelle took her friend along when she went to meet a guy, partly for conversational support and partly to protect herself from wandering hands. And Jo would put up with feeling a gooseberry, partly for the vicarious pleasure and partly because she was jealous. (Not jealous that Michelle had a boyfriend, but that the boyfriend had Michelle.)

It was always Michelle who got boyfriends and this seemed natural to both of them. Sure Jo snogged guys at parties and even enjoyed being groped by some of them, but she didn't get boyfriends.

37

Perhaps because of her freckles, or perhaps because she lacked Michelle's apparent sophistication, no one asked her out. And that was the way she preferred it. She'd far rather go round with Michelle. And if necessary, her boyfriend.

It was typical of their friendship that they both kept the really important news until they were settled on the wall where they always met and the preliminaries of the latest variations in taste were out of the way.

'Guess what?' they both said at exactly the same moment and laughed.

'What?' Again they spoke in unison. And again they chuckled.

'You go first,' said Jo.

'No you,' said Michelle. And Jo knew it was the correct way round.

'OK, guess what?'

'What?'

'Guess . . .'

'Don't, Jo!' Michelle was serious, 'I'm not in the mood.'

'Al-right.' Jo paused dramatically, pushing a strand of her red, bobbed hair back behind her ear. 'I just punched me mum. Right in the face.'

Michelle's jaw dropped.

'Knocked her flat on 'er back.'

'You never!'

'I did. Stupid cow. I'm sick of her.'

'When?'

'Jus' now.'

'I don't believe it.'

'Why not? I punched me dad last week.'

'No, but . . . ' Michelle hesitated. She too wanted the proper effect. 'Guess what?'

Jo over-acted thinking. 'Er . . . you finished with Penny?'

Michelle's 'No!' sounded like 'of course not'. She

paused dramatically. 'I punched my mum. Right in the face.'

There was a moment's silence. Jo knew instinctively that Michelle wasn't joking.

'When?'

'Jus' now. I knocked her flat on her back.'

It was Jo's turn to be dumbstruck.

The two friends were still walking around the estate when it started to get dark.

'What shall we do now?' Jo's role was always to ask the questions.

Michelle shrugged nonchalantly, as she always did. 'I ain't going back there.'

'Nor me.'

The magic of the earlier coincidence had touched them both. Speaking only the most shorthand sentences, occasionally linking arms, the two young women had strolled around for hours, the long summer evening paying tribute to their intimacy.

'What about your stepdad?'

'Na.'

'Na, nor me.'

Suddenly Michelle stopped dead in her tracks and pulled Jo out of sight, behind someone's hedge. She pulled a face: 'Penny's coming!'

'So?'

'So ... ' Michelle hopped from one foot to the other.

Penny was Michelle's new boyfriend. He was the singer in the best, but most disorganised, local teenage band. He was very popular with the young women at the youth club and this had a lot to do with Michelle's interest.

'So I don't want to see him.'

Jo was *made up*.

'Duck!' Michelle pulled Jo down behind the hedge.

'There's a guy at the window,' giggled Jo, pointing up at the house behind them.

'Shh,' hissed Michelle.

Penny was almost upon them, striding up the hill with one of the other members of the band. Their conversation went something like this:

'Where the fuck are they?'

''Ow the fuck should I know . . .'

'Fuckin' 'ell!'

At that moment the man in the upstairs window of the house who obviously didn't take kindly to the invasion of his front garden hammered on the window, gesticulating angrily.

Penny and his friend assumed he was signalling them.

'Fuck's 'e on about?'

'Fuck knows.'

The two lads made an appropriate gesture to the bloke in the window and continued on their disgruntled way. The man scowled and looked as if he was coming to the front door.

Michelle and Jo waited in their hiding place as long as possible and then took to their heels and ran, laughing uproariously as they went.

It was almost dark now and the two teenagers were standing on the wall of the school at the very top of the estate, swinging from the railings, looking out over the whole of Bolton and a stretch of the moors.

They had nowhere to go and though neither of them could articulate it, it seemed quite beautiful.

'I'm leaving,' shrugged Michelle. 'I'm never going back.'

'Me too,' said Jo, 'I'm sick of it.'

The moors looked very dark compared to the shimmering lights of the town.

'We not even got any belongings,' laughed Jo.

'We've got your *My Guy*,' Michelle said, dead-pan.

Jo still had the rolled up magazine in her hand.

'Na. It's shit,' she said and tossed it over the wall.

Then, at a snail's pace they set off. Neither of them said a word, but they both knew where they were going.

To Betty's flat.

As they crossed the playing field, the great display of illuminations behind them, Jo slipped her arm through Michelle's.

'You know what?'

'What?' said Michelle who was just momentarily wondering what Penny was up to tonight.

'I 'ad a weird dream last night. About ... Father Vernon. And a stupid purple balloon.'

'Yeah?' said Michelle, casually kicking the grass as she walked. 'Me too.'

Five's a Bigger Crowd.

'Hiya, Betty.' They both said.

Betty was holding little Lisa who seemed astonished to see the two strangers. Before Betty could say anything, Michelle and Jo had pushed their way into the tiny entrance hall and were gushing over the poor, dazzled microbe.

'She's gorgeous ...'

'How old is she now, Betty?'

'Look at 'er little face.'

'Ain't you beau'iful?'

'Eh, Lisa ... (wink and laugh)'

'Arh ...'

41

Lisa stared at them and wondered what they were saying. Her mom wasn't giving any indication. 'Uh?' she asked and was amazed at the renewed outburst of merriment. All she could do was stare in wonder.

And when the toddler's beauty had been paid sufficient tribute, there fell an uneasy silence.

'What's goin' on?' asked Betty, slightly suspicious of this first visit by the two inseparables.

Michelle looked at Jo, who read her mind and spoke for both of them.

'We got kicked out.'

Michelle added: 'Both of us.'

It was all they needed to say. Betty kept them guessing for a couple of moments then pointed at the stairs with her eyes and the two new-comers went up.

Betty touched her baby's nose. 'It's gettin' crowded ain't it, Tiny?'

Michelle and Jo were shocked when they saw Theresa.

'What've you done to your 'air?' asked Jo.

For a split second, looking at the way she was dressed, Michelle wondered whether there'd been some abrupt change in fashion which she'd missed out on. After all, Theresa Green was somewhat of an authority on style. Definitely not now though. Her hair was greasy and limp. And uncared for. And as for the clothes!

'Where's y' clothes, y' scruffy cow?' Michelle asked.

Theresa knew they were shocked but she wasn't upset. She was pleased to see her two friends. She let them stare in wonder for a time. Then she smiled and said, 'Are you staying?'

They all looked at Betty who was standing by the door.

Betty just shrugged.

*

42

Despite their inherent conservatism, young people have a miraculous ability to adapt to unusual, even dangerous situations. Especially on Sunnymeadow.

It took Michelle and Jo precisely two hours, one packet of chips and peas and a can of Coke each to settle in at Betty's. Theresa slipped out to the chip shop, came back with a carrier bag and a video – and that was that.

There was one large double bed and a cot in the flat between the five of them. It never occurred to them to use the sofa as a bed – no one wanted to be left out – so the four teenagers slept together and managed reasonably well doing a sort of doubles top-and-tail. Betty and Theresa one end and Michelle and Jo the other.

And some nights the baby made five.

There were fights of course, but mostly the arrangement worked out well. A distinct camaraderie developed between them that would have reminded their grandmothers of the air-raid shelters.

Neither Michelle nor Jo thought to question the source of the modest rations of food and entertainment that sustained them. For weeks they lived on a diet of chips, peas, pies, biscuits, crisps, pop and cider. And cigs and vids and bottled milk and Farley's Rusks for Lisa.

'You all live there together?' asked Penny one day, when he, Michelle and Jo were hanging round outside.

Michelle looked at Jo who was perched on the wall beside them.

'Yeah,' said Jo.

'I wasn't askin' you,' snapped the spotted but good looking teenager.

Michelle was wearing the expressionless expression she reserved for her boyfriends.

With his hands in his pockets Penny hopped from one leg to the other for a moment and then gobbed onto the pavement from between his two front teeth.

'Where d' you all sleep?' he ventured.

Michelle looked at Jo and then back into the middle distance.

Jo said: 'Together'.

The look on Penny's face said absolutely nothing at all.

He was still trying in vain to prise Michelle away from her chaperone. But rather than drive the frustrated young lad away, Michelle's habit of bringing along her friend kept him coming back for more.

'C'mon, let's go for a walk,' he said, eyeing Jo malevolently.

'C'mon, then,' said Michelle almost without moving her lips.

The three of them set off down the hill.

One morning when Theresa and Betty were playing with little Lisa, Betty said: 'Is this anything to do with you?'

'Is what anything to do with me?'

'Them two.'

Theresa shrugged. 'I don't think so.'

Lisa was busy filling her nappy.

Betty picked up some of the clutter. 'You gunna tell 'em?'

'What about?'

'Your . . . problem.'

'What d'you reckon?'

Betty shrugged. ''S up to you.'

'What d'you think they'd say?'

Betty looked at her. 'Hallelujah!'

Poor Sinners.

'Hello Father.' It was a young woman's voice. 'I need to talk.'

'This is your programme and God's listening to you – right now,' said Bill with the appropriate amount of feeling. 'It's always bloody females who need to talk,' he thought.

'It's to do with my mom, Father.' She hesitated. 'It's difficult to talk about.'

'God will hear you, my child. If you're listening out there, join us in prayer.' Bill was fiddling with a mountain of cassettes, trying to find the next advert break. Engineer Laura was half asleep in the tiny control room.

'She's not very well, Father. She's got a disease.'

'Is it a . . . serious illness?'

'It can be fatal, Father. It affects her throat.'

'Pray for us poor sinners, Lord. Join me in prayer,' Bill rattled it off. He borrowed heavily from the Catholic mass – little phrases that came in handy. Laura had done the market research. Well over fifty percent of listeners were 'Papists', as Bill liked to call them, and nearly all the callers.

Bill still couldn't find his cassette.

'The thing is, father, she's addicted to sex . . .'

Quick as a flash, Bill pressed the jingle button, but nothing happened. The cassette wasn't in the slot. 'Shit . . .'

A few thousand Lancastrians heard: 'She gets dad to tie her up at night and fuck her with a broomstick. Gives her a terrible sore throat . . .'

There was raucous, adolescent laughter on the other end of the line and then, when the damage was already done, the radio station jingle sang 'Rad-io

Bol-ton Cares . . . ' in sickly four-part harmony.

Bill tried to sound calm. 'Yes, well another little hoax there – and I apologise for being a little slow off the mark, listeners. Let us pray, as we must, for all sinners. Show us the way Lord – the true path of right-eousness.'

In the control box, out of respect for the look on Bill's face, Laura was trying to suppress a wicked grin.

'Next caller,' said Bill avoiding catching her eye.

'Hello Father.' Another young woman. Bill's finger hovered over the loaded jingle button.

'This is your programme and God's listening to you – right now.'

'I've been given the power to do miracles . . . ' claimed the caller.

'Rad-io Bol-ton Cares . . . ' Four-part harmonies.

It was going to be a long evening.

The two adolescents were beside themselves with mer-riment.

'I bet that gave him a sore throat,' he said, literally clutching his sides.

'Pity we can't send someone down there with a sharpened broom handle. Slimy bastard,' she laughed.

He did an impression: 'This is your programme and God's listening to you – right noooowwww!'

They laughed all over again, rolling against each other on the sofa, taking the opportunity to brush their legs together.

Nicola Carson had invited the young man round to get off with him. Her mum was in the house some-where but when her father was out the young woman did what ever she wanted, without a care. Including making obscene phone calls to his pro-gramme.

46

They were laughing fit to burst.

'Oh my God!' she squealed, 'I've done a piss.' She really had let a bit out.

The young man took this as a cue to tickle her vigorously.

Nicola screamed uproariously and giggled: 'Stop it Penny! Stop it . . . you'll make me spend a penny!'

He didn't and she did.

Alternating Current.

Bill's Rover 216/SLi swept into the drive of the family's mock-tudor mansion with a little more fortitude than was usual.

There was a swoosh and the sword-shaped leaves of the neatly placed iris bulbs flinched under a hail of gravel. The car door slammed and the peace of the neighbourhood was momentarily penetrated as the heavy front door banged shut behind him.

The oak of the door was, in fact, pine and the house was not a mansion. Indeed one of the only genuine items in the entire household at that moment was Bill Carson's rage.

'Where is she?' were the first words he spoke to his wife when he burst into the living room.

He wife didn't move a muscle. 'Good evening, darling. Yes, I had a pleasant evening really. Quite enjoyed *Poirot*. Spoke to Marjory on the phone. Sends her love. Peter's looking for a new job. Cathy's doing her finals.' Mrs Carson looked at her husband for the first time. 'And your daughter's walking her boyfriend home.'

There was no point in replying to any of this out

47

loud and so Bill stomped out of the room and continued the conversation alone, in his head, first while pacing round the fitted kitchen and then while poking round his daughter's bedroom.

'Walking her bloody boyfriend home! Who the hell ever heard of a girl walking a lad home? What sort of a lad is he anyway? Lives on that bloody estate, I bet. What the hell's wrong with the woman letting them in the house in the first place? She's been sat on her arse all bloody night. On the bloody phone all night . . . well not all night. She probably passed it over to Nicola. "Here darling . . . you and your boyfriend take this upstairs to your bedroom and do whatever you bloody like with it and then bring it down so I can phone Marjory back . . . "'

Bill was a boiling pot of resentment. He had a knot in his stomach which whiskey hadn't undone and a bloody stream of consciousness.

In Nicola's bedroom he found the handset of the cordless phone on the bed which was rumpled and . . . yes . . . still warm. The room smelt of cigarette smoke and . . . something else. Bill looked around the room at pictures of semi-clad males and even some naked women and sighed.

He was angry. Very angry. Something had to be done and now was the time to do it.

His gaze alighted on some very adult looking black underwear on the floor at the foot of the bed. When he stooped to inspect the article he found it was a pair of soaking wet knickers. Puzzled, he picked them up between his fore-finger and thumb and was just about to smell them when a voice said:

'God is watching you . . .'

Bill gasped.

Nicola was standing in the door way.

Bill quickly crumpled the lace-ware up into his

hand and stuffed it in his pocket. He had his back to the door and calculated that his daughter hadn't seen him. He was a past master at such clumsy deceit and Nicola played along, deriving a keen gratification from the thought that her urine was now wetting her father's pocket.

'Find anything interesting?' inquired Nicola, casually.

'What ancient rules of chivalry demand that a young woman, who may come to God knows what harm on the way back, should walk a young man home at night?' It was all said in one breath.

'Mum said it was alright.'

This was a good answer and Nicola knew it. For a moment Bill was stuck for words. He picked up the handset of the phone and brandished it as a weapon. Nicola stared defiantly back at him.

'Have a good evening at work, Father?' she asked malevolently.

The formality of the address was meant to add insult.

Bill chose his words carefully and spoke deliberately: 'If I thought . . . even for a moment . . . that you were the type of girl to . . . in front of . . . if I thought . . . ' The problem was there was no proof. Yet somehow he knew. At the same time it was so vile and repugnant. Bill realised with a sigh that it was too revolting to be aired aloud. Impossible to bring to the surface.

He fell silent.

He was defeated. Yet again.

The pair of them stood, as they had often done before, facing each other in open hostility. Each one found the other contemptible, despicable, execrable, foul, loathsome, nasty, obnoxious, offensive, repellent, sickening and vicious. There was a perverse balance to their relationship.

49

Bill mistook the situation for a stalemate.

Nicola was in the mood for a kill.

'Poor mother,' she said with mock-concern. 'Such a terrible sore throat.'

This for Bill was the equivalent of a powerful depth charge plunging into his being. The moment it was released it caused a splash. But the flicker of a reaction that Nicola mistook for a direct hit was nothing in comparison to the explosion that occurred several fathoms beneath the surface, when the full horror of the statement had sunk in.

Before his very eyes his daughter's already angular features seemed to contort. Her eyes bulged, the corners sharpening to a point. Her lips parted slightly to reveal a cordon of gnashing, grimacing teeth that mocked and threatened him.

It happened in slow motion.

Bill's hand unleashed itself, lifted high into the air, somehow refrained from forming a fist and slapped the wicked face with such power that it should have smashed the evil thing to smithereens.

What stopped Nicola flying across the room from the force of the slap was sheer hatred. Tears instantly welled up in her eyes and would have squirted across the room but for her pride. The cry was momentary and involuntary. Instantly suppressed.

Two hundred thousand volts of alternating current passed between them as they faced each other and it was a miracle that neither one of them vaporised.

Dads.

'What happened to your eye, Nicola?' asked Father Vernon shifting his position on the stool behind the coffee bar, so as to better mask his furtive glances at the young woman's chest.

'Slimy bastard slapped me,' she replied in her own terms of endearment.

'Let me see that,' said the priest, genuinely concerned. 'Are you serious?'

'You should see his hand,' quipped the youngster coming round to his side of the counter and standing far too close to the young clergyman in his weakened condition.

He was sitting on a tall stool and had to reshuffle his position, this time to avoid pressing his knee between her legs.

'Now that's what I call a shiner.'

Such a close examination of the bruising was unnecessary and Father Vernon knew it. There was something in him though that had changed recently. The young priest had become less diligent in his spiritual accountancy. He had developed an inner blind eye and hadn't said a meaningful confession in weeks.

He was drifting inside and had lost the will to hold on.

Nicola pulled up the second bar-stool and sat facing him, her knees slightly interlocking with his.

'Are you alright, Dad?'

It was Nicola's playful new term for him. '"Father" reminds me of slimy bastard,' she quipped the first time she used it. 'You look mighty pissed off lately,' she said and it was true. 'Don't you wanna talk about it?'

Father Vernon heaved a deep sigh. 'It's nothing,' he lied.

'Come on, Dad, I tell you all my secrets.'

He looked at his young friend and sighed again. He loved the way she called him 'Dad'. It was cheeky and familiar and on a deeper level it reflected a bond that had recently grown up between them. She would pour out her heart and he would listen endlessly. She took little liberties and he let her get away with it. Everyone who knew the girl thought her wicked, but to the young priest she was innocence itself. And he had a shrewd idea of what she got up to.

'It's that bloody housekeeper of yours, Mary, ain't it?' Nicola sighed. 'She uses you, you know.'

'It's nothing to do with Mary,' answered the priest and thought he meant it.

'You should sack her and get me on the case,' said the youngster in all seriousness. 'I need somewhere to live.'

Father Vernon missed the hint entirely. He was thinking about Canon Drinkwater. 'An old priest friend of mine . . . passed away recently,' he sighed. It was the first time he'd actually spoken about it to anyone. 'I'm really going to miss him.'

Nicola was moved. The young priest had confided in her for a change.

Father Vernon badly need to talk to someone and something in him wanted to pour his heart out to this young woman. 'I miss him badly. He was the best friend I ever had.'

Nicola was glowing with pride and love. 'Dad?' she asked. 'Are you gay?'

Inspector Swann was a pompous self-satisfied old git. At least Bill Carson thought so today. Bill's mood had been made worse by the way he played.

'You swiped your way round there,' teased the grey-streaked old copper as they strolled into the clubhouse.

He had a point. Bill had dug divots and excavated

52

the bunkers all the way round the course. He was about to make up for the debâcle in the bar.

'Two large whiskies, please,' he sighed.

'Make mine a shandy,' insisted his friend.

'Come on, Swanny!' coaxed Bill feeling like an alcoholic.

'I'm on a late one tonight,' replied the dutiful Inspector.

When the drinks arrived, Bill knocked his down in one, ordered another and the two men sat down.

'Let me guess,' said the wise old copper, his substantial moustache dripping with froth from his shandy. 'Your teenager's got a new boyfriend, you don't approve, the wife's indifferent, the girl does whatever she wants, including hanging round on street corners with undesirables and possibly even breaking the law on a recreational basis.' He sipped his shandy and went on. 'You never know where she is or what she's going to do next, you confronted her about something last night and she told you were to go in terms you'd only expect to hear in a whore-house.'

'Here's to God's love!' said Bill and knocked back his second drink.

'It's very common these days.'

To change the subject Bill asked: 'How's your little girl?' and immediately wished he hadn't.

'Eve? Delightful. Not so little either. She's only a few months younger than your Nicola.' He listed her positive features rather like a holiday brochure: 'Horse riding, swimming, ballet, reading – she adores reading, studying, Girl Guides. She's a great girl. Young lady, I should say.'

'Pompous, self-satisfied bastard,' thought Bill.

That night as he sat reading the paper before going to work, Inspector Swann reflected on the nature of the family.

53

He looked up from the article he was skimming, gazed into the decorative bevelled mirror on the living room wall and thought how fortunate he was to have such a beautiful, well-balanced daughter.

As he did so the young woman in question entered the room and skipped happily over to him. 'Night Dad,' she said and kissed him on the cheek.

'Night luv,' he muttered, giving little indication of the glow within.

'You are coming Saturday, aren't you?' She was referring to the monthly gymkhana which the old policeman never missed.

'I've arranged for all the criminals in Bolton to take a day off *in lieu*,' he grinned. 'Course I'll be there.'

She still wore her old brushed-cotton panda pyjamas and looked for all the world like an angel.

'Go to bed now, Evey,' instructed the proud patriarch.

'Go' bless,' she said and skipped out of the room.

Inspector Swann lowered his paper and stared at nothing. 'If anything should ever happen to that girl,' he thought and thunder-clouds gathered in his mind.

He spent the next twenty minutes meditating on the causes of war and then went to work.

A Close Encounter.

On his way to work Inspector Swann was obliged to cut across the Sunnymeadow estate.

On his car radio his friend Bill Carson's programme was being broadcast live.

'This is your programme and God is listening to you – right now . . .'

Swann was only half listening. The radio crackled quietly.

A little Irish voice sang: 'Father, I live on the Sunnymeadow estate and I tell you no word of a lie – God the Father visited us tonight. There was a hell of loud noise outside the house and I swear the good Lord himself descended from a giant helicopter. Stark bollock naked . . .'

'Radio Bolton Cares . . .'

Swann snorted disconsolately and turned the thing off.

'What is it about this place?' he wondered. Then he nodded. 'It's the Gaelic influence.'

In his unmarked Sierra 1.8 LX the Inspector felt immune from the dangers associated with the estate by the local constabulary. Police cars were occasionally stoned by youths and it wasn't usual for an officer to answer a call in the area unaccompanied. Especially not at night.

It was therefore something of a dilemma for the dutiful officer when he came upon a disturbance en route to the station.

His usual path was blocked by several youths who were standing in the middle of the road looking up at the night sky, seemingly oblivious to the protocol of road safety.

The old copper sounded his horn with the impatience of a guardian of proper order.

He was about to get out of his vehicle and remonstrate with the illegal assembly when he noticed Nicola Carson standing slightly to one side of the gathering. She might recognise him and tip off the rest of the rabble as to his identity.

He sighed heavily, feeling sorry for his friend Bill. Thank God his own daughter wasn't hanging about in this God-forsaken place.

The policeman thought his best course of action

was to remain in the vehicle, turn around and take evasive action. He was about to execute his plan when there was a blinding flash of light and a fantastic roar of what sounded like jet engines.

'Jesus! ... what the hell ... ' Inspector Swann found himself shouting over the noise. 'This is a serious Breach of the Peace,' he thought.

But upon leaving his vehicle he found the situation was hopeless. The light was directly above him and the noise was literally deafening. For a split second, as he stood there shielding his eyes, he thought it was some kind of IRA attack and his heart missed a beat. But that was just stupid.

The youths were shouting and dancing about, apparently excited by the racket. Perhaps it was some kind of *ad hoc* rock concert. But in the middle of Sunnymeadow? At this time of night? In the middle of the week?

The Inspector found himself comparing the experience with that scene from *Close Encounters of the Third Kind*, when suddenly the noise and the lights stopped and there was dead silence. Which was every bit as disorientating as the previous din.

For a few seconds no one said a word and then everyone spoke at once.

Overcome with curiosity, Inspector Swann decided to investigate. He felt an arm tug his sleeve.

'Hullo,' said Nicola.

'Oh, Nicola ... ' Swann remembered his vulnerability and eyed her accomplices anxiously.

'Oo's 'e?' asked one of them.

'Friend of my Dad's,' she said and the Inspector breathed more easily.

'What's going on here?' he demanded and regretted sounding like a policeman.

There was quite a commotion in the middle of the road.

'That big helicopter came down again,' Nicola informed him. 'Then someone else got out.'

'There's a guy lying in the road over there ... ' pointed out an offensive looking youth. ''E fell out the first time it came down.'

Inspector Swann pushed his way into the small crowd that had gathered.

'Eh, it's Inspector Swann,' laughed a youthful voice.

His moustache *was* fairly distinctive.

'What's going on?' he demanded, trying not to sound intimidated. Or intimidating, which was more difficult.

A nipper piped up: 'The other guy's run off – down towards the church ...'

The throng parted and the policeman's eyes fell on a figure lying face up on the tarmac. He was stark – bollock – naked.

The nipper practically shouted: 'The other guy was only wearing a blanket!'

With a little too much help from the crowd of youths, Inspector Swann had loaded the unconscious, ill-clad individual onto the back seat of his car and was speeding towards the police station.

He should probably have called an ambulance to the scene, but he had felt a little uneasy at the developing situation and thought it impolitic to leave a crowd of youths exposed to the dangers of nudity in the middle of the night.

The offending male was breathing normally, so the present course of action seemed entirely justified. Although he didn't doubt there would be more than a raised eyebrow at the station.

About a mile down the road the man stirred with a moan and sat up.

'Hello?'

Inspector Swann ignored the remark.

'Where are we going?'

'All in good time, sir.'

The old copper felt rather uncomfortable. He wasn't in the habit of talking to naked men.

'Have you seen my friend? I think we've been separated.'

'I'd rather you didn't talk until we get to the station, please sir.'

The naked man fell silent and Inspector Swann switched on the radio. Bill Carson was still on the air.

'. . . God's listening to you – right now.'

The man in the back smiled.

'Father,' a voice crackled, 'I'm worried about my daughter. She's shacked up with a couple of friends at the top of Sunnymeadow and I think one of them's some kind of nut.'

Inspector Swann tutted and switched to a music channel. Was nobody's daughter safe?

'I was listening to that' said the passenger.

Swann shuddered and turned the music up.

A few minutes later the car pulled up on the forecourt of the police station.

Inspector Swann turned round to say: 'Now then sir, I'd like you to accompany me into the station with the minimum of fuss. And you might like to position this cap in the appropriate place, so as to avoid committing any further offence,' when he realised there was no one there.

The naked man had disappeared.

Mary's attack of delirium tremens had long since passed but the poor woman was now caught up in another, equally profound dementia.

Having won a place in her beloved's bed, the afflicted woman would sooner have died than give it up.

So, every night she would act out a scene of lunacy, quite unsurpassed in Bolton's theatrical history. Just enough to convince Father Vernon that she needed consolation, but not quite enough to make him phone the doctor. This achieved, she would slip into his bed and feign sleep.

The main inconvenience was that the alcoholic housekeeper had desperate need of regular poisonous refreshment and a variety of ruses had to be employed to supply the craving.

The insomniac clergyman understood that Mary needed to drink in the night, but didn't suspect that the madness was a ploy. Indeed he didn't pay much attention to the situation, beyond what he saw as essentially a pastoral duty.

And so Mary would pretend to sleep-walk around the house and take a crafty slug from a concealed bottle, or a sip from a camouflaged supply. (Father Vernon had once or twice washed his hair in Tia Maria). And on occasion when they tired of the charade, Father Vernon would pretend to fall asleep and allow her to swig from a hip flask she kept under the pillow.

To Father Vernon the stricken woman's nocturnal presence was a bulwark against sleep, which he dreaded worse than death. And on nights when the priest began to drift off, he was woken almost immediately by Mary, who had what would otherwise be an intolerable habit of rolling over in her sleep and sprawling all over him.

One night Mary was snoring away in a rare outbreak of genuine unconsciousness and Father Vernon was trying not to replay too many of the day's earlier scenes, when there came a gentle knocking on the front door.

The priest looked at the alarm clock. It was two a.m. There it was again.

Father Vernon frowned, quietly got out of bed, straightened his twisted pyjamas and went to answer the door.

'Sorry, Dad . . . Please can I come in?'

Father Vernon's heart leapt. 'Er, of course.'

Nicola was shivering. 'I've taken something, Dad. I'm scared.'

'Drugs?'

Nicola nodded. They were standing in the hallway.

'Shall I call an ambulance?'

Nicola smiled at his over-reaction. 'Noo. I just need . . . company. I don't wanna go home like this.' She shrugged and looked at the young priest imploringly.

'I'll put the kettle on,' he said and plodded into the kitchen.

Ten minutes later they were sipping tea by the fire, chatting away happily.

For once Father Vernon talked at length, telling the eager youngster about his friendship with Canon Drinkwater, how he had appeared in his dream the night he died and how he had been afraid of going to sleep ever since. Of course he omitted the more incriminating details of the dream, but even after this partial admission the young priest felt as if a great weight had been lifted from his shoulders.

Nicola seemed elated, possibly the effect of the drugs, supposed Father Vernon. 'Look why don't you have a little sleep on the sofa and if you start to moan, I'll wake you up,' she suggested.

The poor exhausted man thought there was probably a good reason why he shouldn't, but was too tired to think of it. So he agreed. Though he thought it better to remain seated in the arm-chair.

He gave the young woman a blanket and insisted that she too try to rest and she agreed.

Before you could say 'guide dog for the blind', Nicola said: 'Close your eyes', stripped down to her underwear, and slipped under the patchwork cover which had been made for charity by the Sisters of St Vincent.

Father Vernon couldn't help but notice out of the corner of his eye that the young woman's underwear was, in fact, the same as he had imagined in his dream that fateful night.

He settled uneasily into the over-stuffed chair and found that he was unable to fully close his eyes. Rather he kept his gaze fixed, through the tiniest of slits, on the fidgeting figure on the sofa. He had the uncomfortable feeling that something dreadful was going to happen. What would Mary say if she came down and found them arranged thus?

At first Nicola kept looking over at the supposedly sleeping priest, presumably to see if he'd dropped off. The arm-chair was in the corner and from his position Father Vernon could see her every move.

After about twenty minutes she suddenly kicked off the blanket and began wandering casually around the room in her underwear, examining china artefacts and looking uninterestedly at the old books on the shelf, only occasionally glancing over at the priest, to check he was safely comatose.

Far from it.

Whereas a few months, even weeks ago, even in his dreams Father Vernon would have been horrified to find himself relishing the sight of a semi-clad young woman roaming around his living room, he now felt himself rejoice without even a twinge of guilt. He almost moaned out loud with pleasure and wanted to settle further down in the chair. Instead he sat rigid, not daring to move.

Nicola seemed to be enjoying her near-nudity and kept stretching and yawning luxuriously. Then she began to press herself against various cold surfaces about the room, gasping as she did so and casting furtive glances at Father Vernon, who was ready to ascend straight to heaven.

After a few moments she became interested in a paperweight on the desk. She looked over at the sleeping imposter for a moment and then slid the item down her pants and squeezed it between her legs as if she were testing it for something. Apparently satisfied she hopped back to the sofa and dived under the patch-work blanket.

In the next few moments her underwear appeared on the floor by the sofa and Nicola seemed to curl up into a ball and fidget about, making odd little noises.

At that moment an incredible thought occurred to the priest. It seemed obvious, yet it hadn't struck him before. He had fallen in profound, earthly love with this wily young woman. He pictured them together and liked what he saw.

Then it occurred to him that he was wilfully committing a terrible sin. He remembered his old friend's words: 'The question is: does one act on one's feelings?'

The poor priest's head had begun to spin when he heard Nicola moan aloud. He half-opened his eyes in fright, only to shut them immediately back to voyeur's slits. The blanket had fallen to the ground and Nicola was lying there openly masturbating. At least Father

Vernon assumed she was masturbating. Of course with his limited experience he couldn't be sure.

The paperweight was nowhere to be seen.

There was nothing he could do now except close his eyes completely or watch the awesome spectacle. And close his eyes he could not.

At that moment he noticed with utmost horror that the living room door was slowly opening. In her state of grace, Nicola was utterly oblivious. 'Oh my God – Mary!' thought the helpless priest.

And sure enough, in she sleep-walked.

Father Vernon suddenly and miraculously gained the ability to close his eyes.

A few moments later he felt a hand shaking him gently.

'Father Vernon,' someone whispered. 'Dad, wake up . . .'

The priest opened his eyes.

Nicola was standing there in her bra and pants shaking him gently. Mary was nowhere to be seen.

'Did I fall asleep?' he asked, somewhat relieved.

'Dad, I think there's something strange happening in the church,' she hissed.

'What? How do you know?'

'I saw lights on and I think I heard someone playing the organ.'

The grandfather clock said three-thirty.

'The church is locked.'

'We'd better go and check.'

'No, you stay here.'

She hopped back under the cover and pulled it up to her neck shivering. 'See you in a min.'

Not bothering with socks, Father Vernon donned a pair of brogues that were in the vicinity of the door, grabbed his torch and made for the church. It was a bit chilly outside and the gravel path crunched beneath his feet.

He heard a plane flying somewhere in the distance. And just for a moment, he too thought he heard music. It wasn't the church organ though. It was trumpets and trombones.

A Decent Night's Sleep.

In the church, the fuse had blown and the whole place was dark.

And quiet.

Father Vernon flashed the torch round everywhere and found nothing. He was about to give up when he thought he heard a sound in the old storeroom next to the sacristy.

He pushed the old door open and poked his head round. Someone had tidied the place up. In fact the old clutter had almost completely disappeared.

Then he noticed something he hadn't seen before. In the far wall, behind where the old trestle tables had been stored, there was a door.

A slight shiver ran down his spine and he looked over his shoulder, shining the torch back into the church, cursing the fuse box. Something wanted him to try the handle of the door. And it wasn't his common sense.

He crept across the storeroom and tried the handle. To the priest's dismay the door opened onto a dark, dirty wooden staircase down which he felt he had to go.

He seemed to descend a lot of stairs and it was some time before he reached the bottom.

'Ah, dear boy, it's you.'

Several dim though tasteful lights came on at the same time.

'You had us worried for a moment.'

'Hiya, Dad.'

Father Vernon now knew he was dreaming again, but never-the-less the sight of Nicola, lying naked on a Roman couch, having her body massaged by the Archangel Gabriel sickened him with jealousy.

'A real angel, isn't she?' commented the old man.

'Can't you keep your hands to yourself!' said Father Vernon vehemently, surprised to be angry with his old friend who was now dead and transformed into an Archangel. Not *an* Archangel – *the* Archangel. 'I'm sorry,' he stammered.

'Perfectly understandable under the circumstances,' reasoned the old man. 'Run along, child,' he said to Nicola and she was gone.

'Are you really the Archangel or are you my old friend Canon Drinkwater?'

The question seemed a little out of place.

The old man sighed deeply and looked at the young priest with love in his eyes. 'You've always been special to me,' he boomed. 'I simply couldn't abandon you.'

Father Vernon felt very sad suddenly. 'Aren't you happier now?' he asked.

The Archangel smiled knowingly. 'Ah, dear boy, paradise is lost. There are no angels in Heaven. They're all about you. You are all angels, but you don't know it . . .'

Father Vernon wasn't really listening. He wasn't in the mood for theology. 'Where is He?' he asked.

The Archangel shrugged. 'Oh, He's wandering around somewhere. We were separated.'

The young priest was disappointed. He loved God and wanted to fly away with him. He wondered if He was wandering around naked and once again felt a little jealously.

The Archangel became serious. 'Dear boy, you must

65

listen. Time's running out. This is your last chance. God is angry because humanity has turned away from Him. I persuaded him to try again. Just once.'

For some reason Father Vernon was still angry. 'This is just a bloody dream!' he shouted.

The old man tutted. 'Dear boy. I thought you were a man of faith.'

Father Vernon felt rather peculiar. He wanted to wake up.

Gabriel went on: 'You can hardly blame Him. He won't send family, not after last time. 'You can't just abandon them,' I said. 'Surely anyone can do it, given the proper means. Give them one last chance,' I said. So he agreed.' The Archangel raised his eyebrows, almost apologetically. 'I chose the place, to be near you. He chose the girl. If it fails, all will be lost. You'll be abandoned.'

The Roman couch was rocking and it occurred to Father Vernon that someone was trying to wake him up again. Thank goodness. 'Come to me when you wake up,' said Gabriel, 'I need you to help me.'

'Wake up, Dad . . .'

It was Nicola and he was sitting in the over-stuffed arm chair, covered in sweat.

'Dad . . . You're moaning and mumbling. I think you're having a nightmare.'

Father Vernon was very relieved to see Nicola standing there. She was still semi-clad. 'Wrap yourself up, you'll catch cold,' he said affectionately.

'You should lie on the sofa now,' she said, taking his arm.

Poor Father Vernon was in a state of near delirium. Something was hurting his eyes, terribly.

Before he knew where he was, he found himself lying on the sofa. He could hardly stop himself dropping off to sleep, he was so comfortable and warm and Nicola was lying by his side with her arms and

66

legs wrapped around him, to make him feel safe and secure. And . . . the pain in his eyes . . .

It was sunlight.

It was morning.

Father Vernon opened his eyes and shut them again because the light was so bright.

He was upstairs in bed.

And it was Mary who was wrapped around him.

The covers were down by their feet and Mary's nighty had ridden right up around her neck. His dressing gown and pyjamas were in total disarray and his dignity was seriously at risk.

Father Vernon leapt out of bed with a feeling of acute anxiety.

Mary was beginning to stir on the bed, so the young priest spared her feelings and bolted from the room. He stood on the landing in a daze. He felt sure there was something to do. Something he'd forgotten. He hadn't woken up properly yet and felt an urge to check out the living room.

The room was exactly as he'd left it the night before.

Everything was in its place.

Nicola was nowhere to be seen.

What the hell was going on?

He'd had a decent night's sleep, that's what.

As Good a Time as Any.

Theresa decided she would tell Michelle and Jo her secret.

Breakfast seemed as good a time as any.

They were all in bed eating Rice Crispies, Coke, *Walker's* Salt and Vinegar crisps and *Life-style* chocolate digestives. Betty had a Beef and Onion Pot Noodle. Little Lisa had a bit of everything, but mostly it was smeared on her face and spread all over the bed-clothes.

As usual at breakfast they were arguing over the limited supply of clothes.

Suddenly there was a loud burst of music from Betty's ghetto-blaster over the other side of the room, which drowned out the din for a moment and then subsided.

'What was that?' asked Jo.

Michelle shrugged.

Betty smiled. She had an idea what was coming.

'Betty, you know that Jo Bloggs top of yours ... ' Michelle was interrupted by another burst of music. When it stopped she frowned irritably. 'What the fuck's that?'

'It's 'er!' laughed Betty, pointing at Theresa.

'Pack it in, Theresa!' Michelle assumed Theresa was switching the plug on and off to annoy her.

Theresa said: 'Watch.' Then held up both her hands and clapped them. At the same moment the music started. And when she clapped again the din stopped, immediately.

Michelle frowned.

''Ow d'you do that?' asked Jo.

Little Lisa looked as astonished as usual.

'Clever ain't she, Tiny?' grinned Betty. Lisa beamed and clapped her own hands.

Next, Theresa pointed at the T.V. and it switched itself on. Then she pointed at the light, which fol-lowed suit. And then at the stereo again. And with a wave of the hand she signalled for the volume to change on both the T.V. and the stereo at the same time. And when she clapped everything went quiet.

Dead quiet.

Michelle and Jo exchanged a glance.

Jo said: 'She's got the remote control under the covers.'

Michelle said: 'The light switch ain't got a remote control!'

'Neither's the stereo,' added Betty.

For her finale, Theresa pointed at the door with one hand and gently coaxed it with the other. Even to Betty's amazement the door handle slowly turned and the door began to open, an inch at a time.

There was something spooky about this and they all stared at the slowing moving object, dumbstruck. No one dared to breathe and Michelle and Jo snuggled closer together under the covers.

Betty pulled Lisa onto her knee.

To heighten the effect the door creaked, theatrically, until it was fully agape. Then suddenly it slammed shut with a loud bang causing Michelle, Jo and Betty to shriek aloud.

Michelle and Jo then burst out laughing.

'Careful!' scolded, Betty.

'What the 'ell's goin' on?' demanded Michelle. 'Jo nearly shit herself!'

'No I didn't!' laughed Jo, indignantly, nudging Michelle in the ribs.

'She's got magic powers,' explained Betty, blithely.

'I can see that,' tutted Michelle as though it was the most obvious thing in the world. 'Where'd she get 'em?'

Betty shrugged.

Michelle and Jo looked at Theresa. She admitted she didn't know either with her shoulders.

Then Michelle grinned. 'What else can you do?'

Suddenly Theresa was behind her. 'Boo!' she said and Michelle jumped so suddenly and screamed so violently that Theresa nearly jumped out of her own skin. Poor little Lisa's head nearly came off, she turned round so quick.

'Fuckin' 'ell! Don't do that!' panted Michelle.

Then Theresa was back in her place.

Michelle and Jo were clutching hold of each other, terrified.

'Stop it now,' breathed Jo.

'Yeah,' agreed Michelle.

Theresa looked at Betty.

'What now?' asked the young mother.

Theresa was nonchalant. 'Fuck knows.' She looked at Michelle and Jo. 'You won't tell anyone will you?'

They shook their heads in unison.

Trick and Treat.

That morning they went up to the moors to try a few things out.

They didn't talk on the way up. Theresa carried Lisa and Betty walked alongside. Michelle and Jo lagged behind, Jo's arm through Michelle's. It was as if they were in a trance. They gripped each other but avoided one another's eye.

When they got to the top of the hill Theresa turned to Michelle and said: 'Shall I show you something good?'

Michelle wasn't sure. 'Depends.'

Theresa tutted. 'Betty's done it, ain't you?'

Betty nodded.

'What?'

Next thing Michelle realised that her feet weren't touching the ground. She was hanging in the air about a foot above the grass.

But rather than say anything, she just looked at Jo with a kind of resigned impatience and then back at Theresa, as if to say, 'Yeah – and?'

Michelle's habitual lack of vivacious expression didn't spring from any particular cool — she wasn't tough; she simply had a natural dislike of having her feathers ruffled. Hanging there, motionless — against the background of the sky — her corkscrew perm floating on the breeze, an almost serene expression on her face, she looked the image of a being from a painting by Raphael.

For a moment no-one said a word and all that could be heard was the rustling of the hillside, until Michelle's burnished cheeks suddenly cracked into a grin and the spell was broken.

'You dick 'ead — put me down!' she laughed.

Jo laughed too. 'You don't 'alf look daft,' she hooted.

And Michelle was returned to Earth. 'Give Jo a go at that,' she giggled when she'd regained most of her senses.

Jo ran off shouting 'No way!'

But in the end she did. And as the morning progressed they got more daring until all kinds of levitation had been tried and they'd laughed and squealed themselves to jelly.

Then they collapsed in a heap and gazed up at the sky in wonder.

'I always knew you were fuckin' weird!' said Michelle.

'Cheers,' said Theresa and they drifted into a waking dream.

Little Lisa toddled around happy as pie.

After an opaque period of time Michelle sat up, a slight frown on her otherwise porcelain brow.

'Theresa?' she said, in such a way as to make Betty dimly aware of something impending.

Theresa's 'Umm,' might have come from another planet.

'Why don't you go out and have the time of your life?'

'She's already done that,' said Betty.

Michelle nodded, but didn't lie back down. There was definitely something on her mind. 'What about a palace to live in – or a big 'ouse?' she asked.

'Na,' said Theresa. 'Just wanna keep it quiet.'

'Yeah,' agreed Michelle, doubtfully.

'Don't go and blab it, now,' warned Theresa, still on her back.

'Course not.'

Jo sat up now. And Betty didn't like the look on her face. 'What's it worth?' Jo asked, lightly.

'What's what worth?' asked Theresa, knowing full well.

'How you gunna keep us quiet?'

Theresa remained prostrate. Then, after a suitable pause, she spoke quietly. 'Well – if you both keep your mouths shut I won't do anything like ... ' Suddenly she was inches from Jo's ear ... 'This!' she shouted.

Jo screamed and Michelle jumped.

And Theresa was lying back in her former cloud-watching position. 'Tell you what,' she was smiling as she spoke, 'being as you're blackmailing me . . .'

Jo blushed at this.

'Maybe I'll treat you to something – to keep you quiet.'

Michelle and Jo smiled, cautiously, in case it was some kind of trick.

'You name it,' Theresa said. 'One special treat. But you've got to decide in the next ten seconds.'

The two girls looked at each other.

A slight frown darkened Betty's brow.

Michelle's was the more practical imagination. 'How about a day out in town, shopping. And we can all buy anything we like, all day. without paying.'

Jo said: 'Yeah.'

Theresa nodded. 'Alright.'

Michelle and Jo were made up. There was only one more detail to work out. 'Can Penny come?' asked Michelle, coyly.

'Go on then.' Theresa sat up and turned to Betty. 'You go too Betty.'

'Fuck off.'

'Get some stuff for Lisa,' said Theresa, touching her arm. 'She needs it.'

'Yeah, an' you could get a couple of new shell suits!' Michelle sneered.

Betty said: 'I've already got two.'

Get it Out.

It was much like all the other adolescent parties on the estate.

Someone's parents had gone away leaving the house in the care of their delinquent children. Nothing was supplied by the hosts, except the venue and a poxy stereo.

The lads were in the kitchen drinking cider and beer. A couple of older lads were rolling a joint and a few of the others were hanging round hoping to get a drag.

The girls were either dancing half-heartedly in the living room to music the lads hated, snogging guys their own age who looked two to three years younger, or standing in huddles drinking Thunderbird wine and purposefully looking bored.

It was all very dull. Except in the front bedroom upstairs.

Surrounded by three, thin, semi-clad young men,

73

who looked too young to be of any real interest, Nicola Carson was sitting in a wicker bath chair, naked but for her jewellery.

There were three or four girls grouped around the door trying to look uninterested.

'You ain't touching me till you take all your clothes off!' Nicola insisted.

The tense threesome crouched around the bath chair were desperate to get their hands on the young woman but equally keen to keep their clothes on.

'Get off!' she snarled as one of them tried to touch her. And pushed him over with her foot.

One or two youths poked their heads around the door to see what was going on, as rumour spread around the party, but only these three had the necessary courage to risk getting involved with the beautiful but volatile girl.

'God, you lot are so boring!' she had said several times in a loud voice to the scandalized spectators clustered near the door. But still it was only she daring to expose herself.

'Just get 'em off,' she insisted to the bravest of the bedraggled threesome who was down to his boxer shorts and socks.

Next thing Penny was standing there, his jacket draped casually over his shoulder, looking older, smarter and bigger than anyone.

Nicola smiled, said: 'Hiya, Penny' and walked casually over to him, not showing the slightest shame or inhibition. Or, to be more precise, making a show of not showing the slightest shame or inhibition. Then she kissed him on the lips and he kissed her back. But that was his only movement.

As Nicola sat on the bed the three younger guys hurriedly gathered up their clothes and scuttled out of the room. The disparagers disappeared and the door was closed. The couple were alone.

'You look smart,' said Nicola.

74

And he did.

'I've been shopping,' he said.

The party was almost over by now and Penny and Nicola had made themselves at home in what must have been the parents' bed.

He was sitting up, staring straight ahead and she was lying next to him, her head propped up on her hand.

'Shit party,' she sneered, puffing on a *B & H*.

'Give us a drag.'

She passed him the cigarette.

He flicked the ash onto the carpet by the bed. 'Got a top stereo an' all,' he boasted. 'Personal, with five band graphics.'

'Did you get me anything?' she joked.

'Did I fuck.'

'How much were your trainers?'

'Seventy quid.'

'What!' Her eyes boggled.

'*Fila*.' he explained.

'How much were the jeans?'

Penny looked around the room, as if he were checking to see no one was listening. 'Thirty-nine.'

'You're kiddin'!'

Penny shook his head, blowing smoke from in between his two front teeth and then trying a smoke ring.

'And you got a jacket?'

'An' a top. Two tops.'

'Fuck me!'

'What again?'

''Ow much was the personal?'

'Sixty-nine, ninety five.'

'You're a liar!'

'Straight up!' He flushed lightly. 'I swear!'

'I know that,' said Nicola who was a little bit

miffed. If he'd spent all that why hadn't he bought her anything. She knew she wasn't his girlfriend, but she wasn't a fucking slag.

Something wasn't quite right and they both knew it.

They were silent for a while. Penny felt bad because, even now he wasn't telling Nicola the whole story.

He passed her the cigarette back and ash fell on the sheet. Nicola ignored it. She felt miserable now and wasn't sure why.

'Why didn't you get me anything?'

He sighed. Embarrassed. 'I would have, but . . .'

'. . . you think I'm a old slag!'

'No!'

Clearly an explanation was in order. She wasn't his girlfriend, but he liked her. She was sexy. Different from the other girls. Mad. But a good laugh. She didn't get heavy. Well, apart from now. Definitely not girlfriend material, though.

'You're not a slag.'

'Thanks.' Sarcasm.

He wasn't used to talking. Especially not after sex. 'Look. I didn't really buy any of it.'

'You nicked it?'

'No.'

'What, you magicked it out of thin air?'

He wished he'd never opened his mouth. He hesitated for a moment. 'Michelle bought it all.'

He blushed. They never talked about Michelle.

They never talked about anything really. They just flirted and had sex. Nicola looked at him. She'd had enough of sulking. Probably reminded her too much of her mother. She climbed on top of him and shoved him further down the bed, pinning him spread-eagled beneath her.

Penny breathed a sigh of relief, but Nicola was too curious to let the matter drop.

'So! You have ze girlfriend who buyz ze expenzive prezenz, huh?' she inquired in her best German accent. 'You expect me to belive zat, pig dog! Tell me ze truth, svine!' She showed him a big mouthful of spit and threatened him with it.

Penny was enjoying himself again. 'OK, I'll tell you,' he begged. He thought, 'fuck it, tell her the truth,' pushed her off and rolled on his side to face her. 'Alright,' he said. 'But you won't believe it.'

'Try me,' suggested Nicola, getting into a comfortable position. She could sense something interesting was coming.

'Well, you know Theresa Green?'

'Yeah?'

He rolled onto his back. 'You won't believe me.'

She grabbed him and threatened him with spittle once more.

He closed his eyes. 'Well. She's stayin' at Betty's and she's got magic powers . . . an' to keep Michelle quiet she said you can go out and buy anything you want and you won't have to pay . . . an' Michelle said "can I take Penny" and Theresa said yes an' . . . ' He looked at Nicola. 'Do you believe me?'

Nicola let the spit fall. He tried to dodge but it went in his ear.

'Urh! You . . .'

Nicola was on top of him tickling him viciously. 'You liar!'

'It's true!' he laughed and submitted to the onslaught.

Shopping Trip.

They had to admit the shopping trip had been a great success.

The flat was resplendent, bulging with accessories and full of noise and laughter. The fashion parade, positively fancy dress at times, lasted a full day and a half.

And that was only Jo and Michelle's clothes.

Oh, and little Lisa who had enough outfits to last until age five, not to mention toys.

Betty hadn't 'bought' anything. Well, one pair of trainers, *Reebok* of course, but not too flash. And some knickers and socks. And a year's supply of tampons. But compared to Michelle and Jo's haul, this was nothing.

Michelle had insisted on a scientific approach. She knew only too well that it was the chance of a life-time.

The night before she and Jo had sat down with Penny and written out a list of literally everything they wanted. The list was carefully divided into differ-ent categories and then sub-divided so that nothing could be missed.

Clothes:

Tops.
Shoes.
Knickers.
Trousers.
Socks.
Special underwear.
Jeans

Trainers.
Coats.
Skirts.
Tights.
Silk boxer shorts (for Penny).
Jackets.
Stockings.

Cosmetics:

Eyes. (15 items)
Skin. (33 items)
Hair. (26 items)
Nails. (17 items)
Perfume. Play it by nose.

Electrical:

Etc.

Each new heading was greeted with shrieks of excitement. Most especially the more expensive categories, such as 'Electrical' and 'Musical' (meaning amplifiers, speakers, mixing desks, drum machines, lasers – anything a hard-up teenage band could put to use).

Other categories included: Tapes/CDs; Videos (Esp. *Grease* and *Dirty Dancing*); Posters/etc (visit *Athena*); Sweets/Drinks (at Betty's insistence Theresa had forbidden alcohol); Books (Madonna's *Sex*) and; Furniture (Esp. rugs, new sofa – if there's room!).

When they were finished with the list, or at least when they were too tired to carry on, Michelle declared that it would be necessary to get some transport and delegated Penny to organise something.

The next morning Penny turned up in a battered *Ford Escort* van borrowed from his brother and Michelle wasn't satisfied.

'You'll not even get my make-up in that thing!' she exclaimed. Perfectly serious.

Eventually they persuaded Penny's brother to lend them his licence so they could hire a small removal van (you had to be over age twenty-five). Then they set off into Bolton town centre.

Michelle went first.

Not her usual style. But these were special circumstances.

Very special.

She went straight for the most expensive shop in town and targeted the most expensive item. Which was a silk blouse she thought was "'*angin*'". It wasn't even her size.

Then she walked up to the counter and gave it to the assistant, who smiled kindly while she slipped it gently into a very smart plastic carrier, which Michelle preferred to the blouse itself.

Michelle waited, trembling.

'Thank you,' said the woman beaming at her.

'Thank *you*' said Michelle. And meant it.

As she was about to leave the shop, the assistant called after her.

Michelle's heart stopped.

'Er . . . excuse me!'

Michelle turned to face the music.

'I almost forgot. There's a special offer with that blouse.' The assistant pointed to some silk scarves. 'Any scarf on that rack, free.'

Michelle knew a bargain when she saw one. 'Thanks,' she smiled sweetly. And took the brightest one she could find.

The others were waiting on the corner.

Michelle came running down the road holding the sleek carrier aloft like a trophy.

It was as if Bolton Wanderers had won the F.A. Cup, the Premier League and the European Cup all in one go.

Betty looked like she was facing relegation.

'Better than *American Express*,' screamed Michelle.

The day had been all too short.

At about eleven a.m. they decided to split up to save time. It was a difficult decision to make because showing off each new acquisition to squeals of merriment had been a source of fantastic excitement. But, Michelle decided, they could always show things off later. Which is why the fashion show lasted nearly thirty six hours.

Betty was appalled. She considered the outfits for Lisa a maternal duty. And socks, knickers and tampons were always in short supply. But essentially she was a simple soul.

At first, under intense peer group pressure, before the posse split up for the day, she had been tempted to buy a new shell suit. But on reflection she decided that her existing two were adequate. She did see a top she liked, but somehow she didn't want to be part of the whole thing.

In the end she settled for the new pair of trainers (Her old ones were nearly worn out).

The group had agreed to meet outside *WH Smith* every hour to unload what they had into the van. But they were so over-laden by this time that the interval was reduced to half an hour.

Betty was finished by eleven-thirty and spent the rest of the day drinking tea and eating ice-cream with Lisa. But by four-thirty even Michelle and Jo were flagging.

But Penny wasn't. He was inspired by a plan.

After a couple of hours looking at stereos, clothes and tapes, he decided it was time to check out the really important business.

The music shop.

He poked around the cramped basement for a

while, but Bolton's supply of hi-tech equipment wasn't really the biz. What the band needed was top gear. Not good gear. *Top* gear. The very best. And for that they would need to go to Manchester.

They only just had time.

He put it this way: 'Look. D'you want to see me on the *Chart Show*, or what?' and they were on their way.

It was five o'clock by the time they got to Manchester and Betty moaned all the way.

Michelle was intolerant: 'Shu' up Betty. It's important.'

'I don't think Theresa wants us to go to Manchester,' she said, feebly.

It would have taken a small-scale nuclear attack to stop them.

Penny cleared out *Johnny Roadhouse* in about twenty minutes. 'Enough for three albums and a small world tour in there,' he grinned on the way back. 'Top gear.'

Michelle's cheeks were glowing. She was satisfied with the day's work.

Betty, Jo and Lisa were fast asleep.

Michelle put her hand on Penny's thigh as they drove along. He nearly crashed. Twice.

God Bless Us.

Father Vernon was preparing his vestments in the sacristy for Wednesday's early-morning Mass when he remembered the second part of his dream.

Until now he had only recalled his revelations concerning Nicola Carson.

Not that he had pondered the significance of his realisation that he was in love with the girl – this had been shut firmly out. Rather he had dwelt upon the feelings surrounding her imagined presence in the Presbytery at night. Namely warmth and cosiness. And there was a deep feeling, like serenity, which he couldn't properly identify while fully conscious. Which was, of course, earthly love.

But now Father Vernon remembered his crazy torch-lit trip into the church. How real it seemed. Funny how little details of ordinary life take on special significance in dreams. Like that bit where someone had tidied the store room.

The store room.

The young priest stopped what he was doing and glanced over his shoulder at the sacristy door, as though he was expecting someone to walk through it.

He experienced a peculiar prickly sensation on the back of his neck and shuddered. For some reason he wondered if someone had cleaned out the clutter from the little room next door. And for another reason he hoped they hadn't.

He still had a good few minutes before the Mass, so he decided to have a peep.

He stood outside the storeroom hesitating, like a person about to jump off a diving board. 'Don't be daft,' he thought and hesitated some more.

Then he opened the door and saw the old familiar chaos. There were stacks of metal chairs and boxes of prayer books, old bags of useless jumble every-where and, yes, the trestle tables were in their usual place, leaning up against the back wall.

Everything was as it should be. Of course.

He stood looking at the trestle tables.

He couldn't be certain, but he thought it was an outside wall they were propped up against.

He tried to imagine the exterior of the building,

round the back, by the car park. But he really wasn't sure.

The tables were very long. And he had to admit that it was just possible that there was a door behind them.

He somehow felt that he needed to know one way or the other, so he clambered over a couple of boxes, tutting and brushing dust marks off his trousers. Then he tried to peer behind the table at the end and couldn't. So he pulled the thing to one side.

There *was* a door.

He stood back against the wall.

Shocked.

He looked around the storeroom. The sun was shining through the little window and streaming on to a box of old jumble. Everything was still. And calm. And ordinary. There were particles of dust glittering in the sunlight and all was quiet.

Father Vernon tried the door.

It was locked.

And there was no key.

He breathed a sigh of relief and left the storeroom with a little too much haste.

Five minutes later he had put it out of his mind and was entering the church to say Mass.

He genuflected in front of the altar, turned to face his congregation and realised that no one was there. No one, that is, except Mary who was kneeling in the first pew.

Wednesday morning Mass was usually only attended by a few devotees but attendance had never fallen this low before.

After a moment's hesitation the surprised priest continued.

And it turned out quite beautifully.

There was a certain elegance to Mass which the

young priest enjoyed. The ceremony of the whole thing. And perhaps because it was just the two of them, Father Vernon excelled himself.

There was something deeply personal about the service today. When he declared 'Let us pray', it was as if he were saying 'let us, you and I pray together' which seemed intimate and warm. When he said 'pray for us sinners now', he was referring specifically to himself and Mary, addressing God directly.

The turning of the pages, the opening of the hands, the offering of prayer. This morning all these simple rituals came alive. Father Vernon felt as if he meant every word he said. The Latin phrases, the often repeated verses all seemed rich in truth and meaning. Directly relevant. Poignant even. A rare occurrence in the routine of ecclesiastic life.

Mary noticed it especially. For the first fifteen minutes of the ceremony she was nearly moved to tears and was keenly disappointed when she was overcome by nausea and had to rush to the Presbytery to force down some vodka while she stood over the toilet.

When Mary left, Father Vernon again hesitated. He heard the door close and the bang echo round the building for a moment or two. He was approaching the Eucharist, the most ritualised and dramatic part of the mass.

For the first time in his life he said Mass alone. It was just him and God.

The verse was pronounced beautifully, the movements were performed with grace and the reverence was utmost. The empty church echoed with holy eloquence and, as an extra touch, Father Vernon took a moment out to burn some incense.

The young priest was utterly lost in the ritual. He was filled with an energy he hadn't felt for months and was uplifted to the highest degree. He offered up the wine and was almost convinced of the transubstantiation.

His whole life seemed to pass before his eyes. All his joys. All his sorrows.

He held up the host in his two hands, raised it high and gave real praise to God. At that moment a brilliant shaft of sunlight shone through the window in the roof and poured down on the poor worshipful man.

His hands aloft and his eyes closed, Father Vernon felt the warmth of the sun touch him and it melted his heart. He felt a tremendous surge of emotion. All the suffering of the past weeks, all the anxiety seemed to well up in his chest.

He had to let it out.

There was an incredible bellowing cry. A long and terrible moan as the wretched young priest gave vent to his desolate soul.

And just for a moment, as the ejaculation reached the peak of its crescendo, the young man beheld a light. There was something inside him trying to get out. The tiniest glimmer of hope.

It took a full twenty seconds for the noise to die down.

The enraptured man stood stock still, until complete silence had returned, before opening his eyes and lowering the well blessed host to the alter.

It was then that he noticed Mary had returned to her place in the first pew.

There were tears in the poor woman's eyes and she was marvelling at the priest's appearance. What energy! What passion! It was as if God were shining a light directly upon him.

The band were going to be ecstatic.

Well, half of them were. The other half were going to be sacked.

Penny would have sacked Gibby too, but as Tony pointed out, it was his brother's workshop where they rehearsed.

''E can't do fuck all,' Penny objected.

'Oh aye, so we're gunna pump up the volume in your bedroom!'

Tony and Penny were the backbone of the group.

They were sat in the now dis-used workshop, on a mountain of of hi-tech equipment, resting from the last thirty-six hours of non-stop "jammin". They had yet to tell any of the others the news.

They had all the equipment they had dreamt of for years and consequently no further need of a drummer (Paul), or Willy and his poxy Yamaha Synth. The two had only been tolerated in the first place because of their equipment. Oh, and Willy had been quite handy for dope which he got off his brother.

'What are we gunna do for blow?' Tony moaned.

'Sack it.'

'Oh aye, we're gunna have great rehearsals without a spliff!'

'If we 'ave to,' said Penny doubtfully.

For the past thirty-six hours they had survived on a tiny piece of Moroccan Penny had sponged off Willy.

Tony eyed him, malevolently and then smiled, brandishing his match-box. 'It's just as well I got some in, then, init?' he laughed.

Penny grinned. 'You ... ' He grabbed the match-box, looked inside, saw a healthy lump and handed it back to Tony. 'Skin up, then!'

They were 'on a mission' now, as Tony put it. As far as they were concerned it was only a matter of time before they would appear on the *Chart Show*. The fact that neither of them could write a decent tune was beside the point. They had the equipment, they could both rap, all they had to do was programme the synth's, sequencers and drum machines and that would be that.

'What's 'e gunna do then?' asked Penny.

'Who?'

'Gibby.'

'He can programme the drum machine.'

'No way!' Penny was appalled. 'He can't even shake his dick in time.'

''Ow d'you know?'

Penny wasn't amused. 'We should just sack 'im.'

'We could get 'im to sack the others.'

'No, you're doin' that.'

'Bollocks.'

'I got all the equipment.'

Tony pouted. 'Let 'em stay, then.'

Penny tutted. 'You'll never get anywhere, you.'

'You sack 'em. Willy's my mate.'

Penny knew he'd have to do it. He would have sacked Tony too, but he wrote all the raps. 'What 'm gunna tell 'em?'

'Tell 'em you only wanted 'em in the first place because we couldn't afford a drum machine or a synth.'

Penny grinned. 'Why don't I just say: Look. Guys. Fuck off.'

Tony shrugged. 'Give 'em some of the gear and say fuck off.'

'Fuck off.'

Tony was licking the spliff he'd built and putting the finishing touches.

He brushed loose tobacco from his extremely baggy

jeans, sat up and said: 'D'you wanna hear a master plan?'

Penny tried not to look too interested, though he knew it was going to be a good one.

'Right . . . you don't say anything to 'em . . . you tell Nicola Carson we're sackin' 'em . . . tell 'er not to mention it to anyone . . . she goes and blabs it . . . Paul and Willy get to hear about it, right . . . you know what them two are like . . . they say 'Fuck them' an' sack us.'

Penny was impressed. 'What about Gibby?'

Tony shrugged. 'Tell 'im he can programme the drum machine. It's worth it.'

It was decided.

'I'll phone Nicola in a bit,' said Penny as Tony passed him the joint.

They were getting ready for another thirty-six hours.

'Where'd you get this blow, anyway?' asked Penny.

'Where'd you get the gear?' grinned Tony.

They both said it together and laughed: 'Magiiic . . .'

A couple of hours later Michelle and Jo turned up.

It took a minute for Penny and Tony to notice them over the din.

When they did, they turned off the equipment and came over. Tony was the only person to speak for a few moments.

'Fuckin' wicked!' he laughed and began to build another spliff.

Despite protocol, Penny, Michelle and Jo found themselves grinning. Penny was hopping from one foot to the other and Michelle almost looked friendly. Penny even nodded at Jo.

Then Michelle took the unprecedented step of starting the conversation. 'What do you reckon?' she asked tapping one of the speakers with her foot.

Penny nodded a little more, grinning widely. 'Top one,' he said.

After a moment Michelle abandoned herself to a second comment. She almost laughed. 'And we're just getting started!'

Games.

Betty and Theresa were alone with little Lisa.

'You're mad,' said Betty who was struggling with the infant.

'Hum?'

'There's hardly enough room to change 'er nappy, now!' she moaned.

'What?' Theresa was playing a computer game on the giant screen.

'Look at it.'

'At what?'

'All this stuff.'

'Better, innit.'

Betty tutted and plonked Lisa into her push-chair. 'Forget it.'

'Forget what?'

Betty ignored her and began to struggle through the door with the push-chair. She would normally have asked Theresa for a hand. Theresa saw what was going on, turned the TV off and and came to her aid.

'Where you going?'

'Out.'

'Out where?'

'Nowhere.'

Theresa followed her onto the landing and

watched her as she attempted to bump the push-chair down the stairs single-handed. She tutted and bent down to help.

When they reached the bottom Theresa asked: 'Are you fed up with us?'

With a sour look, Betty said: 'No, I just think you're mad.'

'Why?'

'What happens when the police get on to us?'

'What you on about?'

Betty bent down and pressed her daughter's nose. 'We'll be locked up, won't we, Tiny?'

The little girl seemed to like the idea.

'No one'll know,' said Theresa.

'Oh aye. They emptied the whole bloody shop in Manchester!'

'It'll work itself out,' assured Theresa. She couldn't expect Betty to take it, just like that. 'Trust me.'

Betty tried to knock her down with a look. She nearly succeeded. 'You're just playing games!' she sneered. She quoted Theresa in a stupid voice: 'You've got to decide in the next ten seconds . . . ' Betty was outside the front door now.

Theresa tried to maintain a smile.

'An' you know what really pisses me off?'

Theresa's smile froze. She braced herself. 'Wha'?'

'You're so fuckin' selfish.'

Theresa was shocked. 'I sorted them out, didn't I?'

'Buying friends,' spat Betty.

Theresa stood staring at her friend. If she hadn't been so proud she would have burst into tears. 'What am I supposed to do!'

Betty began fiddling with the buggy, tucking things in and fussing over tiny adjustments. 'Well, 'ow about doin' somethin' for people who really need it?'

It was obvious.

Betty softened. The argument was over. 'I'm going to the shops. D'you wanna come?'

Theresa shook her head.

'See you later.'

Betty smiled shyly and mother and daughter were gone.

Theresa stomped back up the stairs and sat in front of the video game.

She hated Betty sometimes. Especially when she won arguments.

But the thing was, she needed Betty to love her to feel alright about herself. Which was why she couldn't concentrate on the video game.

What the fuck was she supposed to do?

What's so selfish about buying stuff for people? She wasn't buying friends. Betty was jealous, that's all.

Then she huffed out loud.

Maybe she should try and make things better. Sort other people out.

But did that mean she just wanted to buy everyone's friendship?

Fuck knows.

Do something though.

She turned on the T.V., picked up the video game and tried to loose herself.

'Playing games,' she thought vaguely. 'I'll fuckin' show 'er!'

Local Commotion.

There was almost a commotion outside the shops.

A whole gang of elderly people had gathered in the sunshine and were talking, or rather shouting to each other, about the news of the last few days.

As Betty approached a little Irish voice sang above the rest: 'I tell you no word of a lie . . . and this is the God's honest truth . . . there was an almighty racket outside the house and the good Lord himself descended on a rope ladder.'

There was a great communal guffaw and an old woman shouted: 'Next you'll be telling us Jesus Christ was there carryin' a pick axe!'

The old man wasn't to be put off: 'He was stark bloody naked, so he was.'

The was a great chorus of 'Oooo' and much merriment at this remark.

Betty ignored the commotion, parked up the pram and went into the newsagent/post office/off licence/ video library/grocery store combined. The woman in front of her hastily stuffed a bottle of vodka into her shopping bag and stepped back on to Betty's toe.

'Oo! I'm terribly sorry,' she slurred and then exclaimed: 'Oh hello Kirsty, I didn't recognise you.' Mary was the only person to use Betty's real name. 'I haven't seen you in ages. You been away? How's the little baby?'

'She's outside,' winced Betty who was nearly gassed by the fumes Mary was breathing. 'She's not really a baby anymore.'

'Arh. Bless her,' gushed Mary. 'Eh. You seen this?' she added, proffering her copy of the *Bolton Evening News*.

'I haven't had a chance yet.' Betty was holding up the queue.

'Oh . . . ' Poor Mary wasn't doing a very good job of masking her condition. 'I'll go and have a fuss. See you outside.' She did her best not to stagger as she left.

Betty sighed, bought a copy of the local paper and a copy of the *Manchester Evening News*.

When she got outside Mary was only one of a crowd of people gathered round the push-chair sighing, laughing and cooing over her little child. One or two people looked up and smiled and Betty felt a glow of pride.

She took the opportunity to glance at the papers. The headline in the *Bolton Evening News* read: SUNNYMEADOW UFO: GAY ALIEN SCARE. Betty tutted and skimmed the article for something interesting. There wasn't anything. The article concluded that some drunken millionaire playboy had got lost in his helicopter, fallen out, naked, knocked himself unconscious, got himself arrested and then escaped from police custody.

There was a picture of a grim looking policeman with a bushy moustache, who the man had apparently assaulted to make his escape. Underneath the photo were the words: 'Inspector Swann: Homosexual nuisance', which might have given some people the wrong impression.

Betty scanned the rest of the paper. There was an article on the shop-lifting epidemic which she read carefully and nothing much else.

Then she turned to the *Manchester Evening News*. There was no mention of UFOs, or gay aliens. No mention of Bolton at all, in fact. Betty turned the pages, examining the headings, then stopped with a start at page seven. She read a small article entitled: 'End of the Roadhouse?'

Manchester's famous music store *Johnny Roadhouse* faces closure following a bizarre £20,000 robbery.

The owner of the shop who was present at the time of the theft said: 'I shut up the shop at five-thirty and suddenly realised that there was almost nothing left. We employ all the latest security on the premises and have absolutely no idea where it went. Or even when.'

The problem is the shop's insurance company is reluctant to pay out. A representative of the company explained: 'It's not usual to make payment in respect of a claim when there has been no break-in, or any kind of hold-up.'

Police are currently investigating the possibility of a gang of criminal hypnotists.

Betty looked guiltily up from the paper. Some of her daughter's admirers caught her eye and smiled kindly. Betty folded up the papers and put them in the litter bin.

'Ooh. I'd 'ave 'ad them!' exclaimed an old woman.

Mary walked back up the hill with Betty, holding on to the pushchair for support. The poor housekeeper was exhausted by the time they parted company.

'I'll tell Father Vernon I've seen you. I'm sure he'll be pleased to know you're all right,' she panted and Betty was gone.

Mary sat on the wall for a moment to recover what little composure she could before setting off back to the church, which was about ninety seconds walk away.

She watched Betty push the pram up the hill towards their crowded flat and thought 'I'm glad I'm not young today. Gord knows what harm you might came to!' Then she espied a figure a little way off, down the road to the Presbytery.

And blow me down if he wasn't stark naked!

Mary gasped and looked up and down the road for independent witnesses.

And when she looked again, the figure was gone.

She sighed. There was never anyone around when you needed to verify your sanity. And being as there was no one around, she cracked open her new bottle of vodka and took a good hard slug.

And she nearly pulled a muscle in her neck on her way to the Presbytery by looking round and about. But in vain. Maybe she was going mad.

Then, as she lurched up the path towards the house, she noticed something unusual on the path. She bent down and picked it up. 'What's that doing there?' she wondered foggily. 'Must be one of Father Vernon's.'

It was an old door key.

Coq Up.

Bill Carson swung his Rover into the car park of the golf club inadvertently parking it next to Donald Swann's Sierra.

The off-duty Inspector had just finished a round and was crunching his way over the shale to his car, pulling his golf trolley behind him.

Both men were embarrassed to see one another.

The copper was flustered because he'd lied to his friend about his availability for golf that afternoon and Bill blushed at the rejection.

'Oh, hullo, Bill,' blustered the liar. 'They let me off duty at the last minute. I tried to phone you . . . '

'Ah, don't worry. I only came down for a drink,' lied Bill who would now have to wait until the copper drove off before getting his clubs out. 'I saw you in the paper.'

Swann puffed, modestly, relieved at the change of subject.

'What was all that about?'

The Inspector opened his car boot and began to pack his equipment away. 'A typical evening on the Sunnymeadow estate.'

'Weren't you assaulted?'

'Well. All in the line of duty.'

'It said in the paper someone pulled a knife on you.'

'Yes. Yes, quite serious, really.' He was showing off now. 'Homosexual nuisance.'

The old copper seemed uncomfortable on the subject. Bill persisted.

'Stark naked, eh?'

'Not a stitch.'

'Where was the weapon concealed?' asked Bill, genuinely puzzled.

The Inspector gave an amused little snort. And then realised it was a serious question. 'Er? That's a bloody good question,' he said, trying not to blush.

There had been no weapon, of course. The whole story had been invented to cover up the man's disappearance. None of the newspapers had picked up on this inconsistency, however. Bloody good job.

'You know what queers are,' was all Swann could think of.

Bill at last picked up on the man's discomfort and decided to drop the subject. 'Pompous, self-satisfied git,' he thought and wondered why he didn't get himself some decent friends.

'I'm surprised your daughter didn't tell you all about it.'

The Inspector's words hung around in the air for a few moments before hitting their mark.

'Er,' Bill already didn't want to hear what might be coming. 'Really? Why's that?' His voice sounded hurt

97

and pathetic. At that moment Bill Carson wanted Donald Swann to die slowly and painfully. While he watched.

'She was "hanging around" at the scene.' The insensitive old copper was sensitive enough not to add the words: 'with a crowd of undesirables'. But only because it might have given his vindictive game away. His integrity had been called into question, inadvertently, but surely. And this was his revenge.

'Oh, yes. Yes she did mention something.'

It was a lie and they both knew it. And it worked perfectly to bury the Inspector's more widely published deceit.

The rest of the conversation was like walking through a quagmire.

As soon as possible Inspector Swann's equipment was packed away and he was gone. He didn't even remove his golf shoes.

Bill Carson went straight to the bar and used the excuse to get plastered. 'Pompous, insensitive . . .'

Among the debris of the kitchen, Mary had cooked supper for once.

Coq au vin.

Short on *coq*, big on *vin*.

Father Vernon was impressed. In fact he was almost drunk.

'It's delicious, Mary,' he slurped with his mouth full.

Mary was relating the story about the naked man and the helicopter and how she herself had seen the man that very afternoon. Father Vernon was feeling sorry for her.

'I mean, I had a quick look about to see if there was anyone else there, or some youngster who might be shocked. I mean, well any'ow. When I looked back he'd gone.'

'I did see something in the paper. But I didn't pay much attention,' remarked the priest, removing a long grey hair from his mouth.

'I met several people at the shops who swear it's the second coming of the Lord!'

'Well precisely', said Father Vernon.

Mary went on to relate Betty's story. She explained how there were five of them living in the apartment.

'Five? In Betty's little flat?' inquired the priest, his social conscience tingling.

'Well, it's more like four and a half, really. Bless the little angel.'

'Hum, yes.'

'They seem to be managing alright. I mean, they don't know any better these days.'

The priest ignored Mary's philosophical proposition. 'How is the little angel?' he asked.

Mary gushed for a minute or two about little Lisa. Then she got up to fetch her bag. 'I almost forgot,' she said. 'I found this on the front path, just after our naturist got away.' She held up the old door key.

Father Vernon spat his *coq* back *au vin* and stared at her.

Host of Ideas.

The bed was positively kaleidoscopic.

It was an explosion of primary colours and paisley patterns. There were sheets by Next, Laura Ashley pillow cases and God knows where they found the duvet cover. The entire flat was a hotch-potch of pop designs and memorabilia, but nothing could rival the

bed for sheer psychedelia. Especially with the girls'
new pyjamas and Lisa's colourful romper suit.

'Y'need bloody sun-glasses to go to bed now,' Betty
quipped, with little humour.

'You can borrow my *Reybans*, if you want,' replied
Jo.

This morning the atmosphere was a little more
serious (it was more like lunch-time really). Theresa
had announced the night before that she wanted to
talk about something in the morning and Michelle
and Jo were expecting another treat.

'Right then,' said Theresa.

'Shhh!' hissed Michelle, even though no one was
making a noise. 'Go on, Theresa.'

Betty did her best to look indignant.

Theresa prepared to speak. But she was a little
unsure how to begin.

'Betty get hold of Lisa,' Michelle instructed. 'Sorry
Theresa . . .'

Betty was astounded. 'She ain't doin' nothing!'

'She's gunna start making a noise.'

Even little Lisa looked hurt.

Theresa intervened. 'Leave her. She's alright there.'

To confirm her good intentions the little one-year-
old put her hands demurely in her lap and sat dead
still, as if waiting for business to commence.

'Arrh, look at 'er . . .'

'Shu' up, Jo,' tutted Michelle. 'Go on Theresa.'

Theresa looked at Betty who just glared.

'Right then. We've got to decide what to do.'

'What about?' asked Jo.

Theresa was a little worried. 'We're gunna do
something about the world,' she said and checked
Betty's reaction out of the corner of her eye. There
was no scowl, at least.

'What – you mean, like, change it?' said Jo.

Theresa did her best not to nod. It sounded stupid.

100

Michelle and Jo sat and blinked at her.

'What d'you wanna do that for?' asked Jo when she'd thought about it.

Michelle glared at her. 'She wants to do something with 'er life!' she snapped. 'Shu' up and listen.'

'No,' Theresa objected. ' We should all decide. Together. I mean . . . It's not just me, is it?'

'It's you who's got magic powers,' observed Jo.

'Yeah, but we can all do something,' said Michelle. 'Can't we, Theresa?' She nudged Jo in the ribs.

Betty raised her eyes to heaven.

'Well I think we should blow the 'ole thing up and start again,' said Jo when she'd thought about it.

Michelle couldn't believe it and said so with her face.

Theresa was diplomatic. 'I think we've got to start with what we've got, really.'

'OK . . . 'Ow about,' Jo was thinking aloud. 'If we took everyone off to another planet and started again.'

'For fuck's sake, be serious!' moaned Michelle.

'I am!' said Jo and tutted. 'You suggest something then.'

'Alright,' Michelle pouted. And just sat there looking embarrassed. Then sounding a little flustered she said: 'What did Jesus do?'

Jo acted out more surprise than she felt. 'She ain't Jesus!'

Michelle's eyes rolled. 'I know that!' she spluttered. 'It's similar that's all.'

'Yeah except me mum's not a virgin,' joked Theresa, easing the tension slightly.

'Yeah, an' you ain't got a beard,' giggled Jo.

'Not on me face anyway,' added Theresa.

It went on: 'You could handle twelve apostles though, couldn't you,' Michelle grinned.

Betty never said a word.

When they'd told a few jokes that weren't funny

101

and simmered down a bit, Michelle said: 'The point is she can do miracles, right? Like Jesus.'

'Yeah, so?'

'So do some.'

'Why?'

'I don't fuckin' know! Why did 'e do 'em?'

Jo shrugged. 'So people would listen.'

'What to?'

' 'Is bloody stories.'

'Yeah. Tellin' people to be'ave an' that.'

When Jo and Michelle had finished there were some moments of silence.

To be honest no one really had a clue.

'Everyone's got to be nice to each other,' suggested Jo, tentatively.

'That's fine coming from you,' said Betty.

'Fuck off!'

'What d'you reckon, Betty?' said Theresa eyeing her.

'I reckon you've got something planned,' she answered, shrewdly. And she was right.

'Come on, tell us what you think, Betty,' Jo insisted.

Theresa nodded to back her up and Betty knew she'd asked for it.

'Well,' she began, her tone more serious. 'Whatever it is, you should do it round here. Give people a break.'

They all nodded.

'It's right,' said Theresa. 'Look.' She produced a large box from under the bed and waved her hand around above it, as if performing a magic trick.

'What's in there?' asked Jo.

'Open it and see.'

Michelle and Jo exchanged a glance.

Jo opened the box and produced a small white disc of unleavened bread. 'What's this?' she asked.

'Looks like a host,' observed Michelle.

'Suck it and see,' said Theresa, 'I got them off Father Vernon.' Then she broke the bread and passed it round.

'Communion?' sneered Betty. 'We're getting religious, are we?'

'Are we fuck,' said Theresa. 'I just stole the idea.'

Whole Host.

Half an hour later the girls were in a state of ecstasy.

Jo and Betty were dancing on the sofa with little Lisa and laughing merrily away. Michelle and Theresa were discussing the meaning of life in the kitchen area.

Next minute the roles had reversed. Jo and Betty were discussing intimate details of their lives and Michelle and Theresa were dancing round the living area with the delighted toddler.

Then they were all dancing together.

'What's in those things?' shouted Michelle over the din. 'It's drugs init?'

'Unholy communion,' laughed Betty.

'No,' insisted Theresa. 'It's nothing. Just a trick to make people love each other.'

'So long as it don't make people too horny!' laughed Michelle, conservatively.

'It works anyway,' laughed Jo and gave Theresa a heart-felt hug.

Even Betty was grinning from ear to ear.

The music was banging away.

'We should have big parties,' said Jo.

'And Penny can do the music,' added Michelle.

'An' you can do miracles,' shouted Jo.

'Tell people to be'ave,' grinned Michelle.

'Na, just do miracles, an' give 'em one of these,' said Jo.

Suddenly Betty turned down the music. 'There's someone at the door.'

Michelle said: 'I'll go, it'll be Penny' and ran down to the front door. A few moments later she was back. 'Look 'oo it is,' she said.

And in walked Nicola Carson.

As soon as she entered the room the party stopped. Betty turned off the music and the four-and-a-half girls stared at her as if she were the devil himself.

'What you doin' 'ere?' demanded Betty.

'I just came to see if you were alright,' lied Nicola. 'I didn't know it was party time.'

'It's not,' said Betty.

A quick glance around the well decked out apartment was enough to convince Nicola that something was going on. Penny's story had niggled her and she had decided the only way to get to the truth was to investigate further.

'Bloody 'ell, Theresa, what have you done to your hair?' said Nicola, only managing to drop one of her h's.

'Erm . . . nothing.'

'So I see,' said Nicola. 'Suits you.'

Nicola was one of those young women who didn't normally bother with female company and although Michelle had no idea that she had been with Penny, she instinctively felt threatened.

There was an awkward silence.

Nicola tutted. 'What is this? Some sort of private club? Nice telly, Betty. Where d'you get the money for that?' She wasn't expecting a reply. She walked about the flat openly nosing her way round.

The others looked at one another, nervously.

104

'What do you want?' asked Michelle, finally.

Nicola put her premeditated plan into action. 'I was just wondering,' she said casually, suddenly sounding friendly. 'Well, you know my pony ... I never ride it and ... ' she saw the shot hit its mark. Michelle and Jo's eyes lit up. 'It's a waste. And ... does anyone want to ride it in this Saturday's gymkhana?'

Neither Jo nor Michelle had ever ridden a horse in their lives, but they adored Nicola's dapple-grey mare to the point of delirium. It had been the only reason they'd tolerated the girl when they first met her.

They both looked at Theresa, who looked at Betty, who looked at her one-year-old, whose eyes were wide as planets. Then the toddler beamed and a ray of sun peeped out from behind a cloud.

Ten minutes later Nicola had been allotted the sofa and given one of Theresa's special hosts.

And half an hour after that, they were all cavorting round the flat again.

Nicola looked at Theresa. 'What's going on? You're up to something.'

'We're gunna make things better round 'ere,' said Theresa.

'We're gunna have huge parties,' declared Michelle, ecstatically.

'And Theresa's gunna be a star,' grinned Jo.

They all laughed.

Except Betty, who glared away at Theresa, unnoticed.

But Theresa couldn't help herself. She loved the attention.

And Betty loved Theresa, so what could she do?

Prune.

At the monthly gymkhana the ruddy faced Inspector Swann felt as out of place as he looked.

He sported the standard barbour coat, green wellies and Prince of Wales check flat cap, but he felt like a prune in the pickled walnuts.

Perhaps it was his stiff gait. Or maybe it was the way he walked with his hands clasped behind his back as if pounding some marshy beat. Surely it wasn't the broken veins on his cheeks. Though it could have been the pallid skin they adorned.

His ruddy red face just didn't look as healthy and weathered as those of the country folk he emulated and despised. There was a permanent defensive scowl in evidence, which stood out from the benign expressions of ease that surrounded him.

The rank of Inspector was an embarrassment to Donald Swann. He thought it the equivalent of a Sergeant in the army. He was still required to perform menial tasks and his privileges were few. But with years of thrift he had achieved a reasonable standard of living.

He owned a small house in a respectable district (as opposed to a bigger one in an undesirable area) and had made sure that his daughter received the very best in life – including membership of the best stables in Lancashire, which it so happened, backed onto the Sunnymeadow estate. A detail which amazed Inspector Swann as much as it infuriated his delicate sensibilities.

But social grace is social grace, so despite a strange foreboding the old copper enrolled his deepest pride and joy in the East Lancashire riding club and once a month received his reward for a lifetime of dutiful toil. Eve was the best in the club and regularly cleaned up the awards at the gymkhana, making the frustrated patriach very happy.

This Saturday she had already won the dressage and was about to set a very good time over the fences. Her father was brimming with pride and Eve was confident astride her very own horse.

'Now there's an attractive filly,' declared a haughty man standing next to the Inspector.

Donald Swann grew two inches and inflated like a mating wood pigeon. He almost cooed. 'Yes. Yes, she's from the border county.'

The tannoy echoed as Evey thundered past the railings where the two men were standing among the crowd and the father felt a fresh surge of excitement.

'Bloody fine hind legs, what?' The stranger nudged him in the ribs.

The old copper was getting annoyed at the intrusion but felt obliged to reply. 'She likes the soft ground,' he said trying to sound like the owner.

The stranger's eyes bulged. 'I bet she does,' he drawled. 'Horse isn't bad, either, what?' he laughed giving him another nudge in the ribs.

Inspector Swann did a classic double take.

He was thunderstruck.

This upper class swine had been referring to his daughter. 'Very attractive filly ... likes the soft ground ... fine hind legs!'

Given the correct emergency powers the old copper would have arrested the bastard there and then and fed him to the lions. How dare he refer to ... to Evey ... his daughter in that lurid tone. What right? ...

His head was still spinning when he realised the round was complete and the crowd were clapping. The time was announced over the tannoy and the stranger was gone. Evey had disappeared into the contestant's enclosure.

The final contestant had started her round and the suddenly aged policeman stared into space while blood and thunder sounded in his ears.

His own daughter. The man must have been in his forties.

He sighed and his dark meditations were momentarily interrupted by some girlish shouting. The contestant seemed to have some supporters. Very rowdy by the sound of them, too. He tried to see where the unprecedented disturbance was coming from but the young women were out of sight in the crowd.

He squinted at the rider — she did look rather common, not dressed up at all in the right clothes, riding a dapple-grey mare. Looked like the Carson's filly.

The young woman was certainly setting a good time. He strained to hear the tannoy. A better time. Damn it.

The horse thundered past and the Inspector could have sworn the girl shouted 'Come on you bastard!' to the horse as she jumped the fence. But surely not. Not at the East Lancs gymkhana.

There were screams of glee from her supporters as the round ended in a better time than Evey's and the old copper was miffed. As he made his way to the contestants' enclosure he hoped that his little girl wouldn't be too disappointed. *'Little girl?'* he thought and snorted disconsolately. Perhaps he would buy her a new pair of jodhpurs on the way home. But not the tight fitting variety.

He saw or rather heard a couple of young women dashing across to the other end of the field, presumably to congratulate the winner and noted that they too were clad in the same colourful sports clothes and trainers he knew so well from work.

'Bloody undesirables!' he thought.

It took a few minutes to push his way through to

the stables and when he arrived he couldn't find Evey anywhere. For a moment he genuinely thought that she must have been abducted by the swine and was about to launch himself on to some kind of offensive, when he caught sight of her in the paddock.

He stopped dead in his tracks.

She was talking to the trouble causers who were gathered colourfully around, patting the horse and laughing. And smoking cigarettes.

He just had time to see that Evey wasn't smoking before he was upon them.

As soon as she saw him Eve came running up with a beaming smile and threw her arms around him. 'There you are, daddy!'

He was so flustered that he was speechless. In his mind his daughter had been raped and robbed, then molested by undesirables and yet here she was as bright and breezy as an early summer's day.

'It's a miracle, daddy! Jo's never ridden a horse before . . . she borrowed Nicola's . . . and she still won hands down! Isn't it fantastic?'

The old copper looked up from his daze and Nicola Carson was standing there.

'Hello again,' she said politely.

'Eh . . . hello Nicola,' he managed.

He might have known.

'This is Jo, Daddy,' she had pulled him by the hand over to the other girls. 'This is Jo and this is Michelle.'

'Hullo,' blushed Jo.

Michelle blew some smoke and almost nodded.

Donald Swann's bottom lip quivered slightly but nothing came out of his mouth.

'It's so exciting,' his daughter continued, 'Michelle's invited me to a big party tonight. I can go, can't I?' she implored, tugging his arm affectionately without the slightest doubt that she would be allowed.

'Of course you can't go to the party,' he said simply, with no idea of the effect his words might have.

Eve froze.

She wasn't annoyed. She thought she must have misheard. 'I can't go?'

'Of course not,' repeated the surprised man. His word was never questioned. There had never been any need.

Eve looked at her father's face. And for the first time ever, a shadow of doubt darkened her brow. 'I could be home by eleven. You could pick me up.'

'Come on darling, I don't think we want to be hanging round here.' He said it in a loud voice, causing his beloved daughter to blush.

As they walked off Eve looked back over her shoulder at her new friends as they solemnly watched the retreat.

'I don't think you want to be going round with those type of girls,' stated the protector.

Eve didn't say a word. Nor did she speak all the way home. Other than to refuse the offer of a new pair of jodhpurs.

Behold a Man With a Measuring Line in His Hand.

Father Vernon and Mary now had something in common.

A highly developed inner blind-eye.

Mary could stand over the toilet in the mornings shaking like a condemned woman, force vodka down until she stopped vomiting and still ignore the fact of her alcoholism. Father Vernon could sit at his bureau for two days and ignore a feeling of dread that was choking him to the point of sickness, without even once analysing its cause.

He had relapsed into a state of befuddlement. He had not slept again for nights on end and even though he sat at his desk for days, there had been no change in the general clutter and the parish bbulletin was not yet complete.

The priest's life had narrowed itself down to the most niggardly routine. Visits were few and far between, only the dying were granted the pleasure of his company. The youth club was left to its own devices and on some nights the building remained closed entirely as the volunteer workers became disillusioned.

Mass was ill attended, the sacristy was a mess and the vestments needed dry cleaning.

Father Vernon had taken to meandering in the backwaters of the bible and reading the most weighty theological tracts, preferably written in Latin, but always abstract in the extreme. The poor priest was living in a fog of obscure literature. He would spend hours buried in chapters like the Book of Zachariah:

And I lifted my eyes and saw, and behold a man with a measuring line in his hand! Then I said, 'Where are you going?' And he said to me, 'To measure Jerusalem, to see what is its breadth and what is its length' And behold, the angel who talked with me came forward, and another angel came forward to meet him, and said to him 'Run, say to that young man, "Jerusalem shall be inhabited as villages without walls, because of the multitude of men and cattle in it. For I will be to her a wall of fire round about, says the LORD, and I will be the glory within her."'

The dismal man would set himself the task of learning

111

such passages off by heart. Then he would cross reference them to a Jesuit commentary or some other interpretation.

And the total effect of this labour was a dulling of the senses. Even the priest's libido had come under some kind of discipline and on the odd occasion when he drifted off into sleep he would visualise Abraham being tested; Joseph keeping the commandment in the time of his distress; Phineas receiving the covenant of the everlasting priesthood because he was deeply zealous; Caleb receiving an inheritance in the land because he testified in the assembly; and Joshua becoming a judge in Israel because he fulfilled the command. All these and other righteous trivia now inhabited the space once occupied by Sodom and Gomorrah – and of course, his love of the parish.

And just as Mary believed that she drank to live so Father Vernon believed, in as much as he thought about it, that his study was taking him closer to God.

And all this time the key Mary had found sat there on the bureau, driving the priest deeper into his useless meditations.

Then, one morning, he took hold of his copy of the *Catholic Herald*. His intention had been to read a tribute to a notable Jesuit scholar, but as he picked up the paper his attention was caught by a photograph on the front page.

Perhaps he was particularly sensitive that morning. Maybe he was the type of man who can only remain isolated from the world for so long. Perhaps it was just the photograph that set him off.

In the picture a painfully thin black child was walking off into the distance carrying a pail. The caption informed him that the child was looking in vain for food.

Something touched Father Vernon inside.

He looked up from the paper.

Here he was, buried in ... in words and verses ...
stories and psalms. Was he hiding? What was he
hiding from? He looked around the room. What a
disgraceful mess. There were people in the world who
had no food to eat. Children with nothing at all and
here he was sitting in a midden. Why was he living like
this? He was so tired. 'Not too tired to read all day,' he
scolded himself. Why was he tired? Why was he afraid
to sleep? Because he was afraid to dream. Why was he
afraid to dream? Because he was afraid ... of what?

He carefully pictured his last dream images. He
thought of the naked man that appeared as God. He
thought of Nicola Carson and very quickly skipped
to Gabriel ... no, Canon Drinkwater. His old friend.
He felt so guilty. Why? What am I guilty of? He
remembered the other obscene images of his dreams
and his waking thoughts. This was no excuse.

A ray of sunshine came through the window. The
priest remembered the Mass he had said all alone. It
seemed like months ago. He suddenly felt ashamed of
his seclusion. He took a deep breath that was a sigh
and closed his eyes.

He thought of the photograph. He thought of the
young people on the estate. His beloved youth club.
He remembered Mrs Kershaw and her arthritis. The
elderly people on the estate. And finally his thoughts
turned to Betty, the little baby and the rest of them in
their crowded apartment.

He suddenly wanted to stride out into the light
and face the world.

Within twenty minutes the bureau was tidy, the
office was in order, the window was flung open, the
books were shelved, the typewriter was fixed, the
bulletin was complete and Father Vernon was poised,
ready for action.

He grabbed the key off the shelf and strode from
the room.

Down.

Brandishing the key like a weapon, Father Vernon strode all the way to the store room in the church and then faltered.

'What's this key got to do with anything?' he thought. 'Surely I'm just wasting more time.'

He stopped outside the door to the small room. He thought about what he was doing again. A frown appeared on his brow and he wanted to turn back and go about his ordinary ecumenical duties.

'How ridiculous,' he tried to tell himself. But it didn't work. 'The key probably won't fit, anyhow.' But he knew he would have to try it.

He opened the door of the store room and his heart nearly stopped.

Someone had tidied it up.

Father Vernon experienced the most peculiar sensation. His first thought was that he was dreaming again, but he knew he wasn't. He was reminded of his dream, that was all. He tried hard to remember the details, but in vain.

He stared at the empty room. No jumble. No boxes of books. No trestle tables. The room was completely bare.

The door was still there though, where the trestle tables should have been.

He looked down at the key in his hand and swallowed.

His breathing was out.

'Don't be stupid,' he gulped. 'Mary's cleaned up.'

He tried to convince himself of the truth of this for a moment, but he knew it was nonsense.

He took a deep breath and stepped across the room.

He pushed the key into the lock.

It turned perfectly. There was an easy clunk and the lock gave way.

Father Vernon carefully pushed the door and it opened onto a dark descending staircase, as he had expected.

He groped round for a light switch but couldn't find one.

He stuck his head into the gap and listened, but heard nothing. There was a damp smell.

He relocked the door and practically ran back to the Presbytery for his torch.

'Mary?' he called.

Mary was upstairs in the toilet.

He stood near the top of the stairs and shouted in to her.

'Mary – you haven't tidied up the old store room in the church by any chance?'

There was a rasping cough from the toilet, like a choking sound.

'Mary?'

'No . . . No Father.' The was another coughing noise. 'There's just the old jumble in there and the trestle tables.'

'Are you alright, Mary?'

'I'll be fine in a minute or two.'

Father Vernon frowned, vaguely wondering what could be wrong with her and then made his way back to the church.

A few moments later he was poised at the top of the dark staircase, shining his torch down to see what was in the previously unknown basement.

He found himself hoping that it wasn't a Roman couch.

'I wouldn't be surprised if Nicola was down there,'

115

he thought to himself and laughed. 'No, cancel that, I'd die of shock!' He shuddered and began to descend the stairs.

It was very dark. He shone the torch round but couldn't make anything out. The steps were wooden and creaked under foot.

He suddenly became aroused, sexually.

Just for a moment.

But in that moment he remembered the details of his dream that had occurred in the cellar, which was, in fact, very much like it had appeared in his dream. Maybe he'd been down here before. When he first came to the church.

He knew he hadn't.

He remembered Nicola lying on the couch with Canon . . . Gabriel the angel.

Stupid dream.

What was he doing?

He laughed to himself to shake off a fear that was creeping up on him.

He reached the bottom of the stairs.

He shone the torch around.

Nothing much. Just cobwebs and an old work bench with a rusty old vice.

And in the middle of the room an old armchair.

He approached the armchair shining his torch on it.

The material looked red.

He stood stock still.

It was an old Roman couch.

He swallowed. With difficulty.

Then quickly shone the torch around the rest of the room with a shiver running down his spine. But there was nothing there.

Then he shone the torch back onto the couch and stood staring at it. At this moment Father Vernon was trying not to remember his dream because it was making his head spin.

116

Then, from the darkness a voice said, 'Dear boy, hello.'

Poor Father Vernon gasped out loud, span round and shone his torch into the face of his old friend Canon Drinkwater, dressed in his old black suit and dog collar.

Dead Glad to See You.

Father Vernon was still sobbing fifteen minutes later while the sad old Cannon held him to his chest with a grim expression and a soothing, fatherly tone.

All the sadness and distress of the previous weeks flooded onto the old man's lapel and Father Vernon cried like a baby. 'I thought you were dead,' he sobbed. 'I missed you terribly,' he wept. 'I've had dreams . . . I've hardly slept . . .'

And all the while the old man stroked his friend's hair.

'You were a father to me . . . ' stammered the young priest.

'And you a son to me,' replied the Canon.

And neither party dared to move. Father Vernon was afraid he would awaken from a dream and the old man felt as if his life depended on the embrace.

And indeed it did.

In the darkness Father Vernon told his old friend about the events of recent weeks, about his love for Nicola Carson and his worries over his housekeeper. And the old man listened without comment, making only the soothing sounds a man would hum to a child.

And when he was finished they remained still. The

young priest, half-kneeling by the sofa, was comforted by the salt of his tears as they ran into his mouth and soothed by involuntary sobs. The only light emanated from the torch where it had fallen to the ground.

He held on to the reality of the situation with all his might, repeatedly feeling the texture of the old man's jacket against his cheek, but not daring to look up. Until, gently, the old man stirred, taking the priest's reluctant head in his hands. 'I want you to look at me, my son.'

'I can't Father.'

'Please. Look into my eyes.'

Father Vernon slowly did as he was told, fresh tears blurring his vision.

'This will be our last confession,' said the old man with great sadness. 'I hope I have not upset you.'

Father Vernon shook his head.

'It's an unusually burdensome test of your faith, my son. But dreams are so hard to understand, I'm afraid I have to put you to the test in this way. I have to ask you to believe of today what is often difficult to believe of another age.'

Father Vernon sat next to his old friend on the Roman couch and listened as best he could while the old Canon spoke of God's Will and the ways of errant humanity. A favourite theme of his. But changed now. The reflections were sombre, lacking the usual sardonic tone and impious wit. He spoke of how, in despair, God had decided to abandon his precious creation in favour of a new and purer race. Of how humanity were to be tested one last time, on his old friend's request. Of how a young woman and her friends had been chosen. Of how his old friend would try to make the Deity believe again in the world if Father Vernon could help out with the girls. And how, if the experiment failed, humanity would be finally abandoned.

Words the priest had heard before in his dreams.

'Dear boy, you've no idea how I envy you your role,' the old man lamented after some minutes of sermonising. 'Yours is by far the most glorious task.'

Father Vernon was no longer looking his friend in the eye.

'I can see you are full of your old doubt,' observed the Canon. 'And I can offer you no other proof than the girls themselves. Look for them. Offer yourself to them. Give of your true self. That's all you can do.'

Father Vernon had stopped crying now. And had indeed fallen into doubt. But he didn't so much suspect his old friend's words, as his own sanity.

'Look at me before I go,' instructed the old man.

Father Vernon peered through the gloom.

'I am dead. Yet I am risen. Is that really a lot to ask a Christian to believe?' He smiled sadly. 'A brief and final visitation.'

The young man smiled. But couldn't speak, for fear of the sound of his own voice. Then he cried again.

'Dear boy, it's not the end of the world.' The old man smiled again. 'Merely the end of a long and dear friendship.'

Father Vernon sighed heavily and swallowed painfully. He was feeling nauseous and weak.

'You need believe no more than your own eyes,' said the old man. He could tell that the young priest's credulity was exhausted. 'Now go. And kiss me once before you do.'

Father Vernon returned to the Presbytery like a corpse.

'You look like you've seen a ghost!' exclaimed Mary as they passed upon the stair.

For once she was the least pale of the two.

He went into his room and collapsed on to the bed falling asleep almost immediately. Perhaps suffering from shock, perhaps from exhaustion, he remained prone for hours.

He awoke around tea time with tears in his eyes, clutching the old key to his breast.

Playing Host.

It was unlike any other party the estate had ever seen.

For one thing there were no fights. Because there was no alcohol. For another the boys danced as wickedly as the girls. It began at lunchtime when they returned from the gymkhana and looked set to carry on all weekend.

And at mid-afternoon Sunnymeadow party history was truly made as a small crowd of elderly people joined in the fun.

'I do like to shake the wicked hoof,' croaked Mrs Kershaw and (despite her arthritis) waggled like an old iron post.

During the afternoon the party burst its banks and flooded out onto the street below. It was early summer and the sun somehow managed to warm the estate to the point where normally conservative Lancastrians were tempted to remove one or two of their outer garments.

'God's shining his light on us!' declared an elderly reveller. 'If it carries on like this I might take me vest off before the end of June.'

It was quite the most beautiful afternoon anyone could remember.

The word spread, more merrymakers arrived and Theresa went about administering communion. As the effects took hold and the newcomers were touched by the ecstatic atmosphere, so they threw their arms up in the air and danced their socks off.

120

A long extension cable was produced from some-where and Penny and Tony set up their new equip-ment on the grass. They had programmed the sequenc-ers and made some tapes and only the vocals were added live. And when they had performed their entire repertoire (of four tunes) nine or ten times they played other people's records and tapes. They even let one or two others have a go on the synthesisers, including Willy and Paul who'd been sacked from the band.

So long as a good basic rhythm was kept up no one minded what was played and on the whole the sounds were good. Even the elderly folk thought so.

'I like a good old rock and roll,' someone croaked.

'"Tain't rock an' roll, grandad,' answered Penny, indignantly. 'It's rap.'

'Rap and roll, then. What's the difference?' The old man shrugged and continued to shake all over.

'So long as you've had your hip replacement who cares!' joked Mrs Kershaw to a good giggle all round.

Of course the neighbours complained. But Theresa gave them some of the unleavened bread and within an hour they opened up their houses to the party. Front and back doors were unlocked and people came and went as they pleased. The whole of the little crescent was drawn into the festivity.

And for once nothing was stolen.

'It's almost like it used to be when I was a girl,' observed one of the older celebrants.

'"Cept it isn't rainin'!' replied another.

The elderly contingent were the only ones not to participate in the communion. And the truth was they didn't need it. Their spirits were uplifted by the joy and kindness around them. The young people were so friendly and welcoming. There were no drunken scenes to spoil the jollification.

In short, they had a hell of a good time.

And by the time seven o'clock arrived the old folk

were sitting on the wall engaged in the most misty eyed nostalgia. They remembered their youthful summer evenings, the passion wagon to Blackpool, the circus at Belle Vue in Manchester. And then they recounted an A–Z of post-war Bolton cinemas, to laughter and deep sighs.

And then Mrs Kershaw suggested supper and they all went off together with heartfelt thanks and cheers.

Having said their goodbyes, Betty and Theresa sat watching Michelle and Jo dancing with Penny. Nicola Carson was with them and they were all smiling and cavorting like mad monkeys. Well, the others were. Michelle was more dignified.

'You see,' said Theresa, 'it's working already.'

Betty's face didn't budge 'It's a good party,' she said.

Theresa looked at her friend and reached out to smooth the hair behind her ear. 'I really like you, Betty.'

Betty tutted. 'Ge' off.' She blushed. And her face cracked into a grin. Then as if to change the subject she pointed down the road and said: 'Hey, look who it is.'

A tall thin man was making his way up the hill towards the Crescent.

'It's Father Vernon.'

The priest seemed pleased to see the party and smiled to the young people as he approached, many of whom he knew well.

When Nicola Carson saw him she went running over and threw her arms around his neck shouting 'Hiya Dad!' causing the young priest to blush, either with pleasure or embarrassment. He wasn't sure which. Nicola shoved her arm through his and came with him, over to Betty.

'Hello, Betty, er . . . Kirsty, sorry.'

122

'Betty'll do,' said Betty.

'Betty – I heard . . . I wondered . . .'

Betty cut him off and pointed at Theresa. 'That's your man,' she grinned.

Father Vernon looked at Theresa, noted her changed appearance and frowned slightly. He was very unsure of himself. 'Could I talk to you?'

'Do you want to come upstairs?' asked Theresa nodding at the door to Betty's block.

'Watch it, Dad, she's wicked,' Nicola laughed and everyone ignored her.

In reply Father Vernon nodded uncertainly.

'Do you mind, Nicola?' said Theresa. 'I think we need to be alone.'

Father Vernon blushed again and Nicola stomped off.

Theresa turned to Betty. 'Come up, you don't count.'

A Plague on You.

Inspector Swann lowered his newspaper and gazed into the bevelled mirror on his living room wall.

It wasn't long before he would be off to work.

Saturday night. Bound to be busy.

He looked at his watch and sighed.

Eve had been very quiet all evening and she had remained in her bedroom, presumably reading, or sewing.

The doting father desperately wanted to intrude on her privacy. He wanted her to come and read downstairs as she usually did on a night when she was at home.

123

He stood outside her door, but all he could hear was a record playing softly. He curled up his finger to knock but something stopped him.

He tiptoed back downstairs and tried to read the paper.

Surely she wasn't sulking.

Not over a party. Not that sort of party. What could she possibly want with those girls? They had absolutely nothing in common.

At that moment the old copper heard his beloved child go into the kitchen, presumably to make a cocoa for bed. He rose to join her but then thought better of it. She would come and kiss him goodnight and he'd smile warmly and promise to take her somewhere nice tomorrow afternoon.

But where? The country perhaps. No, surely that was a bit dull. It was obvious she was growing up and needed something more exciting. Maybe she could have a go on the assault course at the police academy, or visit the airport – he knew they could tour the control tower if his friend was on duty.

He composed himself in the chair, ready for her.

He heard the teaspoon ringing in the cup which meant she was nearly done.

And then he heard the kitchen door close.

He waited. Anxiously.

'I'm bloody nervous,' he reflected. And sighed, thinking how much he loved the girl.

Then she opened the door a little, said: 'Goodnight Dad,' through the gap and went upstairs.

And he didn't even see her face. Let alone get a kiss.

He stared at nothing and his cheek twitched slightly.

Woe betide any criminal tonight.

If he hadn't been a policeman of some repute you

might almost have thought Inspector Swann was looking for trouble.

He didn't drive through Sunnymeadow on his way to work that night, so much as stalk it in his unmarked Sierra.

'What this estate needs,' someone in his head was saying 'is war. I mean, do they want to stop crime or do they want society to be swallowed up whole. By a plague of locusts?'

He rather liked that idea. He pictured a dark cloud of locusts shutting out the sun and descending on Bolton. Especially those smug bastards at the top of the hill with a swimming pool in their garden. Garden? More like a bloody park.

One row of decent houses in the middle of a vast estate like this. Wouldn't catch him living there. You'd soon be overrun. By locusts.

He visualised a film in which a plague of locusts was driven back by a vast flame-thrower, wielded by himself – the lonely voice who had seen the writing on the wall and who had fought against the odds to get the town to take the necessary precautions in time. But no. It was down to him now. No one had believed him.

Not everyone survived the holocaust, of course and some had accidentally been caught in the cleansing inferno. And he knew exactly who.

Bloody no-one will do anything about this estate until it's too bloody late.

He was thinking about informers and surveillance. He was thinking about helicopter search-lights and roadblocks. Checkpoints and computer tagging. House-to-house searches, dawn raids, saturation policing, riot shields and armoured vans. Guns. That'll be the next thing. It'll be like bloody Moss Side here soon.

He was just beginning to think about the necessary

legal reforms to speed up convictions and the building of new, secure prisons, when he caught sight of something at the side of the road, almost hidden from view. But not quite.

The naked man was standing there.

There was an almighty screech of brakes.

The naked man turned, clearly shocked by the noise. And their eyes met.

There was a second while they both took in the changed circumstances that were suddenly upon them and then they both acted at once.

But Inspector Swann was a bolt of lightening striking twice. He was righteousness scorned. An iron fist descending. A desert storm. A ton of bricks. He was a bat out of hell. A cleansing fire. An avenging angel. He was vengeance itself.

He had never run so hard or pounced so furiously. And he had never taken so much pleasure in the chase.

The naked man had no shoes and was sure to be caught. But still he sprinted and vaulted for his life. He knew what was behind him and the gnashing, growling policeman knew that he knew.

The Inspector wanted to bark like a dog and howl like a wolf as he closed in on his quarry. He was drunk with rage and he knew he didn't have long to wait.

There was a flying tackle in the graveyard of the church and the naked man went down with a yelp. The panting, salivating policeman wanted to bite the man and make him scream, but had to content himself with sitting on his back and twisting the man's arm while he got his breath back.

'You poor fucking bastard,' was all he could splutter. Words couldn't describe what he was going to do. He just sat there shaking his head while the naked man whimpered pathetically.

He was a cat playing with a pigeon.

The wheezing policeman had just begun to entertain some deliciously evil notions of an out-of-court settlement, when there was an almighty crack, a flash of light and a cry.

There was a terrible pain suddenly in the back of his head and the policeman realised with dismay that the flash had been inside his skull and the cry had been his own. He had been struck from behind and was now falling to the ground, at the mercy of unknown person or persons.

On the way down he caught a glimpse of another man wielding a stick – rather old really and dressed in a blanket.

He was still conscious but decided it was best to play dead. 'God knows what sodomy might occur now,' he thought and braced himself.

But none did.

In fact there was an incredible fanfare of trumpets and an arc of brilliant light shone down. For a moment the dazed copper thought he saw the old man floating in the air sporting an enormous pair of wings. He closed his eyes tight.

And it all went quiet.

And when he looked up, there was no one to be seen.

'Very queer,' he thought as he made good his escape. 'Very queer indeed.'

Civil Bloody War.

His head throbbing, Inspector Swann burst into the police station giving the somewhat over-weight Desk-Sergeant a near coronary.

'I want a roadblock on the top of Sunnymeadow, a house to house in the Red Lane area, two or three patrol vehicles in support and a thorough search in the vicinity of the graveyard.'

'Yes sir!' Sergeant Jones assumed Inspector Swann was joking. 'I'll put the station on full alert. Will there be a hot line and an incident room?'

'No I don't think ... ' Swann realised he was not being taken seriously. 'I mean it, damn you. I've just been attacked by a gunman.'

'Sir?'

'Close your mouth, officer. I was set upon by armed men. Naked men.'

The Sergeant hesitated. 'Naked ... armed men?'

'These are highly dangerous individuals, Jones. I want them tracked down and accosted. Before they ... accost anyone else.'

'Shall I call for an armed unit, Inspector?'

'That won't be necessary.'

'But I thought you said they were armed.'

'Did I? Yes. Yes, of course. I don't think the gun was loaded.'

'It's impossible to say that with any certainty, Sir. A gun is a gun.'

'I'm fairly certain it was an air pistol.'

'An ... unloaded ... air pistol?'

'I was struck over the head. There was a gang of them. Two. Two individuals in particular were ... obviously very dangerous.'

'The two naked ones?'

'Yes Sergeant. One of them was wearing a blanket.'

'Sounds very ... ' the puzzled Sergeant searched for the right word. 'Suspicious,' was the one that came to mind.

'All criminals are suspicious,' observed Inspector Swann and massaged his temples.

Sergeant Jones wanted to say 'You seem to attract them, sir – naked men,' but instead he asked: 'Are you alright, Sir?'

'I received a head injury. It was a particularly vicious attack.'

'An indecent assault, by the sound of it.'

The superior officer missed the irony. 'There was no buggery, Sergeant.'

'Buggered your head up pretty badly by the look of it.'

Inspector Swann grinned and there was almost an evil glint from his teeth. 'It's nothing to what they'll get at her Majesty's pleasure, Sergeant.'

The Sergeant smiled. He was looking forward to it.

'Right. You round up the troops, I'll draw up the battle plan.'

Sergeant Jones squeezed the second of his chins. 'There is a slight problem in that department, Sir.'

'I quite understand if there's not enough cover for a house to house. A bit of ... over-reaction on my part, perhaps,' smiled the Inspector. 'Probably due to clinical shock.'

From his expression the bulbous Sergeant looked as if he were trying to help his bowels digest excess fatty tissue.

'Yes, Sergeant?' sighed the exasperated Inspector.

'Well, three of the lads are off with food poisoning following that salmonella outbreak at the Happy Eater on Bury Road; Edmundson and Hughes are away on crowd control; Morris broke his collar bone Tuesday in the revolving door at Safeways – we are suing on that one; and Boughton's wife went into labour this afternoon.'

There was a moment's silence.

'Leaving whom?' inquired the Inspector.

'Well, basically that leaves you and me, Sir. Oh and Mrs Plunkett from Civilian Support.'

129

'And where is the good lady?'

'She just popped out to get the pizzas.'

Inspector Swann looked at this puffy travesty of a law enforcement officer.

'I would have ordered one for you, Sir, but I wasn't sure if you liked pepperoni. I thought we can always send out for more ... ' Something in his superior's eye made him stop and sit up to attention.

'I want Morris down here with his bandages!'

'Sir!'

'I want Boughton here with or without placenta!'

'Sir!'

'I want Mrs Plunkett on this desk ... ' He couldn't think of anything witty about pizzas or pepperoni so he let his quivering lip say the rest.

'Sir!'

'And I want you running round preparing this station for civil bloody war!'

'Yes sir!'

Inspector Swann stormed into his office and slammed the door.

Sergeant Jones thought about mozzarella cheese and spicy sausages.

'Yum.'

Help.

Betty put the kettle on and Father Vernon sat on the sofa. Lisa jumped on his knee and Theresa sat on a kitchen stool.

'It's all mod cons in here,' observed Father Vernon.

'It's the local council,' grinned Betty.

'Oh sure, they're cutting education and providing

young people with videos and ... Jesus!' exclaimed the young priest with a laugh, pointing out their state-of-the-art stereo, C.D. and record deck. 'Even the Bishop hasn't got a system like that! And what's this?' he cried spotting the giant-screen T.V. 'Are you lot working some kind of scam? Or shouldn't I ask?' he said with the wicked glint the young people he knew loved so well.

'Some kind of scam,' Betty muttered.

'Are you out selling your bodies?'

'Look at this,' Theresa said, pulling the control for a video game out from behind a cushion.

Father Vernon loved video games and the two of them played for about fifteen minutes while little Lisa tried desparately to attract their attention.

Then Father Vernon turned to Betty. 'Haven't seen you down at the youth club for a while.'

'You 'aven't been there yourself, I 'eard,' replied the young mother, who always had her ear to the ground.

'No. No, you're quite right,' said the priest, reluctantly recalling the reason for his visit.

Theresa looked at him. 'What did you want to talk about?' she asked, as if she'd read his mind.

'Erm . . .'

'Is it about my special powers?'

Father Vernon was entirely stuck for words and stared at the flickering light from the giant T.V. screen. He felt self-conscious and small and nodded his reply without turning to face anyone.

'Who told you about them?'

'Erm ... Oh, word spreads,' replied the priest feeling uncomfortable with his voice.

'I'm tellin' ya,' said Theresa. 'It's meant to be a secret.'

'Yeah, but not for long,' sneered Betty.

Father Vernon just felt daft. 'What ... sort of special powers are they, Theresa?'

'Do you want me to show you?'

131

'Not necessarily . . . ' The priest gasped as he found himself floating a couple of feet above the sofa. 'I see,' he said lamely. And 'Oof,' as Theresa let him drop back down. Then he buried his head in his hands to hide his feelings.

He would far rather have been told that Theresa had seen a statue of the Virgin Mary moving, or that she had suffered an immaculate conception. He hadn't so much sought proof of her miraculous powers as some means of doubting them successfully.

'Satisfied?' asked Theresa.

Father Vernon nodded. 'What are you going to do?' he asked when the colour returned to his cheeks.

Theresa shrugged her shoulders. 'Spread the word.'

'She's gunna go round doing miracles,' interjected Betty. 'Tonight's the first one.'

'And talkin' to people,' added Theresa.

'And givin' people drugs.'

'It's not drugs!'

'What's not drugs?' asked Father Vernon with a frown.

'These, you gave me.' Theresa produced a handful of hosts.

'Oh, those,' laughed the priest. 'They're alright. They haven't even been blessed.'

'I wouldn't be so sure,' muttered Betty.

Theresa tutted. 'I just give them to people . . . to be friendly.'

'It's a nice idea,' said the priest, radically.

'Try one,' said Betty with a look at Theresa.

Theresa scowled at Betty and then, to cover her embarrassment, held one up to Father Vernon, as if she were at Mass. 'Body of Christ . . .'

He grinned and took it on his tongue.

'We're going to change the world,' she announced, simply.

Father Vernon almost laughed aloud at her naivety. But he was too used to holding back his feelings and too good a youth worker to let himself down like that. He looked at her through the gloom and was struck by a proud vulnerability.

Maybe he was influenced by the indisputable evidence of levitation – or perhaps he was seduced by youth's apparent personification of possiblity. Whatever it was, his cynicism died away and for at least a moment something in him believed the girl. 'I'm sure you are,' he mumbled.

'We are,' she asserted confidently.

Then after a few more moments spent summoning courage and fighting common sense, Father Vernon said: 'I'd like to help.'

Theresa eyeballed him. 'How?'

'Any way I can.'

Then Theresa smiled, hopped off the stool and gave him a hearty hug.

'We're gunna need it,' Betty huffed.

'We're gunna get it,' assured Theresa.

'You will have to be careful,' offered the young priest, his cheeks hot.

'I know!' pouted the miracle-maker.

Father Vernon grinned. He couldn't help but love cock-sure youth. 'Do you know what?' he laughed. 'I feel like letting my hair down, for once.'

Betty and Theresa exchanged a glance.

And a few minutes later he was cavorting around outside with the others, happy as pie.

'He's lovely,' said Theresa, as she and Betty stood looking out of the window at him.

'He's mad, said Betty. 'What's he wanna help us for?'

Mary Magdalen Maloney had just put the kettle on for a hot toddy when there came a hammering on the Presbytery door.

'Good evening Madam. Inspector Swann.' He flashed his I.D. 'We have reason to believe that a dangerous criminal may be hiding in the vicinity of the church.'

Mary was more surprised by the presence of four uniformed police than by news of a potential threat to her safety.

'There's dangerous people everywhere these days,' she declared. 'Rapist or murderer?'

'Possibly both,' replied the Inspector.

'They just can't make do, can they?'

'Sorry?'

'In my day a rape was a rape and a murder was a murder. You don't know where you are any more.'

'Er . . . quite,' agreed the Inspector.

'I've experienced a bit of nudity myself recently.'

'Really?' His eyebrows flinched.

'Yes, on the wall there, just down the road.'

'I see,' said the worthy officer dubiously. 'Can we come in?'

'Oh. Yes please.'

The four policemen filed into the hall.

'Ohh! Were you attacked by the murderer?' asked Mary of the officer with his arm in a sling.

He shook his head.

'There was an incident at Safeways,' explained Sergeant Jones.

'Is nowhere sacred?'

'Apparently not, Madam,' said Inspector Swann. 'I was set upon myself this evening by a man in the graveyard.'

'In my experience graveyards are never safe after dark,' exclaimed Mary. 'Put the willies up me they do!' She put her hand over her mouth, looked at the junior officers and almost giggled. She rather relished this manly intrusion. 'I was just about to make a hot t . . . cup of tea. Will you join me.'

Sergeant Jones was quick off the mark: 'I only drink alcohol on duty, thanks, Madam.'

Mary didn't get the joke immediately but was just about to laugh when the Inspector growled, 'Thank you, Sergeant!' and glared at him.

Then to Mary's surprise, one of the men put his head in his hands and began to sob. Sergeant Jones put his arm round his comrade's shoulder. 'His wife's having a baby,' he explained.

One or two hairs on Inspector Swan's moustache stood to attention.

Mary was moved by the sight. 'It's nice to know that a sensitive man can wield a truncheon,' she sighed. 'When's the little angel due?'

'She's in labour as we speak,' said Sergeant Jones. 'Never mind Boughton, there's always next time.'

Inspector Swann wanted to stamp his foot and bellow like a drill sergeant.

Mary was genuinely impressed. 'That's real dedication to duty, that is. You should award this officer a medal, Inspector.'

The Inspector's lip quivered but he couldn't find words soft enough to address a lady.

'He's on the warpath,' explained Sergeant Jones.

'It's about time somebody was,' said Mary.

'Do you have a hanky?'

'Oh, yes. *Kleenex*. The real man's tissue.'

This was too much.

'Atten-shun!' screamed the Inspector.

The three policemen stamped their feet in unison and stood erect.

135

Mary jumped out of her skin.

She wanted to stand to attention, too. 'Oh, you did give me a fright,' she laughed.

Inspector Swann ignored her.

'Right. At the double. Outside. Search the grave-yard, search the church building, report back here in nine minutes. GO!'

The three men shuffled out muttering among themselves.

'Never mind, Boughton, it might be a protracted labour . . .'

'She's never going to speak to me again . . .'

'Och, mind me arm . . .'

'Bloody freezing . . .'

'We can send out for pizza when we get back.'

Inspector Swann looked at Mary.

'You're a very forceful man,' she observed.

'I do my best,' he replied. 'Now then, is the vicar at home?'

'We don't have vicars here, Inspector. Strictly communion and cassocks.'

'Pardon me?'

'This is a Catholic church and Father Vernon isn't at home.'

'Will he be long?'

'He's gone to see some young girls. At the top of the hill. There's some kind of party going on up there.'

'Yes. We're going there next,' said the Inspector.

'Oh, well you'll see him, then,' said Mary.

Down the A666.

After work, while his daughter frolicked with a Catholic priest in Sunnymeadow, Bill Carson's Rover 216/SLi shot down the A666 to Manchester.

It didn't happen that often these days, but tonight Bill was possessed of dire need for relief and once the decision had been made to pick up a girl, it became just that. A need. His heart was beating in his chest and lust was pounding in his trousers.

He knew where to go.

There are two areas of Manchester where prostitutes walk the streets. Behind a well-known city centre hotel off Piccadilly Gardens and on the streets of Whalley Range.

Normally Bill was more careful and visited a massage parlour during the afternoon. But tonight he felt reckless and untouchable. And there was something thrilling about driving round taking your pick.

There was nothing he wanted in Whalley Range. The streets were too dark and the girls were in pairs. Bill didn't have the nerve to approach more than one woman and he couldn't get a decent look anyhow. He circled again, but no.

Off to the city centre.

Over the Mancunian Way, up the back of Piccadilly and into 'the village'.

It was busy.

People for sale. Male and female. Well, for rent.

It was too busy.

There were ten or twelve women on the hundred yards of Minshull St. and five or six others scattered around the back streets.

On his first run Bill could hardly take anyone in.

'Too bloody many,' he thought.

There was one black woman he would have had straight away, but she was standing with another woman and was altogether too conspicuous.

'Why the hell's she standing there? How does she expect anyone to stop?' he wondered angrily.

He was in turmoil. He didn't want to circle too many times for fear that someone would know his intention. Which was obvious. But somehow he wanted the women to think of him as above it all. He wanted to keep his desire secret from all but the woman of his choice.

Which is called shame.

And anyway, what about the police? Hadn't seen any. But you do hear . . .

On his second time round he saw her.

He was going too fast to stop and too fast to be certain she was definitely what he wanted.

'Damn!' he thought and felt his heart contract.

He had to go round again.

'She'll be gone!' he worried.

Next time round she was talking to another woman.

She was definitely what he wanted. Young enough. And small. Why didn't he stop? Why's she talking to her?

He sped round the block again with an unhealthy pulse rate and a pit in his stomach.

She was in the right spot. Not too near the crowded area and near enough to a side street. He wouldn't have to stop on the main drag.

This time the other woman was talking to someone. The girl he wanted was alone again and she peered into his car, giving him a big smile.

But he still drove past.

'Shit! She'll definitely be gone!'

He put his foot down.

'I'll crash in a minute, doing this,' he thought as he accelerated.

Round he came again.

She was on the corner. Alone. It was now or never.

He pulled up just round the corner and stopped. She saw him and walked towards the passenger door. Bill unlocked it and waited. So far so good.

She stooped by the window and said something. Bill signalled for her to get in, but she just stood there. He leaned over and opened the door.

'Get in,' he breathed.

She did so.

He looked at her and she said: 'Hiya.' And when he didn't know what to say she said: 'Alright?'

Bill nodded and she closed the door.

'Turn your car round, please.'

'Er . . . O.K.' Bill wanted to discuss terms but did as he was told.

He drove not knowing which way to turn and made a fool of himself at the junction. 'Sorry . . . ' He signalled to a disgruntled driver. 'How much is it?' he asked, distractedly.

'In the car?'

'Yes.'

'Ten, fifteen and twenty.'

'Right,' said Bill not really knowing what she was talking about. 'Do you know somewhere?'

'Yes. Turn right here, please.' She smiled at him and he relaxed slightly. She was nice.

He thought about it for a moment and decided it probably wasn't a good idea to go where she suggested after all. He had heard stories about people being mugged by prostitutes' friends.

'Er . . . do you mind if we go somewhere I know?'

'So long as it's not out of town,' she replied still smiling. Professionally.

'Right,' he said, wondering where on earth to go. He hardly knew the city.

They fell silent.

She was quite young. How young? He didn't dare to ask.

He wanted to look at her, but he didn't want to turn his head for the shame. He wanted to ask how she became a prostitute. Ask who she normally went with and if they were all as nice and polite as he was. Is she clean? Will she take all her clothes off in the car?

It was a bit too quiet for Bill's comfort.

His heart beat had slowed down and he wasn't so full of lust now.

She was nice though. Young enough to be his daughter.

He looked across at her. Just for a moment.

Then he sighed and turned on the radio.

'Do you like music?' he asked feebly.

'Yes,' she said and smiled again.

Eve of Discovery.

It was eleven-thirty p.m. when Eve arrived at the party.

She was in good time for Theresa's debut.

People were still arriving in droves, attracted by the lazers and enticed by word of mouth.

Eve was greeted by a nod from Penny, a wink from Tony and shrieks of delight from Jo, Michelle and Nicola Carson.

By this time Michelle had got organised and she and Jo were selling cans of Coke at extortionate prices. Betty moaned about this but Theresa let them get on with it. Why should she stop them? How could she?

Eve was surrounded and given a free can.

'How did you get 'ere?'

'Did your dad change 'is mind?'

'He's at work all night,' beamed Eve.

It was the first time the poor girl had ever gone against her father's word and she had very mixed feelings. Among which were elation, excitement, exhilaration, jubilation, even intoxication on the one hand and fear and guilt on the other. The one side far outweighed the other.

'Dad! ... Dad come over 'ere,' shouted Nicola to Father Vernon, who was busy dishing out Theresa's hosts.

'Is that your Dad?' asked Eve, wide-eyed with it all.

'I wish he was,' laughed Nicola. 'Dad, this is Eve. We met her today at the gymkhana.'

'Hello, Eve,' said Father Vernon. He grinned and took a host from his pocket, holding it up to the smiling girl. 'Body of Christ,' he joked and popped it onto her tongue.

Eve removed the host and asked: 'What's this?'

'It's a gift from God, to welcome you to the party,' laughed the handsome young priest.

'Suck it,' said Nicola.

Father Vernon wasn't taking the communion at all seriously. It was his way of making conversation and joining in the fun. He put the general euphoria down to a mixture of God's love and youthful exuberance. His own high spirits he put down to his new-found mission.

He was glad to cast off the isolation that had nearly suffocated him over the past weeks and let his hair down. His place was among the young and he was here to stay. He understood their ways and loved and accepted them, unequivocally. And they loved and accepted him back.

'It's not drugs, is it?' asked Eve nervously.

Father Vernon threw his head back and laughed.

Eve looked at Nicola.

'He's a priest,' she explained.

Eve put the host in her mouth and sucked it.

Twenty minutes later she was kissing Tony.

It was the first time she'd ever kissed a guy properly.

And it tasted better than horse riding. And swimming. And ballet. And reading. And the girl guides. Better than all of them put together.

She loved Tony's clothes. They were the baggiest jeans she'd ever seen. And his T-shirt was the best.

'It's Cotton Rich,' he explained. 'That's my stage name, too.'

She loved his stage name.

And his hair.

And his lips.

''Ow come I've not seen you before?' asked Tony during a break from the action.

'I don't know,' grinned Eve. 'I don't think I've ever seen myself before!'

They laughed and then kissed for ten minutes non-stop.

Then they danced like crazy.

Then came Theresa's bit.

Penny had built it up well on the mike and Tony managed to get a spotlight shining onto a makeshift platform. There was quite an atmosphere of anticipation, though no one quite knew what to expect.

Theresa climbed up on to the precariously balanced planks that had been shoved on to some crates at one end and a low wall at the other. She said a few words, but no one could hear. Penny gave her the mike and jumped down to join Michelle and Jo in the crowd.

She didn't look very impressive in her drab clothes,

with her hair hanging limp and Betty felt herself blushing already.

'Go on ... ' Michelle hissed, to encourage her.

'Hello!' her voice boomed out over the P.A.

Then she started.

'Listen everybody ... we've all got to love each other. And make the world a better place ...'

The dismay was almost tangible.

'I believe God has given me special powers so that people will listen to me.'

'Oh fuck ... ' Michelle cringed, hiding her head in Jo's shoulder.

'Shut up and get on with the magic!' shouted someone.

Theresa knew it was Penny.

'I'm serious ... with my powers and real love we can change the world ...'

There was a general murmur as everyone tried to cover their embarrassment. Some people walked off.

'Just get on with it!' the voice repeated. Tony laughed.

Even Father Vernon, standing among the crowd found himself blushing and staring at the ground.

Betty had to turn away. She pretended to rock Lisa gently. It was way past her bedtime and the little beauty had fallen asleep in her mother's arms.

'Okay ... Okay,' said Theresa at last, turning a little pale. 'If it's a miracle you want ... there you go.'

Suddenly Penny screamed and found himself floating in the air above the assembly. He blushed so deeply you could have had him pickled with salad.

'Put me fucking down you ... ' was all the wit he could muster.

Michelle and Jo nearly lost control of their bladders and everyone who knew him laughed and scoffed at the spectacle.

His arms flailed helplessly and he let out a series of wails and yelped like a poodle. And when he begged for mercy, Theresa let him down. None too gently.

A few moments later the music struck up and the youths danced on as if nothing had happened. Theresa tried to continue with her speech but she was drowned out by the din.

Afterwards some people thought there was some kind of trickery with ropes involved and the others didn't give a damn.

The first thing Betty said was: 'What's all this God shit!'

'It's what I believe!'

'Bollocks!'

Then the others came up laughing.

'What did you think?' asked Theresa.

'Top ... ' laughed Michelle. 'You should have spun 'im round and made 'im sick, though.'

'I nearly pissed meself!' giggled Jo.

'What about what I said?' asked Theresa, flushing.

Michelle tutted.

Jo said, 'Shit.'

A little later, perched on the wall, Father Vernon recalled his recent dreams.

Sitting there, in the darkness, in the night air he was struck by the strangeness of it all. Of his imagined meeting with Canon Drinkwater. Of what he had just seen and heard.

Surely it was his imagination?

'Maybe I'm going mad,' he thought.

Then he caught sight of Nicola Carson. She waved to him and he waved back, smiling to himself. 'If only she knew what I thought about her sometimes,' he reflected. 'What if her father knew!' he added, perhaps to hurt himself.

Then he thawed a little.

'Well,' he thought, 'if I am going mad, at least I'm not alone.'

Then he saw blue flashing lights along the buildings and heard someone shout. 'It's the cops.'

Pulled Up.

They had been driving round for nearly a quarter of an hour and Bill was lost.

'Do you know somewhere?' he asked after all.

She pointed. 'Take a left here, please.'

'I don't really know Manchester, that well.'

'It's best if the customer chooses the place,' she smiled. 'They trust you then.'

'Yes,' said Bill. He would have to take the risk.

He sat back and put himself in her hands.

'Take a right here, please.'

She was very polite. Formal, but friendly.

Anonymous.

'Straight over, up there, please.'

She was sitting forward now, looking out of the window, presumably for a turning.

'Nearly there, now.' She turned and smiled at him.

Bill felt a new shiver of excitement.

'How old are you?' he managed to ask.

She looked at him guiltily. 'I'm nearly twenty,' she assured him.

It was a fairly decent area. Large Victorian houses loomed in the darkness among towering trees.

'There. Turn down there, please.'

They turned down a driveway into what looked like some kind of sports ground. There was a smallish wood between the houses and the car park where they stopped.

'Pull up here, please.'

Bill was almost disappointed to park up. The anticipation had been thrilling and now the atmosphere would die as terms and conditions were discussed.

He killed the engine and turned off the headlights.

It was very quiet.

They turned to face each other and she said: 'What do you want?'

God damn bladder. 'I want a piss, actually.'

He got out of the car wondering if it was a good idea to leave her in there alone. 'Got to have a piss, first,' he thought.

There was no one around, so he stood at the rear of the car on the driver's side, where he could keep an eye on her.

As he splashed the shale he noticed a car had appeared at the end of the driveway to the car park. Its headlights were switched off, but Bill thought nothing of it.

Poor fool.

'Someone else wants to come down here,' he mused.

The car reversed back up the drive and disappeared.

'Sorry, mate,' he thought and got back into the car.

'What do you do?' he asked.

'Everything.'

'Yeah? How much is everything?'

'Twenty for a full strip, then add five pounds for each extra: oral; straight sex . . .'

'I see,' said Bill.

'What do you want?'

'I'm not sure.'

He didn't know whether she was clean enough for sex. He was dithering, badly.

146

'Come on, I haven't got all night.'

Her impatient tone was a turn off and Bill was now worried that he wouldn't be able to get an erection.

'Erm . . . sex, please . . . I'm British.'

She didn't get his joke.

'That's twenty-five.'

No 'please' now.

Bill sighed and reached for his wallet. She began to remove her jacket.

Suddenly Bill saw two men in the woods, about thirty yards away.

'Shit! What's that?'

He thought for a moment that he was going to be mugged by friends of hers, but she looked worried too. They both froze. The men were heading towards them.

Bill switched on his engine and the two men stopped and then hurried off in the opposite direction.

'Couple of queers,' he thought, but something told him to get moving.

'What shall we do? Do you think it's the police?'

She was looking out of the window with her arm half out of her jacket. 'If they were cops they'd have come over.'

He put the car in reverse and moved a few yards, not sure what to do. He sat there. Why did they hurry off like that?

'Let's go,' he declared. It wasn't safe.

He put the headlights on and drove towards the entrance.

One of the men had run onto the road in front of them. He was walking straight at the car, holding something out. An I.D.

'Oh my God,' he said. 'It's the police.'

In Charge.

There was an almighty chorus of disapproval as the music was turned off.

Inspector Swann informed Penny that he'd be arrested if he continued. The noise, however, remained unbearable as the youths began hissing and hollering. The night air was filled with a racket that soon reached threatening levels.

Eve was hiding in the crowd, her eyes wide with fear and excitement.

'Are they going to arrest us all?' she asked of the girl standing next to her.

'What, four of them?' the girl laughed.

Eve laughed along.

'One of 'em's a cripple,' added the girl.

'And the other one's a fat bastard!' yelled someone else. Loud enough for Sergeant Jones to hear.

Eve could see her father talking to Penny. Tony was there too.

Tony was less passive than his friend. 'What's the matter? Don't you like the music. How about some classical, you could have a waltz,' he shouted, defiantly. Penny grinned at him.

The Inspector flushed, angrily. 'That's enough of that. I'll 'ave you down the cells.'

'Oh, they're 'avin' a rave down at the police station.' he called to anyone who could hear.

The Inspector's moustache itched. He tried to ignore the loudmouth. 'Who's in charge here?' he said to Penny.

'I am.' laughed Tony.

'I'm warning you, young man.'

'We ain't causing no trouble!'

'We've had complaints.'

148

'Yeah? Who from?'

'Er . . . the church,' he lied.

'Oh yeah?' Tony laughed.

Penny was blushing but enjoying himself.

Overtaken by curiosity and daring Eve had pushed her way to the front and was half hidden behind the front row of onlookers. She had borrowed a peaked cap and a red spotted scarf which she wrapped round her nose out-law fashion, just to be sure her father wouldn't recognize her.

The general disturbance was still intimidating the old policeman. Lights were flashing and everyone was screaming and wailing.

'Eh, Father . . . ' called Tony. He beckoned Father Vernon. 'This copper reckons he's had complaints from the church.'

'Are you in charge here?' asked Inspector Swann when Father Vernon joined them.

'No, I'm just a guest,' said the priest.

'Can't you get them to stop making that racket?' shouted the copper, over the din.

'Perhaps if you put the music back on?'

Inspector Swann looked at Father Vernon in disgust. 'I'm afraid I can't allow that, sir. It's causing a disturbance.'

'That's a shame. We haven't had any trouble.'

'Not yet you haven't,' spluttered the old policeman. 'But if that noise doesn't stop right now I'm going to start some! I'll be back in five minutes,' he warned and stomped off.

As he pushed through the crowd of youths, the Inspector took Sergeant Jones by the arm. 'I'm going to sniff round. You check the serial numbers on that equipment.'

Tony had no idea that Eve was the copper's daughter of course. And when she came forward to join him he gesticulated at the retreating policeman, as

149

any right-thinking youth would have. 'Fuckin' dick 'ead,' he laughed.

At that moment you could have knocked Eve down with a feather. She had just seen her father behaving like a spoilt child. He had been bad-tempered and rude. Hadn't he even threatened violence of some kind?

In the night air, in the crowd, with the lasers flickering and the lights flashing it seemed as if she had been transported to another world.

And indeed she had. A world of youthful possibilities. And kindness. And excitement. And her own father seemed dead against it.

Cop That.

Five minutes later, when Inspector Swann returned, the situation was getting out of hand.

People were dancing, waving their hands in the air and throwing their arms round each other. Everywhere the old copper looked teenagers were kissing.

The music wasn't so loud now, though.

'We decided the best thing was to turn it down,' explained Father Vernon, as the Inspector stormed up to them.

In her outlaw disguise, Eve was now standing right next to Tony, thrilling to the defiance. Her father didn't know her from Adam.

'Off!' ordered the fuming copper. 'I'll confiscate all this equipment in a minute.'

There were a few minutes of negotiations while the music continued, during which Inspector Swann remained intransigent.

Poor man. He was giving his best performance of obnoxious provocation. He had been attacked, the security of his family had been threatened, he had been frustrated by a naked man, defied by youths, hindered by a Catholic priest and on a gut level he required some kind of compensation.

Like an arrest.

It was perfectly natural.

If only he'd known his daughter was watching the show.

Eve wanted to rip off her colourful mask and shout: 'Daddy, don't be so bloody stubborn!' But of course, she couldn't. Instead she stood there and underwent a profound personality change.

Her blood boiled in a way she had never known before and unfortunate new areas of consciousness were forged, as her thoughts turned in on themselves and previously unshaken truths were confounded, transformed by the scene playing itself out before her eyes.

The final straw came from the priest.

'I know,' he said suddenly. 'I'll open up the youth club and we can transfer the whole thing down there. I think that way we'll avoid the sort of disappointment that could lead to trouble, don't you?'

'I'm sorry, sir, but I'm sure people in the area of the youth club won't like that one little bit.'

'Oh no, don't worry, the club is right back off the road, there are no houses in the area.'

'I'm afraid you'll need a licence. It'd be an illegal gathering otherwise. I can't allow that.'

'No. We've done this before. It's perfectly legal if you don't charge a fee. We checked up last time. All they need is my permission.'

*

151

And if Inspector Swann hadn't been on the warpath, it would have passed off without further incident. Perhaps Eve would have recovered her old self and life might have returned to normal.

But in his frustration the old copper was easily provoked.

Pulling Eve after him Tony followed the worthy officer and as they disappeared behind the van he called after him. 'Better luck next time, Inspector.'

Inspector Swann turned round sharply, marched back to him and under his daughter's watchful eye, took the boy by the scruff of the neck and snarled: 'Watch your fucking step, you little bastard!'

Tony, partially for Eve's benefit, replied: 'Oh yeah . . . pig!'

The Inspector's eyes bulged. The futility of the evening and the frustration of the whole situation was suddenly overwhelming.

His lack of a decent career, the idiots down at the station, the earlier assault, the bastards in the big houses on the estate with the swimming pools in their gardens, the swine at the gymkhana, the locusts, the danger to his daughter, his beloved daughter who wouldn't even speak to him because she wanted to attend a party like this one.

All this welled up in him and he butted the vile youth so hard that the poor lad's nose exploded with blood.

He instantly regretted it.

Tony cried out and laid into the old copper with all his puny might, punching and kicking him wildly.

Sergeant Jones came running over and grabbed him.

'Stick him in the van,' snapped the Inspector, who knew they would now have to beat a hasty retreat.

Luckily, the only witness to the incident was the stupid little girl with the red scarf round her face who was now screaming abuse and kicking him.

152

Inspector Swann grabbed her arm near the shoulder and squeezed with all his manly force. She screamed in pain.

He pulled her up, close to his face. 'Mind your own fucking business, you stupid little bitch,' he spat.

At this moment Father Vernon appeared, having suffered a pang of remorse over his assertiveness.

Oblivious, Swann pushed the girl roughly to the ground and made his exit.

Come Uppance.

'Would you step out of the car, please, sir.'

'Certainly, yes.'

For a glorious moment Bill Carson thought he was only going to be breathalysed. For once he was stone cold sober.

But it was only a moment.

'Sergeant Knowles, Vice Squad.'

It was too horrible to be true. Yet it was happening.

He stepped out and followed the officer to a space in the beam of the headlights, where another man, presumably a policeman, stood waiting.

Knowles said: 'Who's the woman?'

'Er . . . she's my girlfriend.'

It sounded pathetic. She was wearing the shortest of skirts and looked as common as muck. He was smartly dressed, much older than she was and obviously well off. As soon as they looked at her they would know. All he could do was pray for a miracle.

None came.

'How long have you known her?'

Bill was almost crushed by shame. His head was reeling.

'Actually, we only met tonight,' he stammered.

The two policemen looked at one another.

'Where did you meet her?'

'In one of the pubs in Whalley Range.'

'Which one?'

He didn't know any pub in Whalley Range.

'Er . . . I'm not sure what it's called.'

The officer exchanged another look with his colleague. And then played his trump card.

'What's her name, then?'

Bill was dumbstruck. He didn't know. Why hadn't he asked her? It was a dead give-away.

There was a moment's silence.

The two men looked at Bill. They wanted to hear him say it.

He obliged: 'I don't know.'

The second man, who hadn't spoken until now said: 'Excuse me while I go and corroborate your story with the girlfriend,' and walked over to the car.

Bill wanted to vanish into thin air.

Knowles said: 'You picked her up off the street and brought her down here for the purpose of procuring sex, didn't you?'

'No,' lied Bill hopelessly.

Knowles was suddenly very aggressive. He almost shouted. 'Oh yeah! You picked her up from Minshull street, in the city centre. We watched you. Then you drove around for fifteen minutes. We followed you. Then you came to this secluded spot. She's a prostitute. Isn't she?'

Bill wondered whether he would have to suffer the ignominy of being arrested and taken to a police station. He pictured his wife's face. He thought of Nicola. He shuddered.

'Isn't she?'

154

'Yes. Yes. She's a prostitute . . . ' He wanted to add something else, by way of mitigation, but there wasn't anything.

The policeman was suddenly polite again. Friendly almost. He produced a clipboard from somewhere and said: 'I'm afraid you'll be summonsed to appear in court and charged. It's a standard fine.'

Bill suddenly felt grateful to him. For not shouting any more.

'You're not going to arrest me?'

'Oh no. It's not an arrestable offence, don't worry.'

Bill wanted to put his arms around the officer and hug him.

'Can't you just . . . let me off with a caution?' he inquired.

'I'm sorry, sir. You'll have to go to court. If I do it to one person, I have to do it to everyone else.'

Bill flushed hot at the thought of attending court. Would he have to admit it out loud, in front of everyone? Or could there be some kind of postal plea? He didn't dare ask.

'We're trying to clean up the streets altogether,' the policeman explained. 'We've been out for weeks.'

'What about . . . some kind of . . . on the spot fine. In cash.'

The officer grinned. 'Sorry sir. Now can I take down some details. If any of this proves to be incorrect we'll be calling on you in person.'

'Yes, yes.'

'Car registration . . . ' He read it out. 'Is that correct?'

Bill sighed. 'Yes.'

'Name?'

When he told him the officer said: 'Well, well.'

The other man looked up from his position by the car door, where he was questioning the young woman. 'Preacher man? . . . Oh dear.'

*

On his way home, Bill replayed the scene a thousand times in his imagination, each time coming up with a different way out.

He should have driven off straight away as soon as they spotted the men in the undergrowth and then dropped her off. But he hadn't known they were police.

He shouldn't have gone there in the first place.

If he'd asked her name. He could have said he was just talking to her. Researching some paper on harlots.

If he'd said nothing, how could they have proved anything? But if he'd have refused to talk they would have known it was suspicious.

And so on, until he was blue in the face and palpitating dangerously.

Getting Even.

Sergeant Jones was a decent sort really.

He had seen what happened to Tony and would lie about it in court, but at least it made him feel bad. He knocked on the cell door and came in. 'Room service,' he quipped.

Tony tried not to grin.

'I've got you some Pizza,' he said coming into the cell. 'I assumed you like pepperoni.'

Tony sighed. 'Thanks.' He found it impossible to be unfriendly to the fat Sergeant. He'd helped him clean up his nose, made him a hot chocolate and helped him feel better about his two black eyes.

'Your equipment up there, was it?

Tony hesitated. 'Er . . . no.'

Sergeant Jones was casual. 'Your mate's, eh?'

'I dunno.'

The fat copper shrugged. 'Your mates'll think you're a bloody hero.'

'You saw what happened, didn't you?' said Tony.

'Only with my blind eye.'

'What's going to happen?'

'You'll be charged with assaulting an Inspector.'

'He hit me first!'

Sergeant Jones looked at the young man, sadly. 'This isn't a television programme, you know. Which is a shame. Because we can all act. Especially in court.' He sighed. 'Now eat your pizza and behave.'

Inspector Swann had cheered up.

Having given vent to his feelings he felt like a new man. Boughton had been allowed to return to the hospital, the bandaged constable Morris had been sent home and the good Mrs Plunkett let off early. The appearance of the naked man that evening had been erased from his memory forever and the subject conveniently dropped by his staff.

He and Sergeant Jones had ordered pizza and it had been Inspector Swann's idea to order one for Tony.

The tea was made, the video had been set up (*One Good Cop*) and the Inspector was just about to take his first bite of *Super Supreme with Spicy Sausage*, when there was some kind of disturbance outside.

He listened again. And sure enough, there it was again. Shouting.

He stepped outside and his jaw dropped.

There were thirty to forty (possibly more) youths gathered on the pavement outside, shouting in unison. They were being lead by the bitch with the red scarf over her face.

Who did they think they were?

When they saw him they began to holler in that same threatening manner.

For a moment he thought they were going to mob him.

Then they began to chant together. His name.

'Inspector Swann . . . police brutality.' Or something like that. 'Something, something innocent.'

What the fucking hell . . .

He caught sight of the priest. What was he doing there? Surely he wasn't demonstrating with the rest of them.

He dived back into the station in a cold sweat.

Sergeant Jones was on the telephone.

'People are complaining about the noise, sir.'

Inspector Swann stood there. His head span. Storm clouds gathered.

'I want that little bitch!' he snarled.

On the pavement outside there was a party atmosphere.

Sure, they were angry about Tony's arrest. But demonstrating outside the police station was great fun. There was no doubt about it.

Michelle and Jo wandered about the crowd selling their cans.

Nicola Carson was standing with her arm through Father Vernon's.

Betty was showing off a highly astonished Lisa to a crowd of admiring teenage girls.

'Poor little thing. Woke you up in the middle of the night, didn't we Tiny?'

Theresa was standing next to Eve singing her heart out and shouting with the crowd.

Up on her pedestal (a drinks crate she'd carried from the youth club), Eve was in that glorious state where anger and euphoria unite to produce a sensation of invincibility.

Her scarf around her face, her fist in the air, she was singing and shouting with all the force of right-eousness, leading the protest from on high. In this condition she could have entered the gates of hell and wrestled the devil.

In the space of an hour everything she had ever known had been stood on its head and her whole being was now engaged in a holy jihad. She was on the other side of the fence suddenly and would stand with anyone she found there.

The demonstration had been decided upon at the youth club. Eve had suggested it and everyone agreed.

For Eve it was an uprising.

And then out came her father, in full battle dress, wielding his truncheon, with a very serious looking Sergeant Jones in tow. Well, he was doing his best.

Their appearance had the effect of greatly increasing the noise level.

Inspector Swann's original plan was to rush out and nab the ringleader ('the bitch') and rely on the demoralisation that would inevitably set in to discourage the remaining demonstrators.

Sergeant Jones had argued against this course on the grounds of health and safety. They were, he reminded the Inspector, Sunnymeadow youths and therefore unpredictable.

'And there are only two of us,' he pointed out.

'Humm.'

And so diplomacy was decided upon.

And they couldn't get anywhere near Eve without causing a serious threat to their personal safety, so they made for Father Vernon.

'Right, I want you out of here in two minutes flat or we'll be making arrests,' threatened the diplomat, his moustache bristling.

'Hello there,' said Nicola, still hanging on to Father Vernon's arm.

Inspector Swann ignored her.

'I'm afraid I'm only here in the capacity of an observer,' said Father Vernon.

The Inspector's face must have asked why on earth he needed to observe anything, because Father Vernon added: 'I saw what happened before.' Meaning, of course when he'd man-handled Eve.

But Inspector Swann thought he was referring to the incident with Tony.

He was stunned. And embarrassed. And horrified.

He looked at Sergeant Jones who understood his superior's feelings and empathised with his eyebrows.

'What's the charge against Tony?' asked Father Vernon.

Inspector Swann hesitated.

'Assaulting an Inspector,' advised Sergeant Jones.

'Thank you, Sergeant. I'll handle this.' He eyeballed the troublesome priest. 'There's been no formal charge as yet. Now I suggest you pass on the message to this ... these ... people, that the pavement has to be cleared.'

'Or else you'll be making arrests?' asked Father Vernon, nervously.

'We'll be back out in ten minutes to ... assess the situation,' said Inspector Swann, in as threatening a manner as possible. Then he marched back into the station under a hail of jeers and hisses.

Father Vernon relayed the message as best he could and the youths took up a chorus of 'We Shall Not Be Moved'.

Ten minutes passed and nothing happened.

Except a lot of shouting.

Then the door to the police station opened and out walked Tony with his two black eyes.

There was a great cheer followed by scenes of jubilation.

'They dropped the charges,' he beamed.

'You should sue him for assault,' said Eve.

160

They cleared the pavement.
And went back to the party.
And by morning Eve was back in her bed.
Asleep and dreaming.

Squealer.

Mary was devastated.

'What do you mean 'they're moving in'?' she asked when Father Vernon broke the news.

The young priest looked into his Rice Crispies, philosophically. 'There's a time when you have to open your doors as well as your heart, Mary. Every good Christian knows that. And I think the time has come.

'All five of them?'

'Six now, if you include the baby.'

'The baby? I thought . . . will mother and child be coming? Surely they want somewhere to them-selves?'

Father Vernon sighed. He'd known it wouldn't be easy to explain to Mary.

'They're going to use the flat as a base of opera-tions.'

Mary's lips moved but no sound came out.

'They're starting off a business. Of sorts.' It was only half a white lie. 'And until something more suitable turns up they'll be living here with us.'

Mary badly needed a drink.

'Well . . . if it's mother and baby . . . I'd be prepared to offer them my room,' she tried.

Father Vernon's spoon, laden with Rice Crispies, stopped short of his mouth. He had never been very

161

good at addressing issues directly, and now was to be no exception.

'I've been meaning to talk to you about our sleeping arrangements,' he said and shovelled the cereal into his mouth.

To Mary these words were like the sound of one of those first world war bombs known as 'squealers', which would let off a high pitched scream as they flew through the air to let you know you were about to be blown to pieces. She wanted to dive for cover.

'I think,' he snap, crackle and popped, 'I think we should revert back to our usual routine at bed time. You've shown . . . a vast improvement in recent weeks and . . . and I think it's about time.'

It was very awkward to talk about. There had, of course, been no previous discussion of either Mary's condition or the social arrangements. Things always happened to them by default. They had stumbled blindly into their situation. The rules were unspoken, but none the less clearly understood by both parties.

This attempt at planning by Father Vernon was the first direct mention ever, of anything that had passed between them. It was brutal and felt like violence to the poor alcoholic.

It was true, too. Mary had badly neglected her role of invalid in recent weeks and taken her place in the priest's bed for granted. She cursed herself to damnation.

'Yes,' she said and left the room at the next opportunity.

About time.

That night Mary took a turn for the worse.

There were hallucinations, spasms, convulsions, twitches and an outburst of delirium.

There were cries of anguish.

162

There was agony, distress, misery and torment.

There was sweat and bile and tears.

There was even some blood (she scratched herself so hard she bled.)

Her eyes rolled, her limbs jittered and her body shook.

And the worst of it was that she was only half acting.

The horror was real enough.

'Don't leave me Father,' she cried at the height of her suffering.

She grabbed the lapels of his dressing gown and implored him. 'Please, Father. Help me.'

She wanted to shout: 'I love you,' and crash into his arms. She wanted to kiss his mouth. And hold him tight.

Forever.

She broke down and cried like a girl. She wailed and sobbed and blubbered. Clutching at him as though she were hanging from a cliff edge. Clinging for dear life.

It was very convincing.

So convincing that Father Vernon became gravely concerned.

For the first time ever he pondered his own role in the affair.

('What part have I played in all this?' he wondered.)

He felt a terrible surge of guilt.

Had he made matters worse by looking after her himself when he should perhaps have sought professional help? Things were worse than he thought. Her condition had deteriorated seriously behind his back. She might be fatally ill.

Why had he not thought of this before?

He looked at the wretched woman as she squirmed on the bed.

He felt a sudden stab of anxiety. A terrible thought

occurred to him. Whilst she disintegrated, he had used Mary for his own comfort.

'Oh my God!'

He said it out loud.

The stricken woman was suddenly still.

'What is Father?' She caught the urgency in his tone.

'Mary, I'm most terribly sorry. All this time I ...'

He stopped. What was he saying?

Mary waited. What could possibly be about to happen? All this time he ... what? What was he sorry about? The girls moving in?

She lay there, panting awfully. Not daring to move in case she missed the rest of his sentence.

'All this time ... what, Father?'

'Nothing, Mary. I'm sorry. I was thinking out loud.'

She lay still. She almost forgot where she was and what she was doing. His words went round and round in her head, making her dizzy. All this time he had wanted her? Could it be true?

She waited.

And waited.

And then, possibly due to her long exertion, she fell asleep.

Father Vernon checked she was alive and breathed a sigh of relief.

First thing in the morning he phoned for the doctor.

Mary objected at first, but when he insisted, she opted to try and convince the doctor to confine her to her (or rather his) sick bed.

The doctor was convinced alright.

Afterwards he spoke to Father Vernon privately, downstairs. Rather as if were talking to the mother of an ailing child.

'She's very sick,' he said over his pince-nez glasses. 'Has it been going on long?'

'I'm afraid so,' apologised the priest. 'We were . . . she was reluctant to call for help.'

'They always are,' declared the medic as if he were talking about some kind of specimen. 'She's a chronic alcoholic too by the smell of her. I dare say her liver's shot.'

'What shall we do?'

'I'm going to commit her into compulsory psychiatric care,' he announced. 'She's a danger to herself.'

Father Vernon was surprised, but somehow slightly relieved. 'You can do that, can you?' he asked.

'I can't but I know a man who can.'

'Oh,' said the priest. 'When . . . when will you do it?'

'Right away,' said the doctor. 'Can I use your phone?'

She put up such a fight that in the end they had to strap her on to a stretcher and take her away.

She spat and spluttered and ground her teeth so hard that one of them broke.

And when they took her down the drive from the Presbytery there was such a terrible scream that the birds took flight from the trees. The horrifying cry should have turned the sun black and the sky red.

But it didn't. It didn't make any difference at all.

'Noooooooooooooooo!'

When he heard it, Father Vernon had to clutch the doorframe for support.

'Don't worry,' assured the doctor. 'It's always like this.'

Inspector Swann hated Manchester at the best of times, but he especially disliked Chester House, the police headquarters, to where he'd been summoned.

Not only were all the officers there senior to him in rank, but they were younger in years, age-wise and service-wise.

And they were a bunch of pen pushers.

As far as the old copper could tell they spent their days walking briskly around the building with clip-boards under their arms, attending meetings and starring in press conferences.

Somewhere in his being he was disappointed that the IRA had never targeted the building with a rocket launcher. 'That'd shake the bastards up a bit,' he'd muse.

Divisional Commander Whitehouse had an office on the eleventh floor. It was one of a suite of well-furnished offices reserved for the top brass and Inspector Swann sneered at the soft carpet under his feet as he stepped out of the lift.

'You won't get bunions pounding this beat,' he thought.

He'd never met the Divisional Commander and had heard little about him since he'd been appointed six months ago. The Bolton Constabulary were a little behind the times really and Inspector Swann didn't make a habit of gossiping with his men. Which was a shame, because if he'd known before-hand, he might have paid more attention to the report he'd submitted describing Saturday night's fiasco.

'He's probably some fuddy-duddy old bastard,' thought the provincial retard as he stood in front of the office door.

He was just straightening his uniform and preparing to knock, when the door was flung open by a very smart giant in full uniform, with a lot of metal on his cap and a clip-board under his arm.

'Ah Swann,' he snapped. 'You're four minutes late. I was just coming to look for you.'

Inspector Swann was utterly overawed and stood staring at the imposing figure that filled the doorway and blocked out the sun.

'Well don't just stand there man, come in.'

The Inspector almost marched into the room and stood to attention. He half expected the Commander to say 'at ease'. Instead the great man indicated a chair with his spade-like hand.

The chair was so low and luxurious that Inspector Swann nearly fell back and lay down. It took him a moment to adjust himself into a semi-respectable position. In the end he perched like a demure school girl on the edge of the seat with his knees pressed primly together.

As always, when he became nervous, his moustache began to itch.

'Your reputation precedes you, Inspector.'

'Sir?'

'I was warned in advance about your moustache.'

There was no accompanying smile and Inspector Swann waited anxiously for a cue.

None came.

After some moments silence, during which Inspector Swann felt he was failing some kind of test, the huge Commander laughed. Inspector Swann took it as a cue and smiled. Thinly.

'Yes. And your sense of humour. I was warned about that too.'

'Yes, sir,' was all the poor Inspector could say.

Suddenly all trace of humour disappeared from the giant Commander's face. He slammed his clip-board down on the desk and sat down with a flourish. It was all Inspector Swann could do to refrain from jumping out of the window.

'Now then.' A thin file was produced from somewhere and the Commander opened it carefully, smoothing out the papers with his palm. Inspector Swann noticed that the man had very precise control of his enormous hands.

'Last Saturday night.'

'Yes, sir.' Inspector Swann shifted his uncomfortable position slightly. A shuffle that didn't escape the Commander's notice.

'I have here two conflicting reports.'

'Sir?'

The Commander gave him a withering look which said: 'Don't keep saying 'Sir' all the way through this interview, because I'll find it very tiresome.'

Inspector Swann wanted to say 'Sorry sir, I won't say that again, sir,' but didn't.

Every word the Commander spoke was individually chosen. 'One of the reports – highly consistent and carefully considered – is written by a Catholic priest and has an accompanying letter signed by the Bishop of Manchester, the Right Reverend Stanley Grove-Clifford.' Inspector Swann could hear the breathing from Commander Whitehouse's nose. 'The other report – rather inconsistent and hastily constructed, was submitted by yourself. And counter-signed by one Sergeant Jones.'

The was a moment of silence during which Inspector Swann's being was nothingness. Then the Commander said: 'And this (he was pointing at the bottom left hand corner of the second report) unless I'm very much mistaken, is a small lump of . . . mozzarella cheese.'

The silence that followed was one of the most uncomfortable Inspector Swann had ever experienced.

Commander Whitehouse sat back in his chair,

placed his chin between the thumb and forefinger of his right hand and regarded the motionless Inspector with what could almost have been relish.

By the time the Commander opened up his hand and said: 'Well?' Inspector Swann had held his breath for so long that he'd gone dizzy.

'Er . . . conflicting, sir?'

'Conflicting, Inspector.'

The Inspector swallowed. 'In what way . . . conflicting, sir?'

The game was over. The Commander stood up and raised his voice in the most intimidating manner. Which actually wasn't very loud at all. 'In every way, damn you!' He was pacing around, looking out of the window and back at the terrified Inspector. 'The priest alleges that you head-butted a young man and assaulted a young woman.'

'I was attacked. The young man was injured when his head . . . when I was forced to restrain him.'

'Like it says in your report!'

'Sir.'

The Commander sighed. 'If that's the case, Inspector, why was he later released without charge?'

'Because of the demonstration, sir'

'And why was there a ruddy demonstration, outside a police station, in the middle of the night, in the first place, damn it!'

'Er . . . because . . . they were trying to intimidate us.'

'And was this Catholic priest, whom I believe you spoke to on the demonstration, also trying to intimidate you?'

'It was complicated, sir . . .'

The look on the Commander's face stopped him in his tracks.

'Not in your damn report it wasn't. It was all quite straight forward there. Inspector. No complications there. Inspector.'

169

He hung his head in shame. 'No sir.'

'How do you think I feel when I receive a complaint from the public, regarding an officer's conduct, supported by the Bishop of Manchester and I look up the report on the incident and find this.' He held up the piece of paper, complete with mozzarella cheese.

'Yes, sir,' sounded highly inappropriate.

The Commander sat down and calmed down. The main part of his point having been made. He sighed.

'You've been making rather a name for yourself lately haven't you, Inspector.'

'Sir?'

'Chasing naked men around the streets. Or was it aliens from space?'

Inspector Swann blushed to the roots of his moustache.

'Yes, sir,' he mumbled.

'It's a terrible responsibility sometimes being a policeman, isn't it, Inspector?'

Inspector Swann, oblivious to what was coming, perked up a little. 'Yes sir.'

'You'll be quite glad to take a little break from duties, then, won't you?'

He was thunderstruck. 'Sir?'

'We're sending you on a little refresher course, Inspector, down in Kent.'

'But . . . refresher course, sir?'

'Training, Inspector. Community realations, youth liasion. They've got all the latest stuff down there.' The Great man winked. 'Riot control, counter-insurgency. Should be right up your street.'

'But, sir, my daughter.'

'What about her, Inspector? Housewife as well are we?'

'No sir,' he lied.

'How old is she?'

'Nearly sixteen, sir.'

'Oh, I'm sure she can look after herself for six weeks.'

'Six weeks?'

'That's right, Inspector. Seven days a week for six weeks. It's very intensive. Might lick you into some shape.'

'But . . . who'll be in charge at the station?'

'Sergeant Jones, of course.'

'S . . . ' His jaw dropped. 'Er . . . when does the . . . training course start, sir?'

'First thing Monday morning.'

Chip Off the Old Block.

The night after Mary was taken away, Father Vernon had the first of a series of dreams that disturbed him throughout the summer.

Blasphemy is one thing, but systematic, organised profanity is quite another, especially if you believe, like he did, that dreams are the consciousness of the soul.

But, the priest decided, if he was eventually to return to some kind of normality he must face his fears and sleep through the night, come what may. So he cast himself on to his bed and fell asleep almost immediately.

There was some catching up to do.

And catch up he did.

Within a very short time he had had sex with practically everyone he knew – and some he didn't. The entire youth club writhed and pulsated as one. One young woman he knew was having sex with ten young men in a series of vaginas that had sprung out all over her body.

171

He and Nicola were wandering round watching people and holding hands.

'I've never seen that before,' said Nicola. 'I've got a vagina under my arm, but I've never made love with it. I usually pretend it's my armpit.'

'Very original,' laughed the priest.

'Will you tickle me there?' Nicola asked and Father Vernon was just about to oblige when he saw the Archangel Gabriel approaching, dressed in a shell-suit.

'Dear boy, no time for that now.'

'That's not like you,' grinned Nicola.

'Duty calls,' replied the Archangel and he and Father Vernon were in Bolton town centre. Father Vernon felt a little out of place, being naked.

'I know how you feel,' remarked the Archangel. 'He was just the same – walking round starkers. I had to borrow these suits from a washing line.' The Archangel stopped. 'How do I look?'

Father Vernon didn't want to hurt his feelings. 'Fine.'

'You always were a diplomat.' The old man pointed at some striped material. 'You could always put your pyjamas on, you know.'

Father Vernon's pyjamas were lying at the side of the road. 'I must have left them there' he thought. 'Where are we going?'

'He wants to talk to you. I suggested taking human form, to show Him what it's like. But it's not going well. He's getting frustrated.'

They came to a chip shop, down a quiet side street. God was in there, dressed in his own shell-suit, which Father decided made him look quite magnificent.

'He's very proud. He insisted on getting a job, to pay his way.' The Archangel shrugged. 'I've got a cash card.'

There was quite a queue considering that the shop was out of the way.

'The women love him,' observed the Archangel. 'Well, He is rather attractive, don't you think?'

Father Vernon thought Him the most beautiful man he had ever seen.

'He can't help it, he just does everything right.'

They were the only men waiting in the queue.

When He saw Father Vernon God was cross. 'What was the demonstration about?'

Father Vernon was somewhat taken aback. He didn't know what to reply. .

The Archangel nudged him. 'You'd better explain.'

'Erm, there was a bit of trouble.'

'So I heard. Did you turn the other cheek?'

'There was a young lad, unfairly arrested.'

'By whom?'

'An over zealous officer.'

'A friend of yours,' put in the Archangel.

God stopped what He was doing, pouring some chips from a bucket into the fat. He pursed His lips. 'Did he have a moustache?'

'Yes.'

God threw the bucket into the corner and growled angrily. 'I ought to have wiped him out!'

Some of the women in the queue sighed appreciatively at this manly out-burst, a couple of others looked anxious. Father Vernon was shocked. He looked at the Archangel who gave him a tired look.

'We have go through the proper channels,' sighed the old man.

'So does he,' snapped God, shoving the chips around violently and splashing His wrist with hot fat. 'Ouch!' He wailed. 'Damn this body to Hell!'

A couple of the women took God into the back of the shop to fix up His arm. Gabriel took Father Vernon by the arm and led him out.

They were immediately back among the revellers at the youth club. Even the walls had sprouted vaginas now.

'You see my problem?' shouted the Archangel over the din. 'He's frustrated because He wants everything done properly, yet it's very hard to do.'

Father Vernon was distracted already. He wanted to explore the building. And find Nicola before morning. 'What shall I do,' he asked.

'Whatever you can,' replied the angel.

'Anything. Anything at all,' agreed the priest and returned to his beloved flock.

A Dressing Down.

'Where the hell is she?' demanded Bill Carson as he burst into the livingroom.

He had been filled with anxiety all week, awaiting his summons from the court and was in the mood for a fight.

'Oh, hello darling. Yes, I had a lovely time at bridge, thank you. The Carmichaels send their regards. June said we must go for dinner one night, soon. Mark's doing very well at school. But Harry's firm are having difficulties . . . ' His wife looked at him for the first time. 'And your daughter's upstairs in her room.'

'What?' He was almost shocked. He hadn't seen her all week. She hadn't even been home at night, which was a serious breach of the increasingly ineffective rules. He leapt up the stairs and burst into her room.

She was standing there in her underwear and Penny was sitting on the bed. It was the middle of the afternoon. He was momentarily thrown off course.

'What the hell ...'

'Father! I'm getting changed!'

He looked at Penny whose face hadn't even flinched.

'Where the hell have you been all week? You haven't even stayed here one night!'

'I've been out.'

He stood there, staring.

Penny moved his head for the first time and looked at him.

'Has she been at your house?' Bill asked somewhat more politely.

Penny shook his head.

Nicola was rapidly pulling on her clothes.

'You just came home to get changed, did you?'

'Yes, as a matter of fact.'

She was stuffing belongings into a little ruck-sack at the same time. Very hurried.

'I was on the verge of calling the police.'

Silence. Packing and dressing.

Penny casually turned the pages of a magazine.

Bill stood there, flabbergasted.

'Come on, Penny.'

She was pulling on a jacket, stuffing her feet into some shoes, trying to zip up her bag and leave all at the same time.

Bill grabbed her arm. 'I demand to know where you're going. I'm your father.'

'Drop dead,' she said, pulled herself free and continued on her way. Penny followed her.

She stopped at the top of the stairs. 'And let's get one thing straight. I may have come out of your penis some time in the distant past, but you ain't my dad now.'

They stared at each other for a moment. Both

recalling the time he struck her, since when their relationship had been an outright disaster. Then she made off down the stairs.

'Do you mind if I use the phone?' he called after her. She'd left the handset on the bed.

'Be my guest,' she shouted and slammed the front door.

Bill kicked around in her room for a few moments and then picked up the phone and began to dial.

'What a bloody mess,' he thought.

He surveyed the scene while he waited for a connection.

He saw a packet of condoms left quite openly on her chest of drawers. 'She's going to wind up in trouble that girl,' he thought. Then he snorted miserably. 'Like her father ...'

Someone answered.

'Swanny? It's Bill.'

'Oh, hello.'

'Are you alright? You sound a bit ... low.'

'Oh, I'm alright.'

'Listen. I wondered if you could meet me for a drink tonight. I've got something I need to talk to you about.'

'Tonight?' The old copper didn't sound too keen.

'Just for twenty minutes or so, it's quite important.'

'Er ...'

'I suppose it could wait till Monday ...'

'No, no. I'm away next week.'

'Oh. Anywhere nice?'

'No. Not really.' There was a sigh.'Yes. Tonight's fine. At the golf club?'

'How about eight?'

'Um. I'll see you there.'

'You sure you're alright?'

'Yeah, yeah. See you later.'

'O.K. Bye.'

Bill frowned for a second. His old friend didn't sound too happy at all. He wondered if this was the right time to speak to him.

'There's never going to be a right time,' he lamented.

He put the phone back on Nicola's bed. Then snatched it back up. 'What am I doing?'

He was just about to leave the room when his eyes alighted on something odd among the debris of the bed. He smoothed a crease in the covers to reveal several white discs of unleavened bread.

He picked them up and stood looking at them.

'Don't tell me she's going to a Catholic church,' he thought and quickly dismissed the possibility. 'How odd.'

He paused for another moment, gazing in astonishment at the hosts, then put them in his jacket pocket and left the room.

Parting Shots.

Swann was doubly depressed.

Not only was he about to be whisked away, God knows where, to do God knows what for six weeks, but his beloved daughter hadn't spoken to him all week. She hadn't even flinched when he told her he was going away.

He gazed at the bevelled mirror on the livingroom wall and sighed. He'd even miss the next gymkhana.

He felt a sudden stab of anxiety at the thought. What if the swine were there? And those damn girls, inviting her to parties?

He thought about Nicola Carson. She'd been there Saturday, with that damn Catholic priest. Which brought him round to pondering Bill Carson's request for a meeting.

'I wonder what he's after. Bound to be something,' he mused. 'It's about time he brought that daughter of his under some control'.

At that moment Eve came into the room and stood looking at him, almost coyly. It was as if the very tip of the sun were peeping over a mountain. He wanted to say something to her, but he was overawed.

'Daddy,' she said. 'I want to apologise for my behaviour. I've been beastly all week.'

There was a faint stirring of hope. He thought he heard a cello tuning up, ready to weep a sonata.

'Oh ... ' he shrugged casually and was about to forgive her everything when she cut him off.

'No, Daddy. It's not fair. I've been sulking all week because you wouldn't let me go to a stupid party.'

'It was for your own good, Evey.'

'Yes Daddy, I know. That's why I'm apologising. And it really isn't your fault.' She sighed, heavily. 'Women ... women have these problems ... sometimes.' She looked down. 'Once a month.'

The old copper blushed. 'Yes. Yes, of course.' The cello struck up. Women's problems. Of course. She was a woman. A real woman. He beamed. 'I assumed it was something like that, darling. I didn't want to say anything.'

'Of course you didn't. You're very understanding. I just didn't want you to go away thinking ... I didn't want you to worry about me while you were away.'

She came over to hug him and the old copper nearly burst into tears.

'Nothing of the sort,' he said.

As they hugged a funny little pattern of wrinkles appeared on the young woman's forehead. Rather as if she had just bitten into a lemon.

When he'd recovered his composure, Swann said: 'Darling, I won't be here for the next gymkhana.'

'I know that Daddy, I don't mind, honestly.'

'It's not that, Evey.' He expressed his reluctance with a sigh. 'It's just that ... it's for your own good ...'

'I won't go, daddy. Don't worry.'

The old copper smiled. She was such a good girl.

Woman.

'Two whiskeys please.'

'Make mine a double.'

'That's better, Swanny. Two large whiskeys, please,' ordered Bill.

They were standing at the bar in the golf club house. Donald Swann heaved a sigh but gave nothing away with his face.

'Having a hard time of it?'

'I'll say. There was nearly a riot, Saturday night.'

'On Sunnymeadow?'

'Where else.'

The drinks arrived. Bill paid.

'Your daughter was in the thick of it,' Swann said and knocked his drink down in one. 'Same again, please.'

Bill was immune to such shocks by now. Almost. He knocked his own drink back and said: 'And again,' to the barman.

He stopped the copper getting his wallet out. 'I'm getting these,' he insisted and the old copper knew his friend was in some kind of trouble.

'Where are you off to?'

'Sorry?'

'Next week. You said you were going somewhere not very nice.'

They were sat on an old leather sofa now, with a

179

bowl of peanuts on a shining wooden table before them.

'Oh just some training.'

'So you can teach old old dog new tricks, eh, Swanny?'

The copper made an expansive gesture. 'It's a promotion really.'

Bill raised his eyebrows. For once he was happy to listen to his old friend's boasting. 'Very good. You've waited long enough.'

The off-duty Inspector looked at him. It hadn't been intended as an insult.

'I mean, you've worked hard,' added Bill, by way of compensation.

'It's a whole new world. There's a lot of new technology. New techniques. I'm moving up to counter insurgency.'

'Why, are they expecting a revolution in Bolton?' Bill laughed. And wished he hadn't.

'As I said. There was nearly a riot on Sunnymeadow last Saturday.'

Bill caught the implication. 'Yes. Yes ... Nicola was there, you say?'

He didn't really want to know.

'And several hundred others. Youths.'

'Isn't it always the youths,' observed Bill, feeling depressed all of a sudden. It wasn't going well at all. How was he going to ask now?

'It's none of my business,' said the old copper after a lull.

('Oh my God, here we go', thought Bill.)

'But you really ought to have a word with that girl of yours.'

'Umm,' ummed Bill.

'I don't want to worry you, but if matters had got any worse she may well have got herself arrested.'

'What happened, exactly?' asked Bill wearily.

'They practically stormed the police station.'

'What!'

'There were bloody hundreds of them. Someone might have got killed.'

'Were there many arrests?'

'Er . . . Only one as a matter of fact.'

'I see,' said Bill in such a way that made the old copper feel uncomfortable. He remembered the interview at Chester House and his stomach contracted slightly.

'Yes. I was personally commended by the Divisional Commander for the minimum use of force.'

'Of course,' said Bill 'The fewer arrests the better, I suppose.'

'Absolutely,' declared the old liar and cheered up a little.

'What was Nicola's role in all this?'

'Yes, well. It's rather hard to know at this stage. But I can tell you this much. She seems to be rather fond of a certain Catholic priest.' The words 'Catholic priest' were spat from the old copper's mouth.

Bill frowned. 'Oh, yes?'

'Yes, she had her hands all over the fellow and I have to say, he looked to be rather enjoying himself.'

'Umm,' said Bill darkly.

'Runs some kind of youth club. But I tell you . . . there's something not quite right about him.'

'Really? Like what?'

'Well, it's only a hunch at this stage. But I intend to find out more about him. He's got a certain look about him. He's young. And Irish.'

'Papist, eh?' Bill put his hand in his pocket and produced the hosts for inspection.

'What are they?'

'I found them in Nicola's bedroom, this afternoon.'

'Her bedroom?' A picture was beginning to develop in the old copper's criminally investigative mind. 'Let me see.' He took one of the hosts and held it up to the light. Smelt it. Then put it in his mouth. 'It's fresh,' he said.

'Really?' said Bill and tried one himself.

All For One.

About twenty minutes later Bill Carson and Donald Swann began to feel very good indeed.

'You know what?' said Swann. 'I feel like letting my hair down.'

'Yeah? Did you have anything in mind?' asked Bill Carson. 'I have,' he thought.

'Let's drive round somewhere. Have you got time?'

'Nothing but,' grinned Bill. He hadn't broached the subject that he had in mind, yet, but as the effects of the hosts took hold, he started to feel less worried about the whole affair.

'How about Manchester?' asked the old copper.

'Your car or mine?'

Five minutes later they were heading down the A666, feeling even better still.

The old copper was driving. 'I'll tell you what,' he said, feeling very talkative. 'I love my daughter that much I'd commit any kind of murder to protect her.'

'The way things are going, you may have to,' said Bill blandly.

'Love's a strange thing,' said the old copper.

Bill had a different kind of love on his mind right now.

'It's a shame you've got no real relationship with

Nicola. I'm sure she's a great girl underneath it all.'

'It's just a phase they go through,' asserted Bill, hopefully.

'Not my Evey. She still calls me daddy and tells me she loves me. She told me that today. This very afternoon.'

'You're a lucky man, Swanny,' said Bill and for once he didn't resent him for it. 'Where shall we go?'

'Let's go and look at the whores.'

Bill looked at his friend in astonishment. 'Great mind's think alike,' he said.

Quarter of an hour later they were driving down Minshull Street, feeling positively ecstatic.

'Look at that type there,' said the old copper, pointing at a black woman, wearing the shortest skirt in the world.

The car nearly mounted the pavement.

'I wouldn't touch that with yours,' laughed Bill untruthfully.

'I would,' said the old copper and laughed for the first time in about three weeks. 'Let's go round again.'

He swung the car round to do another tour.

'You've got to be careful round here, Swanny. They're watching the place.'

'Don't be ridiculous, I'd know about it if they were.'

'I'm serious. A friend of mine was caught picking someone up here, last weekend. By the vice squad.'

The old copper tutted. 'You don't pick anyone up here! This is just to get you in the mood. You go somewhere else for that.'

It was a night of surprises for Bill Carson. He was seeing a different side of his old friend. And he liked what he saw. It suited his purposes.

'There's an old hotel, on the Wilbraham Road.

Only it's not a hotel,' winked the off duty Inspector and caused a dangerous situation to develop on the road in front. A passing van sounded it's horn. 'Have you got any money on you?'

'No,' said Bill. 'But I've got my cash point card.'

'Was it Cynthia Payne who said "You can never talk to a man 'till he's been de-spunked"?' asked the old copper, later, with a coarseness Bill had never heard before.

'Probably,' replied the preacher-man.

'So what did you want to talk about?'

The two men had visited the hotel that isn't a hotel on the Wilbraham Road and were now enjoying a drink in an upstairs club, somewhere off the Oldham Road in Manchester city centre.

'Well you know that friend of mine I was telling you about, who was caught by the vice squad, last Saturday night . . .'

'Oh no.' The old copper grimaced. 'It was you.'

'Brilliant deduction, Holmes.'

'It's nothing to worry about,' sighed Swann. 'It's a standard fine. Sexual Offences Act.' Then the penny dropped. 'Ah . . . Your career!'

'Precisely.'

'You've been summonsed?'

'I'm going to be.'

Swann said: 'Leave it with me.'

'Can you do something for me?'

The off-duty Inspector nodded and looked hard at the degenerate preacher-man. 'Can you do something for me?' he asked. Apparently serious.

'Sure. Anything. What do you need?'

'An ally.'

Bill was puzzled. 'What kind of ally?'

The old copper sighed. 'I'm worried.'

'What about?'

'Things.'

Bill nodded. Then made a mock-Tudor bow. 'Your humble servant.'

The two men looked into each other's eyes.

Swann said: 'I'm serious.'

Bill Carson said: 'So am I.'

---

52. In the House.

Father Vernon was in his element.

In two short weeks his life and that of the parish had been transformed.

From early morning to last thing at night the Presbytery was a hive of activity and the young priest was at the centre of it. There were now seven people in residence but everything was in harmony. There was a preponderance of colourful new decorations throughout and the house had become a home once more.

The walls were covered in posters of every shape and size and Michael Jackson, Jason Donovan, Richard Gere, Madonna, *Take That, East 17,* Winnie the Pooh, The Little Mermaid, Bart Simpson, or Thomas the Tank Engine watched everything Father Vernon did.

He even added a few touches of his own. Including an old Van Morrison poster in his bedroom.

There was no stumbling over bottles, or getting drunk on shampoo and no cleaning up to do after anyone but himself — and occasionally little Lisa, whom the young priest adored. He would bounce the little mite on his knee for hours and hush her to sleep with lullabies, when Betty was too tired.

The household was united. They felt like comrades and friends, thrown together by circumstances to face the world and all it could turf at them.

The original four – Betty, Theresa, Michelle and Jo took the living room and established their bedtime foursome (and occasionally four-and-a-halfsome), in their luxurious psychedelic bed. Nicola took Mary's old room upstairs and Father Vernon was left on his own again.

Which suited him fine because he slept like a baby.

And dreamt like a demon.

Even by the first Wednesday things had begun to change for the better and the early morning Mass was packed.

It was Betty's idea originally.

They should make soup every day and distribute it among the elderly people on the estate, at lunchtime. She had met Mrs Kershaw and the others at the party and danced and chatted with them for most of the afternoon, finding their company preferable in some ways to that of the younger revellers who had shown up.

They needed help and Betty was only too glad to oblige.

Father Vernon thought this was a grand idea and he decided to help out with the distribution himself, whilst at the same time doing some publicity for the Wednesday morning service – after which they would put on a coffee morning (which turned into a bit of a sing-song and dance).

The parish was positively throbbing.

One afternoon Eve had appeared to a rapturous welcome.

No one had seen her since the party and when they opened the door she was standing there in her red, outlaw scarf. There were screams of delight and hugs.

'I thought you only borrowed that?' shouted Nichola over the din.

'It suited me,' beamed Eve.

Soon they were all sitting round the kitchen table drinking coke and munching crisps. They were all dying to know what had happened when her father got home.

'Shhh . . .'

'Well,' began Eve, brimming with pride. 'I didn't speak a word to the bastard all week.' She got the word 'bastard' from Nicola, whom she adored. 'I couldn't believe it . . . he never said a word about anything.'

There were grins and scowls all round.

'I could see he was worried about me . . . He thought I was sulking about not being allowed to go to the party! I wanted to show him my bruise and say somebody had beaten me up – see his face.'

'Bastard,' said Nicola.

'Anyhow . . . .' Eve paused dramatically. 'He's gone away for six weeks! . . .'

There was a collective cry of joy.

She almost had to shout over the din: 'When he told me he was going, I thought I'd better play very safe. So I went up to him . . . put on my best hurt little girl act and said: (here she put on a silly voice and quoted herself) Daddy, I'm ever so sorry I've been sulking . . . I know I've been beastly, but I've got . . . you know . . . women's problems . . .'

There were squeals of laughter.

She went on. 'And I want you to know I'm terribly, terribly sorry. So please don't worry about me while you're away, Daddy.'

They all laughed again.

Father Vernon was reading the *Catholic Herald* in

his study, upstairs and wondered what could possibly be giving them all so much pleasure.

At the beginning of the second week, Michelle called a meeting to discuss the future.

Father Vernon was invited but declined to attend. He decided that his role would be strictly pastoral. They were part of his flock and other than that he would mind his own business.

They would do what ever they decided themselves and he would assist them as best he could, making suggestions when he saw fit. Especially if he thought they might be of benefit to the parish. That was his decision and he stuck to it. And he was proud because he thought it radical and democratic.

The priest heard that there was some fierce debate in the meeting, but noticed that they were all the best of friends afterwards. Except perhaps Betty. But she often seemed removed from the others – distant somehow.

Later that day he read the minutes which had been taken and typed up by Nicola who had done a business admin class at school.

He saw that Michelle had been put in charge of finances (opposed by Betty but carried).

Theresa and Jo were to organise more public shows.

Nicola was to help Betty in the parish.

'What do you think, Dad?' asked Nicola when he'd finished reading.

'Very interesting,' he replied.

'Is that all you can say?' she laughed.

'Yes,' he said and smiled. 'That's all I can say.'

Something to Say.

One morning Betty found Theresa down on her knees in prayer.

Poor Betty was dismayed but not surprised. 'There's some carrots need chopping in the kitchen,' she said without ceremony.

Theresa ignored her.

'Or are you busy polishing the floor?'

Little Lisa ran over and jumped on Theresa's back.

Theresa pretended to come out of a trance and Betty plonked herself down on the sofa.

'Oh, hi.'

Betty expressed herself with a barely detectable scowl — which Theresa could have detected at a hundred yards.

'I was praying,' she explained, trying to hide her self-consciousness by fussing over Lisa.

'I thought you were practising for when the police pick you up.'

'Very funny.'

Theresa wanted Betty to acknowledge that she'd seen her praying. Betty's instinct was to leave it and hope the fad would disappear of it's own accord, like Theresa's brief membership of the Anti-Apartheid movement and her crush on Madonna.

'I was asking for God's guidance.'

'Did 'e tell you to wash your 'air and change your clothes?'

Theresa looked away. 'Actually, 'e didn't say anything.'

Betty wanted to be contrary, so as to avoid taking her friend seriously. ''Ow d'you know it's a *he*?'

'I don't,' replied Theresa seriously.

Betty was forced to resort to silence.

189

Theresa went over to the writing desk in the corner and made a show of opening the bible she had obviously been reading. This was too much for Betty to ignore.

'She thinks she's Jesus Christ now, don't she Tiny?'

'Bollocks!'

'Oh, sorry – no, Tiny, I think she thinks she's God!'

Theresa tutted and closed her bible. 'Pissorf!'

'You're such a bloody show off!'

'I'm just looking for something to say.'

'Who to?' asked Betty with some indignation.

'People.'

'What bloody people?'

Theresa shrugged. 'Everyone, when I do a miracle.'

'Magic trick, you mean . . .'

Theresa said *Whatever*, by tilting her head.

'I'm sure they're gunna listen to you!'

'They will when they see what I can do.'

Betty laughed, heartily. 'Yeah. Everyone listens to Paul Daniels, don't they.'

''E don't say anything.'

''E's got bloody brains.'

Theresa was crest-fallen and could no longer hide it. 'It was your bloody idea in the first place,' she moaned.

'What was?'

'To do something.'

'Fuckin' wasn't!'

'You said I was selfish.'

'You are.'

'I'm . . . I thought we were trying to help people.'

'I thought you were trying to be a big star.'

'It's not about that.'

Betty shrugged nonchalantly. Or tried.

'I know what I'm doing!'

'Is that why you're asking God for help?'

190

'Fuck off.'

They fell silent, while little Lisa perused the bible, tearing out the odd page she fancied.

Then Betty wondered why she was so irate and softened up. 'Do you really want to help people?' she asked.

'Yeah.'

'Well, come and chop the carrots, then.'

Theresa sighed and stood up. 'You dick 'ead,' she laughed.

'Cheers,' said Betty. 'Luv you too.'

And she did.

Central Performance.

If they hadn't been made of stone, the lions on the steps of Bolton Town Hall would surely have yawned.

Like Sergeant Jones.

He almost preferred being on duty to shopping on a Saturday afternoon. Especially with his whole family. It was bad enough with the wife, but when the kids and her mother were there it was unbearable.

'We'll go off and buy an ice-cream,' he said.

'Ah, go on. Leave me 'ere in me wheel-chair, then. I'll talk to meself.'

They were standing outside *Boots the Chemist*. The off-duty Sergeant was under instruction to 'look after mum and the kids', while his wife nipped in.

'Yeah an ice-cream!' squealed the kids and tugged him off towards the caravan. The fat man looked at his mother-in-law over his shoulder and pretended that he was powerless over the children.

She scowled and they escaped.

'Back in a min ...'

The caravan only sold hot dogs so the plump children dragged the not-so-reluctant father off across the huge square in search of sweet refreshment.

There was some civic event or other winding up on the steps of the Town Hall and a small television crew were having difficulty with a group of youths who were jumping in front of their shots and generally interfering.

All over the square forlorn groups of youths and elderly people fought against boredom, smoked cigarettes and shoved down starchy snacks. In the stone hut at the far end of the square there appeared to be some sort of open air jumble sale.

It was England at its finest. A picture of natural law and municipal order. Sergeant Jones sighed sleepily.

Without Inspector Swann life was sleepy.

For some reason there hadn't been any crime on Sunnymeadow lately.

And certainly no major dramas.

Maybe he should make a few arrests to keep up appearances.

He bought the kids an ice-cream, and a double ninety-nine with extra sauce for himself. They were strolling back across the square when he was accosted by a young woman.

''Ere, try one of these.' The young woman trust a small white disc of what looked like a novelty sweet into his hand. 'It's free ... ' she said and winked. Then accosted someone else. 'There's a show on,' he heard her say.

It looked like a sacramental host. With a cross on it.

'Can I have one Dad?' asked his little son.

Suddenly there was the sound of music and a

crowd of unpleasant youths who were gathered round a couple of amplifiers began dancing. In the street. In broad daylight. And some elderly people appeared to be joining in.

He felt someone tug his arm. 'Can of coke for your kids, mister?'

Two young women were standing there. One with a make-shift tray round her neck, containing soft drinks and the other with a money belt round her waist, like a market stall holder.

'Have you got a licence for that?' inquired the fat man, as much out of curiosity as anything.

The two girls exchanged a glance and laughed.

The red-haired one said: 'Course we bloody 'aven't!' tutting. 'D'you want one or not?'

They could tell by the look on his face he didn't.

''E's had too many already by the look of 'is belly,' said the other one,. with great cheek and they both ran off, laughing.

Another young woman approached and gave him a second host. He frowned and pocketed them both.

He realised he was standing amidst some considerable jollification and at the same moment caught sight of the young man they had arrested on Sunnymeadow, with the broken nose. He was standing with a pretty young girl he thought he recognised from somewhere, over by the amplifiers.

He suddenly felt the need to make his presence discreet.

'Come on, you two. Time to go and find Mummy,' he said, turning round to find his two youngsters had gone missing.

If there had been a camera there, Sergeant Jones would have turned and looked into it, like Oliver Hardy. But there wasn't, so he contented himself with a deep sigh.

And then he saw them. One was in the arms of the

girl he vaguely recognised and the other was just being picked up by the lad with the broken nose.

'Why is life so complicated?' pondered the off-duty ice-cream licker and was just wondering what to do when he realised that the two youths were talking to his wife and mother-in-law, who was sitting there in her wheelchair.

The really strange thing was that his mother-in-law was smiling nicely and chatting away. She hated most things, but especially young people. What had come over her?

Then there was an announcement over the small public address system. It was the same bunch alright. There was that spotty youth on the microphone, with whom Inspector Swann had remonstrated. People like that should be confined to their own areas.

'Where's that bloody Catholic priest?' he wondered. But the troublesome cleric was nowhere to be seen.

The blushing youth was shouting about some kind of event that was about to take place. People began to jostle for a position close to the front and despite a fear that a dangerous situation was developing, Sergeant Jones' curiosity got the better of him.

Even the bloody television crew were hovering around. And when spotted, they were ushered to the front by the two girls who had illegally tried to sell him a soft drink. He looked back over the crowd into the square. Surely there was a policeman somewhere in the town centre?

The rest of the square was almost deserted. People were attracted by the commotion and everyone wanted to see what was going on.

Then a strange looking young woman climbed up on to some kind of platform and just stood there. The music stopped and all that could be heard among the assembly was a subdued murmur of anticipation.

Most of the youths that were involved climbed up and stood behind the mysterious girl.

Then a very peculiar thing happened.

The man standing next to him floated up into the air above the crowd and seemed to just hang there. Some people cheered. Then the man seemed to come to his senses and realise what had happened. As he did so his arms began to flail helplessly and he began to jerk about as if he had lost his balance, which greatly increased the level of amusement in the audience.

Next thing, he was floating forward and came to rest on the platform, next to the Sunnymeadow youths, who grinned wickedly and smiled at him.

All he could do was show that he was the good-humoured sort.

The strange girl began to speak to the crowd.

Listening to her the Sergeant thought: 'Surely they're not religious nuts. Not from Sunnymeadow . . .'

Then the young woman was interrupted by shouting from down in front of the stage and an old woman began to climb up on the platform.

It was his mother-in-law.

The man who had been levitated bent down to help her, but she brushed him off. She had got out of her wheel-chair, unaided and was standing there, a little unsteadily for sure, but independently.

She raised her arms aloft and shouted: 'I'm cured! . . . I can walk! I just climbed out of me wheel chair . . . and I can walk!'

Next thing, the television crew had taken her to one side and were doing an on-the-spot report.

The Sergeant thought it was time to rejoin his family.

His wife was holding the children.

'I bloody told you she could walk,' she said.

195

Sergeant Jones wanted to have words with the youths who were responsible for the disturbance.

So did the television crew.

But they were nowhere to be found.

The amplifiers were gone and so were they.

Chosen.

'This is your programme and God's listening to you right now.'

'Hello Father, I can't walk and I need to know where that girl is. The healer.'

Bill Carson was getting annoyed. 'God is the great healer. You must have faith in the Lord, my son.'

'Oh, I know that, Father. But I'd like to find her anyhow. Do you know where she is?'

'I'm afraid not.' Bill tried a different tack. 'Do you have a . . . serious condition?'

'Oh I'm confined to a wheel-chair.'

'And do you have faith?'

'Well I've seen her on T.V. a couple of times and I believe she can do it, yes. Several people have been cured, haven't they?'

Bill sighed and looked at his engineer.

Laura raised her teacup to him in salute.

This was the fifth call on the subject that evening and he'd only been on the air for half an hour.

'I think there's a tremendous religious revival just now,' observed the caller, unchecked. 'I mean a man in Rochdale saw an angel at the rubbish dump, Wednesday, and according to my cousin in Runcorn an old lady ascended straight to Heaven a few weeks back . . .'

'Yes, there are all kinds of rumours . . .'

196

'Oh, they're not just rumours, Father, it's God's honest truth ...'

Bill surrendered and sat back from the console.

'It's the British, you see. We've been chosen by God. I mean the bloody Pakis round our way can't be doing with it ...'

'Rad-io Bol-ton Cares ...'

Bill wasn't so much defending ethnic minorities as finding a good excuse to get rid of the caller. And the theme.

'The English are raving mad!' he thought. 'Thank God I'm not one of them.'

He raised his eyebrows at Laura.

'Let us pray, listeners, for tolerance among people of all creeds and colours. Pray for the spirit of understanding. Next caller, please.'

There was a crackle and some heavy breathing. Bill was ready with his jingle.

'Hello, Father,' croaked a woman's voice. 'I'm in hospital and I need to talk.'

'Uh-oh,' thought Bill and said: 'This is your programme and God's listening to you right now ...'

'I'm all alone in the world ...'

The voice was slow and painful. Each word seemed like a terrible effort.

'... I've been abandoned by God and I'm all on my own.'

'God will never abandon his children. You have only lost contact,' said Bill and felt quite glad to be talking to a normal human being.

'No, Father. He's completely abandoned me. I'm really stranded.'

'You sound very hurt.'

'My heart's broken, Father.'

'Can I ask your name?'

'It's Mary. We have spoken before, Father, you told me to pray for God's love ...'

'Yes?'

Something was stirring in Bill's memory.

'But He let me down. Abandoned me. And now I'm in a loony bin.'

'Do you mean a home for the mentally disabled, Mary?'

'Full of bloody loonies.'

'Have you prayed, Mary?'

'No I haven't!'

'Are you very angry?'

'Of course I'm bloody angry! I looked after that man for five years and what do I get for it? Locked up!'

'Which . . . man was that?' Bill was frowning.

'I can't tell you his name, Father, I still love him. I don't want him to know.'

'Was it . . . a professional person?' Bill had a feeling he remembered her now.

'A Catholic priest, Father . . . Threw me out. Took in a lot of girls.'

Bill sat up in his chair. Catholic bloody priest. Young girls. 'Er . . . which hospital are you . . . staying at?'

At that moment there was a terrible hissing and crackling. Bill shot a look at Laura who was wrestling with the controls in the engineer's box. She shrugged, puzzled by the interference.

Mary was very indistinct . . . 'get out of here . . . *hiss/crackle* . . . get out . . . *ccrrr* . . . back . . . *ssss/ ccccccrrr* . . . mine . . .'

Then there was a series of whistles and whines and suddenly someone else was on the air and all Bill and Laura could do was listen in horror.

'Special announcement . . . special announcement . . . calling all supporters. There will be a miracle tomorrow. Repeat . . . miracle tomorrow . . . Call this number to find out where . . . call this number tomorrow morning . . .'

Bill recognised the young woman's voice and his blood boiled as the number was read out.

'Sssssccccrrr . . . see you there . . . ssscccrrr . . .'

Bill was back on the air before he knew it. 'Can't you jam the fucking thing,' he accidentally broadcast and saw Laura cringe. 'Oh! Er . . . hello? Mary?'

She was gone.

'Oh, I apologise for the interference listeners. We seem to have lost Mary for now. Let us pray for her in her hour of need.'

His face was red as blood.

Mass Spectacle.

Sunday Mass had become something of a spectacle.

People suddenly travelled from miles around to be there and in a few short weeks attendance reached record levels.

Extra pews were carried in from the back of the Presbytery where they had languished since the church was first opened and seats were crammed into the aisles at both sides, yet still people had to stand during all three services.

In the end Father Vernon was forced to borrow a small public address system from Penny, so as to make himself heard and even toyed with the idea of adding an extra service to the itinerary.

On the forth week, a coach party turned up from Manchester and out stepped, or rather, hobbled, fifty-two elderly people from four rest homes that had clubbed together for the trip.

God knows how the word spread.

But there was an incredible dissemination.

A promulgation.

Which led to a proliferation of the congregation.

And the truly remarkable feature of the supplementary population was its age range. Or rather, make up.

The old and the young.

Father Vernon was uplifted in the extreme by the addition to his flock of what seemed like hundreds of local youths. Normally irreligious, previously antagonistic young people now unself-consciously packed the pews.

Many of the youths weren't Catholic, of course, but to Father Vernon this didn't matter in the least. In his capacity as a youth worker he understood that such formalities hinder successful community development. And after all, he was, essentially, a radical.

Admittedly the youths were restless during the litany and the Eucharist, which the enthusiastic clergyman found himself hurrying through, but by the time communion came around, they were positively jostling for position. And on one occasion so many hosts were distributed that, by the end, they had to be broken up and administered in fractions to ensure everyone received the Body of Christ.

And then came the true miracle of the new services.

Once the communion ceremony was concluded and the usual incantations recited, the party started. It was worship, the like of which no one had ever known. A real tribute to the glory of God. And, of course, the grace of humanity.

Musical instruments were produced — hand-held percussion; bongos; castanets; drums of all shapes and sizes. Anything that could be banged or rapped. Plus: banjos; clarinets; fiddles; a glockenspiel; a flugelhorn; flutes; gongs; guitars; a piccolo; pipes and trumpets. One week someone even produced a hurdy-gurdy.

Fantastic rhythms were invented and strange hymns improvised.

Devotees of all ages held hands, singing at the tops of their voices and the whole congregation danced to the strange enchanting rhythms.

The celebrations went on well over the allotted time and the Sunday morning rota had to be amended to allow for the elongated services to run their unpredictable course.

In between the unorthodox hymns, worshippers would sometimes add their own meditations to the ceremony, standing up and proclaiming God's love to shouts of 'Amen'.

People who had previously been convinced of their intonality sang like larks. People lately rigid wriggled like snakes. Cynics became romantic. Bigots were humbled. Sloths were energised.

One old lady was so moved during a service that she told everyone afterwards she had sat next to God and the Archangel Gabriel, dressed in track suits.

To a large extent Father Vernon lost control of the ceremony. Indeed he handed it over.

One Sunday he proclaimed from the pulpit: 'This is your church and and you, each and every one of you, must treat it as your home. That is the way God intended it.'

When he came back for the next Mass, young people had adorned the place with posters and hung brightly painted sheets, previously used at discos, from the walls and arches, giving the church the feel of a fluorescent grotto.

The young priest was worried in case of a reaction from the old people and decided the best thing was to take a vote at the end of his sermon.

There wasn't a single dissenting voice and during the closing celebrations, as a spontaneous act of approval, Mrs Kershaw again waggling like an iron post, led the congregation in a bizarre conga round the church, weaving in and out of the vivid new decorations.

As Father Vernon watched the ecstatic procession go by, he was almost overcome by the thunderous percussion and by the strangely harmonious cacophony, that resembled the Vienna Boys Choir singing with the football crowd at Old Trafford on a Saturday afternoon.

He caught sight of Nicola Carson tagging along at the end.

She called him: 'C'mon, Dad!' and he couldn't resist.

In his full battle dress (as he called his vestments) the happy priest took hold of Nicola's hips and joined in the conga with the rest of them.

As he half-hopped, half-stumbled down the centre aisle singing uproariously as he went, he caught sight of a man, sitting, unmoved in the back row of pews. The man was looking straight at him wearing something of a startled expression.

Father Vernon was just thinking to himself that this was the first proper adult he could remember having seen at the services, when Nicola stopped dead in her tracks. She took hold of the priest's hand and led him over to the stranger. Over the din he heard her say: 'Dad, this is my father.'

The Lot.

A lot can happen in six weeks.

Especially when your father is away.

Eve lost her virginity – or rather gave it away gladly, told Tony she was her father's daughter,

202

learned how to give head while working her way studiously through The Joy of Sex, got drunk for the first time and broke the bevelled mirror on the living room wall.

'That was his Mums,' she lamented picking up the pieces. 'He'll die, when he finds out!'

'Good riddance,' spat Tony. 'Bastard.'

'Yeah. Yeah, good riddance,' said Eve who'd forgotten herself for a moment.

One afternoon Michelle caught Nicola snogging Penny.

And that night she slept with him for the first time.

In the end she enjoyed it more than she thought she would and spent the next five nights with him. And for a whole week afterwards they were inseparable.

Jo became intensely jealous and highly resentful towards Nicola and one night attacked the girl with her curling tongs, but no damage was done.

In the end Nicola promised she would never kiss Penny again and Michelle returned to the fold. She'd had enough of Penny's constant company by then, anyway.

'Couldn't keep his hands off me!' she moaned to Jo afterwards.

'They're all the same,' Jo said, wondering why Michelle hated it so much.

At the same time Nicola Carson and Father Vernon became firm friends.

Before bed, watched over by Van Morrison, Father Vernon would read to Nicola from the armchair in the corner of his bedroom, while she sat on his bed. Nicola had borrowed one of Michelle's thick towelling dressing-gowns and every night she curled up, comfy as a mouse, taking in every word he read.

The books were very different from those that had preoccupied Father Vernon during his recent studies. He read old favourites from his student days, when he had been encouraged to read widely from secular literature by his old mentor, Canon Drinkwater.

In four weeks they got through: *Thérèse Raquin*, at which Nicola screamed aloud and squirmed on the bed; Dickens' *Hard Times*, in which Nicola cried at the sad bits, passionately hated Mr Bounderby and cheered at the end when he has a fit and drops dead in the street; and *One Hundred Years of Solitude* during which the entranced young woman expected it to rain flowers.

After *Thérèse Raquin* was finished and before they started *Hard Times*, Nicola patted the bed and said: 'Sit over 'ere, Dad, I can hardly hear you over there'. So he did.

After *Hard Times* and before they started *One Hundred Years of Solitude* she said: 'Can I get in while you read, Dad, I get a bit cold sometimes.'

'Course you can,' he said.

After *One hundred Years of Solitude* Nicola asked: 'Aren't you cold, Dad?' and he got under the covers while they started *Great Expectations*.

And every night, when he couldn't possibly read any more, Nicola hopped along the landing to her own room and they both fell asleep.

Perchance to dream.

Meanwhile Betty's soup kitchen expanded at a rapid rate.

She suggested to Father Vernon that special collections be made at the crowded church ceremonies and an appeal for money be put out with the parish bulletin. The extra funds could be used to provide better meals than just soup.

204

The appeal got a fantastic response and huge donations were received.

The money should really have been paid into the general funds of the Catholic church, of course, but Father Vernon was so pleased with the improvements to parish life that he decided to act independently.

He agreed to 'deal with the Bishop' on the question. Which basically meant keeping it quiet. No harm was being done, he reasoned, indeed a lot of good things had come.

All donations were requested in cash or postal orders to 'keep things fluid', as the enthusiastic young priest put it to supporters.

Perhaps the biggest change was in Theresa's popularity.

By the time Inspector Swann returned from his sojourn, Theresa was quite a star. At least in the North West and requests flooded in for her to open supermarkets and appear at sundry private functions and although she never accepted an invitation she was said to have appeared everywhere from Sainsburys to the roof of Liverpool Cathedral.

And of course journalists were on the lookout for the base of operations. So stealth and careful planning were the order of the day.

Miraculously photographs and T.V. cameras seemed incapable of capturing their faces on film – which greatly intensified the enigma and raised curiosity to near-hysteria. And, of course, helped to keep their identities secret.

When Theresa appeared in public, tight organisation was required.

For now, if the slightest indication was given of a

public appearance, the motorways of the North West became jammed within hours.

Coachloads of physically disabled raced against each other to be first to arrive at the scene. As soon as the announcement was made by cutting into Bill Carson's show, giving a Vodaphone number to contact for details, there was a region wide scramble.

Interested people, nothing to do with the Sunnymeadow youths, organised some kind of telephone network to alert people as soon as the location was discovered and a mobilisation took place with incredible efficiency.

Sites, well away from Sunnymeadow, were carefully reccied before hand so that Theresa and the others could escape by entering a building or vehicle and disappear without trace before anyone caught up with them.

At the gatherings hundreds scrambled for a chance to attract Theresa's attention, to demand healing or favours.

And not everyone was disappointed.

But most were.

Betty's flat was the base of operations.

It was a hive of activity.

In a few short weeks it had become the nerve-centre of a sophisticated clandestine organisation.

Except for Michelle's desk, the whole place was cluttered with debris.

There were boxes piled on boxes of soft drinks and hosts (which Father Vernon had been persuaded to order for them); crates and planks leant against the walls; a small but powerful PA system was stacked in the corner; papers and assorted office equipment were strewn everywhere; and, of course, a brand-new video system was kept in pride of place to replay their exploits, taped from local T.V. news coverage.

They had a vodaphone to publicise public appearances and huge donations were collected at events.

Michelle saw to it that money matters were kept straight by keeping careful records. The cash she kept well hidden. And only she knew where. (Well, and Jo)

'I can account for every penny,' Michelle boasted one day.

'I bet you bloody can,' answered Betty with considerable scorn.

Michelle and Jo's private money making schemes weren't going too well.

Selling cans doesn't make a million – especially when they are on sale in nearby shops and to Michelle and Jo the idea seemed a little tame after their mega shopping trip, but the trip had been a one off so they had to make do. They only made a few quid on Theresa's outings, but they remained optimistic about the future and for the present their overheads were negligible.

The estate was buzzing.

Several youths in the area had left their jobs and now spent their days helping out round the office and organising in the area. There was food to be distributed and special squads were created to help keep petty crime at bay. In fact many of the squads were made up of the petty criminals themselves, so they knew what they were doing.

From cash raised by Theresa's appearances and a contribution from diverted church funds, pocket money wages were paid to helpers and more got involved every day.

And of course food was provided by the 'soup kitchen', which was a fairly large scale food co-op by now, providing three meals a day for anyone who wanted it. And a surprising number of people were happy to pay for it, especially among the pensioners.

In short it was almost too good to be true. And certainly too good to last.

Sex and Religion.

Father Vernon and Nicola were rolling on the sofa in the living room at the Presbytery.

It was the first time he had actually made love to the girl and he was shocked by the way it happened so quickly and unexpectedly. She was talking to him and clutching him to her at the same time.

He just wished they could have been alone, although the others didn't seem to be taking much notice. They were all sitting in bed drinking tea and eating crisps.

It was rather like floating on air, he remarked to himself.

Next thing the Archangel Gabriel was kneeling next to them and the others had disappeared. Except Nicola, who was still sighing and panting happily.

'You're doing very well for the first time,' remarked the Archangel.

Father Vernon was flattered, if not slightly embarrassed.

'I just popped along to tell you the bad news,' said Gabriel with a puff. 'He's been sacked. From the chip shop. No-one's seen Him for days. Never turned up one morning so they had to give Him the push. I'll let you know as soon as I hear anything.'

*

Father Vernon remembered he was having a nap in his study when he was disturbed by Theresa.

He seemed a little flustered.

'Are you alright, Father?' asked the young woman.

'Yes. Yes, I was just having a peculiar dream,' replied the priest.

'What about?'

'Oh, this and that,' blushed Father Vernon. 'Did you want to see me?'

Theresa sat down, as invited. She too blushed slightly. 'I want to talk to you about God,' she said.

'Ah.'

'I can't talk to the others about it.'

'It's easier to talk about sex, these days,' joked the priest.

Theresa smiled.

'Fire away.'

'Well . . . ' She tilted her head. 'Where do you think my powers come from?'

Father Vernon's sigh came from a long way away.

'Do you think they come from God?' she ventured.

'Everything comes from God,' said the priest almost automatically.

'Bollocks,' replied the girl.

They both laughed.

'Don't play the school teacher. I wanna know what you think. You must think something or you wouldn't have invited us to stay.'

'Well if you must know I invited you to stay because of over-crowding.'

Theresa sat coyly back in her chair. 'Come on. What d'you reckon. You're the expert for God's sake.'

Father Vernon knew he would have to stop fooling and offer some proper spiritual guidance. But the problem was, it wasn't at all clear in his own mind. And while it was locked away inside, it remained a manageable mystery, or at least possible to ignore.

He took a breath. 'I think you have to decide for yourself what it all means, Theresa.'

'Oh that's a great help.'

He smiled, pathetically. 'I mean, in a way, what we think of it isn't important. What matters is what we do. It's how you use your powers that counts.' He looked up to gauge her reaction, which was neutral. 'If you assume they come from God and use them well, to help people as best you can, then what harm can you come to?'

Theresa thought this over for a while. 'What do you think we should do?' she asked eventually.

Father Vernon blinked. 'Whatever you think best.' He smiled. 'You will anyway.'

Now Theresa smiled. 'Thanks,' she said and stood up. 'Is that it?'

'That's all I'm gunna get. I can tell.'

He grinned.

'The Gospel according to Father Vernon,' she laughed. Then she came over, kissed him on the cheek, said 'God bless,' and skipped out of the room feeling a little sad.

A few minutes later, in their bedroom, Theresa put the bible she had been reading back on the shelf. ''S up to us,' she thought.

A Peak in Lancashire.

Stories create themselves, whether we like it or not.

A climax is inevitable. Things peak. Turning points arrive. You look back and see that there was a moment after which things were never the same again.

For Theresa this probably took place on Rivington Pike.

Things were never better – things were never worse than on Rivington Pike.

The Pike is about five miles from Sunnymeadow and rises above the Bolton suburb of Horwich, just up from Lord Leverhulme's Chinese Gardens.

It's characteristically strange, graffiti-embellished, urinous sandstone tower is perched on an sudden bump in the hillside. From the tower you can see the moors stretch out to the edge of the world and count six broadcasting masts.

Well, you used to able to, Now the windows have been bricked up so you need a bulldozer to get to the top.

The Chinese Gardens, (now owned by North-West Water) are hidden by rhododendrons. They are criss-crossed by a maze of paths and winding gullies down which local children dart and squeal, often plunging by accident into bushes or the well concealed ornamental swimming pool, now sadly strewn with rocks and debris.

The event had been well publicised and was due to begin at one o'clock in the afternoon. But, by nine o'clock in the morning, over a thousand people had gathered and the usually tranquil setting already resembled a shambolic jamboree. For generations the spot has been used by gypsy travellers on Good Friday to sell odds and sods and candy floss to local people. Today enterprising local traders (including Jo and Michelle) descended in droves and were peddling everything from toffee apples to 'made in Malaysia' religious paraphenalia.

Inspired by a stall selling small plastic replicas of Theresa, complete with stringy hair and baggy clothes Michelle was struck by the idea of selling bottles of 'holy water' along with their cans of Coke and Tango.

211

She bought some bottles of Lucozade, scraped off the labels, emptied out the contents, nipped to the pool in Lever park and that was that. By the time the others arrived to dish out the hosts Michelle had sold five bottles at five pounds each.

'It's a fuckin' miracle,' she told Nicola.

By the time Theresa arrived at ten-to-one it was like Woodstock without the acid. It was impossible to estimate the number of believers that attended. All that can be said for sure is that there were too many. You couldn't move for wheel-chairs, zimmer frames, folding chairs, picnic lunches and people. Loads and coach-loads of people. People everywhere. More than anyone could remember ever having seen before. And more kept coming.

Penny had hired a generator but even his PA was powerless over the vast expanse of people and only those within a certain radius of the Pike itself got to dance.

Theresa was overwhelmed at first. And worried for the safety of her followers. She could see disabled people being pushed up the steep incline towards the summit and she saw one old lady fall out of her wheelchair and cry out in pain.

People were jostling for position and shouting at each other to make room or sit down so they could get a better view of the make-shift podium. Theresa resisted the temptation to intervene for fear of being accosted.

It was Penny's idea – they asked his brother to organise some bouncers. Mainly to protect the equipment, but as it turned out they were needed to protect the stage area itself. By the time Theresa reached the top there was quite a struggle in progress. But when she clambered up onto the platform and Penny made the announcement an eerie silence fell across the whole gathering.

Even the children shut up.

And whereas the music had travelled only a matter of a few yards – seeming muffled and indistinct – every word Theresa spoke was clearly transmitted and heard by the whole assembly.

In truth it only lasted about thirty seconds, but to Theresa it seemed to have lasted for hours. It was her greatest speech ever and everyone was touched by it. Perhaps it was the result of so many people acting as one and concentrating so much attention at the same moment, maybe it all seemed more poignant in retrospect, especially in view of what happened immediately afterwards, or perhaps for once, Theresa caught the mood of the moment with her words.

Whatever it was for at least thirty seconds there was such an atmosphere of unity among the gathering that later Michelle congratulated Theresa. 'I thought you was serious for a moment!' she laughed, as she counted the proceeds of her day's work. 'I almost felt religious!' Which was odd because for the first time Theresa hadn't mentioned God at all.

This is what she said (and, don't forget, she was nervous, so it didn't come out quite right): 'Today is a special day . . . ' she paused between each sentence, which greatly intensified the impression of the silence. 'This is what happens when a lot of ordinary English people get together on a sunny afternoon. Six weeks ago none of this was possible, but now look. (Some people clapped here, though they weren't quite sure why) I've been given special powers. We've all got special powers. All of us. But what matters is what we do with them. And if we do the right thing, what harm can we possibly come to?'

At this point one or two people near the base of the rise stood up out of their wheelchairs. These were

213

all people who were able to do so normally, but it had an electrifying effect on the assembly. Theresa's last audible words were 'It doesn't matter what we say – it's what we do that's important ... ' the rest was lost. The spell was broken.

Quite how it descended into a stampede and then a near riot is unclear. But, certainly, people began to push forward in large numbers and fight among themselves. And many people, unfortunately, got on the wrong side of the bouncers. And, certainly, one or two people were assaulted (though it was never properly established who hit who first) And, certainly, there was a stampede.

And several people (two of whom fell out of wheel-chairs) ended up in the swimming pool in the Chinese Garden and four people suffered broken limbs.

Theresa, Michelle, Jo, Nicola, Eve, Penny and Tony were lucky to get away at all.

And, certainly, the police arrived too late. And acted inappropriately. And probably the real cause of the stone-throwing on a nearby estate that evening was a crowd of youths unconnected to the events on Rivington Pike.

But whatever happened. Things were never the same again.

Sunshine and Rain.

Father Vernon and Mary Magdalen symbolised something to each other.

To the young priest, his former housekeeper was guilt personified; her undoing was his doing; she represented neglect of duty; the fallen, or rather the pushed; his self-obsession. She was a victim of his carelessness and callous disregard for others.

Her own part in the descent was overlooked as the poor man now used her as a stick with which to beat himself up. Which meant, of course, that he still failed to see her as an independent being.

For Mary, Father Vernon represented the garden from which she had been cast out for her sins. He was reward denied. Paradise lost. And ultimately, her excuse to drink.

When he set eyes on her, sitting in a chair by her hospital bed, Father Vernon's spirits gave way to the most profound malaise. He was instantly depressed and felt choked by self-loathing.

When she saw him, Mary was uplifted to the highest degree. She was taken out of herself and transported to a leafy glade of serenity. Drugged up, as she was, she even imagined he had come to release her from her confinement, as well as her suffering.

Mary stood, a little unsteadily, held out her arms and they hugged, awkwardly. Mary held on tight and Father Vernon tried to ease himself from her grip. He felt as if he was holding a corpse. She felt as if she were making love to her long lost betrothed.

'How's things?' he asked as he subtly pushed her away.

'Oh, not too bad. I survive.'

'Have you had many visits?'

'No Father. Not one.'

This had been the wrong question to ask. Father Vernon made a mental note to organise a visiting rota. Why hadn't he thought of it sooner?

Self obsession.

'How's life at the Presbytery?' asked Mary, basking in the sunshine of his presence.

'Crowded,' answered the priest before he could stop himself.

A cloud passed over Mary's face. 'Yes. Keeping you busy, I suppose?'

'There's no peace for the wicked, Mary.'

'Oh I don't know, I get plenty of quiet down here.'

Father Vernon looked at her, trying to ascertain how serious she was. He sat down and changed his tone. It was difficult to know how to react. Did she really believe she was wicked?

'You're not ... there's nothing ... there's no sin involved, Mary. Alcoholism is an illness, it's widely known ...'

'I'm not an alcoholic!' snapped Mary, 'I've been ... depressed.'

'Yes. You need to rest.'

'I've had plenty of rest. I'm ready to get back down to some hard work.'

Father Vernon looked out across the gulf that separated them. He sighed and changed the subject. 'Well, Mrs Kershaw sends her regards and said to tell you she'll be visiting sometime next week.'

'Oh I'll be well away by then. But thanks anyway.'

Father Vernon tried as best he could not to confound the poor woman's expectations, but at the same time he didn't want to encourage her delusions. So he skirted issues and chatted his way round obstacles for the remainder of the visit and Mary was too drowsy to know the difference.

When he stood up to leave, the fact of his imminent departure struck Mary as a terrible blow, as if torrential rain had suddenly interrupted an idyllic, country scene.

The picnic was going to be ruined. There were provisions to be wrapped, a whole spread of delicacies to be returned to the hamper. There were precious belongings scattered everywhere.

'Don't leave yet, Father,' she stammered, reluctant to abandon the feast. 'The sun'll be out shortly.'

216

'Yes, it is looking brighter, isn't it?' said the priest, looking out of the window at the clouds and slowly backing away.

There was a kind of yelp as Mary dived into his arms. Clinging desperately to him. 'I'm coming with you,' she sighed.

'Erm . . . I don't think so, just yet, Mary. Soon perhaps.'

'Take me away!' she begged.

Father Vernon was looking round the ward for help. A male nurse saw them and came over.

'I'm a prisoner here. They torture me! I've been raped! And sodomised! Don't leave me!'

There was a scuffle that was pretending not to be a scuffle for a few moments and another male nurse hurried along. The struggle became more desperate.

In the end the poor, guilt-ridden priest had to literally tear himself free and escape from the ward at a trot while the two nurses restrained Mary. There was such a blood-curdling howl as he finally left, that his legs turned to stone and he had to limp down the corridor.

While he calmed down, he had a cup of tea with an orderly who assured him that such behaviour was perfectly normal among newcomers.

But it still took him ten minutes to stop trembling.

On his way out of the hospital, as he perused a leaflet on *Care in the Community*, he saw a man he recognised enter the building and head for the reception desk.

The man nodded at him a little frostily and turned his back rather quickly, obviously not intending to enter into conversation.

It was Nicola Carson's father.

Father Vernon frowned and set off home, riddled with several kinds of guilt.

Set Back.

In the small hours of that night Father Vernon's moral well-being suffered a further setback.

He was busy at the youth club, as usual at that time, but tonight he found himself unable to love any of the youths that presented themselves to him. Instead of making love he found himself defiling them in the most obscene manner.

And the worst of it was that he was enjoying it. Indeed, the more degenerate his behaviour became the sharper was the pleasure he derived. And all the time the pleasure hurt him somewhere. But the pain itself was the most exquisite sensation. And the more he felt it the more he was driven to debauchery.

Until there was no stone unturned and the youth club was awash with discharge and excreta. And all the time Nicola clung to his naked back, clawing at his skin, groaning mischievously.

Suddenly the Archangel Gabriel was at his side. 'Dear boy, I'm surprised. I thought this sort of behaviour was quite beyond you!'

Father Vernon was surprisingly unabashed. 'There's something inside me wants to come out,' he replied.

'So I see,' remarked the old man. I didn't know you had it in you.'

'Neither did I,' said Nicola.

'Neither did I,' said Father Vernon, slipping around in the mess and chuckling madly.

'Dear boy, this is no time for laughter. I've found Him.'

Father Vernon went cold.

And they were in an old building which Father Vernon didn't recognise. It looked like an old warehouse. And smelt much the same as the youth club had. Only more stale.

'It's not so glamorous down here,' observed the old man.

'Where are we?'

The old man knocked on a door and they entered.

God was sat there, among some old blankets.

Father Vernon stared at him.

'He lost His job,' said Gabriel.

God hung His head.

'And His flat – it came with the job.'

'It's nothing to be ashamed of,' assured Father Vernon. 'No one works in my parish. We don't think anything of it.'

'That's not why He's ashamed.'

Father Vernon realised there were two women over in the far corner. He looked at God.

'They're very beautiful, don't you think?' He said, feebly.

They weren't really Father Vernon's cup of tea.

'I'm so weak,' He went on. 'The shop was always full of women.' Again He looked down, His long eyelashes fluttering. 'When I spoke to certain of them I got this odd sensation in my stomach.'

Gabriel was solemn as Hell, for once.

'That's perfectly understandable,' stammered Father Vernon, searching for something to say. 'There are no sinful feelings. It depends on how you react.' He looked at Gabriel for support.

The old man grimaced and shook his head.

'That's just it,' God lamented. 'When I mentioned it to the women they said they could do something for me. If I visited them at night. Somehow I knew it was wrong. But . . . ' He stopped and put His head in His hands. 'I couldn't stop myself.'

'He didn't open the shop for a week,' explained the Archangel. 'So they sacked Him.'

219

'We're all sinners,' offered Father Vernon.

'That's what's worrying Him,' said the old man.

'I'm looking for a new job,' announced God. 'Do you think there's anything up your way?'

'Very unlikely. You could come to the church and get cleaned up. Stay with us for a while ...'

'I don't want charity!' He declared. 'I want to stand on my own two feet. With the rest of them.'

'He's very independent minded,' remarked the Archangel.

God looked highly dejected. 'I've got an interview later ...' It wasn't very convincing.

The two women in the corner giggled and God blushed.

'Better leave them to it,' said the old angel. 'Sin's His only consolation right now.'

Then they were back at the youth club and Father Vernon was looking for Nicola. He too needed consolation.

Coming Home.

On his way home, Inspector Swann was filled with a peculiar dread. Somehow he expected things to have changed.

He was changed, for sure.

He was fit, refreshed and in a curious way he was grateful to Commander Whitehouse (Commander Shithouse) for the experience of the last six weeks.

After all, he was a conscientious copper with a genuine desire to serve and protect society from the danger of subversion — and infestation — and the intensive training course had refilled him with zest for his work.

His mind was ablaze with new ideas and his spirit was steeled.

On the return journey he drifted into his dreams.

How could he have been so far behind the times? Had his head been buried in the sand? Had he been blind to reality all this time? He had more responsibilities than most, for sure. Perhaps that was it. Had he been like a woman, his life wasted on domestic trivia while the world span out of control?

It was a whole new police force. A whole new philosophy. He felt like one of those ancient astronomers who had puzzled over strange, unpredictable variations in the movement of stars only later to discover that it was the earth that revolved and not the heavens. Suddenly, previously baffling phenomena had become the central planks of a new argument.

And he had studied hard. And trained like a Trojan.

He had been schooled in the Irish question. In fact he had been given answers to the Irish question and could now formulate his own hypotheses which were borne out by events.

He had met such luminaries as the former Chief Constable of the Metropolitan police, with whom he had been most impressed.

He was warned of new forces at work in society. Subversives. Insurgents. Political activists. Agitators. Impostors. Immigrants. And of course, communists, which they all were in the end anyway, even if they didn't know it.

He had learned about the struggle against such characters in the former colonies from the men who had led the fights themselves. No pen pushers, these, but real, battle-hardened . . . soldiers. Yes, that was it. Soldiers.

And he had made new friends. Who sympathised

with him. Understood his difficulties. Men with similar experiences. From similar backgrounds. His own kind. Who would not turn against him.

He had learned how, in Ireland and elsewhere, the police had taken over the role of the army and that, to maintain liberties, similar methods would, one day, have to be employed on the mainland.

One day soon.

He learned that from tiny acorns of dissent, dangerous, calamitous situations quickly grow. And society is eaten away.

But, most important of all, he had learned how to cure the pestilence as well as diagnose it.

He had been taught how to fight. Learned the tricks of the trade. And taken them in. Swallowed them whole. Heartedly.

And been refreshed.

Made ready.

Briefed.

Let in on it.

From the top.

By the top brass.

And it was music to his ears.

A well-respected general from the British army told them: 'At times of great difficulty the law is merely a propaganda cover for the disposal of unwanted members of the public.'

He liked that. And made a special note of it.

'Where there is an uprising we must work to isolate the genuine subversive element.'

He made a note of that, too.

'We, like Mao, must become the guerrilla. Fighting to win the hearts and minds of the people.'

He liked that, especially.

He was in good company. These people were on the warpath, too.

His favourite idea of all was the 'dirty tricks'

campaign. Beating them at their own game. Using whatever means necessary. It had a feel of revenge about it that he enjoyed.

Round and round his head it all span until he drifted dangerously across the lanes of the motorway. Mixed in with a kind of passionate fatherly love it all became a spectacular adventure. A made-for-T.V. stunt show with fire and brimstone.

'Once the confidence of the people has been lost it is difficult to regain.'

He was coming into Bolton at last. Speeding down St Peter's Way, under the huge iron bridge and up between the green, green, grassy banks of home. He decided to cut through Sunnymeadow, for the sake of time. And curiosity.

As he neared his patch, his thinking slowed down. He was expecting a degeneration. Bracing himself, almost. But when he turned off the Bury Road it all looked much the same.

They weren't dancing in the streets as a part of him had expected. No. As dreary and drab as ever. Perhaps it was just the dusk.

'What a God-forsaken place this is,' he thought as he turned down a side street to sneak past the church and the youth club.

Then he saw some people up ahead. Youths. Standing in the road.

Flagging him down.

There appeared to be some kind of barricade across the street.

The youths who approached were wearing masks. Not altogether unlike those worn by the bitch. That night.

He stopped his car. A large vein bulged under the collar of his shirt and his temples pulsed as he unconsciously ground his teeth.

When he wound down the window, the nearest

223

youth said: 'It's just a spot check. Where are you going?'

'*Spot check?*' he managed to ask rather than shout at the top of his voice.

'We're keeping an eye on things. It's our estate and we don't want shady people coming down 'ere, doin' shady things.'

'Isn't that up to the police?' he asked, heavily, glad to be out of his uniform.

The youth was grinning under his outlaw mask. 'You ain't from round 'ere, are you?'

When he didn't answer, the youth demanded: 'Where you goin'?'

The Inspector nearly growled. 'Home. I'm coming home.'

The youth eyed him suspiciously. For a moment the copper thought he'd been recognised. He sighed. 'It's a short cut,' he said by way of conciliation.

The lad's accomplice said: ''E looks alright.'

Then, after a moment, they stood aside, without further comment and let him through.

As the raging Inspector drove off, a cloud entirely blocked out what was left of the sun.

Girls Talk.

'Comfy?' sneered Betty.

'Umm?'

'Sure you've got enough to do?'

Theresa was playing a video game at the Presbytery. Everyone else was out. Lisa was helping Betty carry a great big basket by swinging from it.

'Give yourself a break, Betty.'

Betty came and flopped on the sofa. Lisa climbed on top of her and pulled her nose.

'Ge' off!'

Theresa could see Betty was tired and took Lisa off her. 'Come 'ere, you.'

'How's tricks?' asked Betty with some sarcasm. 'Saved the world yet?'

Theresa ignored her and tweaked Lisa's nose. 'She's got a sense of humour your mum, ain't she Tiny.'

Betty puffed. 'I read about Rivington Pike.' (Betty had refused to have anything to do with the public appearances.)

Theresa ignored her.

'Cured a few people there, didn't you? Or did you leave that to the hospital.'

'Leave it out.'

Betty felt she had to quote the worst headline: "Miracle Girls Run Riot".

Theresa tutted. 'It wasn't a riot.'

Betty sat back on the sofa. Theresa prepared herself for a confrontation.

'How long is it before we get into serious trouble?' said Betty.

Theresa grunted. 'What, for giving food to pensioners?'

'And the rest! You're running an illegal business,' answered Betty. 'A bloody big business an' all.'

'It's not a business, it's lookin' after people.'

'Do you know how much is involved?'

Theresa hadn't got a clue.

'I know we don't see much of it.' Betty looked at her little daughter. 'Do you want a job, Tiny – accountant?'

She did.

'Michelle's doin' all that.'

Betty's eyebrows made known her feelings on the subject. 'Michelle's the one who's workin' the real miracles,' she jeered.

225

"Aven't you got enough?'

'Plenty,' said Betty indignantly.

'What's the problem then?'

Betty lapsed into sulk mode for a few moments and then changed her tack. 'And what about them bloody masses?'

'My greatest creation,' grinned Theresa.

'So you give 'em all drugs. That the idea?'

'It's not drugs.'

'It's the same bloody difference.'

Theresa didn't reply. She sat back and regarded Betty, who carried on moaning:

'They're eating them like cornflakes in the office. Some of the lads are selling them by the box!' She threw up her hands. 'And what would bloody Father Vernon say if he knew the truth?'

Theresa stopped herself interrupting. Betty was letting off steam.

The shell-suited young mother took a breath. 'And another thing . . . I saw the bloody shows on T.V. And another thing . . . them poor bloody cripples. You cure one or two of 'em. What about the others? 'Tain't bloody fair!'

Theresa was grinning.

'It's not bloody funny.'

Apparently little Lisa didn't think so either.

Theresa sighed. 'I 'aven't done a miracle in weeks.'

Betty looked at her. She wanted to say 'What?' but she'd heard alright.

'Honest.'

Betty hesitated. 'What about the cripples? The ones who got up and walked?'

'I've never cured anyone in my life. Ever.'

'But . . .'

Theresa shrugged. She didn't know either. 'I just turn up and they do what they like.'

'What about the 'osts?'

'Yeah, well, at first. And the first couple of masses, yeah. But . . . I haven't touched 'em in weeks. I haven't done anything for ages. Well, apart from disappearing occasionally.'

Betty looked at her little daughter. Then she grinned. Slowly. 'You dick 'ead!'

'What?'

'Why didn't you tell me?'

'You never asked.'

Betty grabbed the control box for the video game. 'Give us a go on that,' she laughed.

Little Lisa ran up to Theresa and jumped on her.

'Ooof!' Theresa gave the little mite a hug and Lisa pulled her ear. 'I'm stickin' with you now. They can do what they like.'

Betty was concentrating on the game.

Theresa watched her for a moment and then reached out and pushed the hair back behind her ear.

Betty winced. 'Ge' off!'

Fair Shares.

Michelle had taken her first evening off for two weeks.

She and Jo were strolling around the estate at a snail's pace and so far communication had been largely telepathic. The sun was casting long shadows that fell across their path.

It was the first time the two girls had been on their own together for a while. Jo seemed to spend most of her time with Penny these days, while the two of them waited for the odd morsel of Michelle's company.

227

Jo broke the silence. 'Me mum asked me what was going on. Up at the church. She's getting suspicious.'

Michelle hardly awoke from her meditations. 'Yeah? What did you tell 'er?'

'I told 'er to fuck off and mind 'er own business.'

Michelle grinned ever so slightly and they relapsed into a pleasant silence. Jo had her arm through Michelle's. Michelle was running figures through her mind and adding up sums. Jo was running through a fantasy about telling her mum what she was really up to, just to see her face.

What would she say if she knew that her own daughter was causing one of the biggest stirs in the local papers and on the region's T.V. for years? There had even been a small item on the national news the week before.

They were swinging on the old school railings, at the top of the estate, overlooking the town and a stretch of the moors when Michelle made her little announcement:

'Me and Penny are getting a flat when all this is over,' she said, trying to sound casual.

Jo looked at her friend and her ears went red. Luckily they were hidden under her ginger hair. 'What do you mean – when this is all over?' What she really wanted to ask, of course, was, 'What about me!'

Michelle shrugged, without moving. 'Well, ain't gunna last forever, is it?'

This was news to Jo whose attention didn't span much beyond the visible horizon. 'I know that,' she lied, feeling lost, suddenly.

'We're lookin' at one tomorrow.'

'Haven't you got to go on the council list? You're not even pregnant.'

'We ain't gettin' a bloody council flat,' pouted Michelle, indignantly. 'We're getting somewhere nice.

Not round 'ere, either.'

Jo was hurt. And perplexed. 'How you gunna afford that? Don't you need a deposit?'

Michelle didn't reply. She just stared out across the moors.

Jo looked at her. 'We've not sold that many bloody cans. An' I thought you only made fifty on that snide water.'

Still Michelle said nothing.

'That's about a hundred and twenty all together. Well 'alf of that's mine.'

'Yeah, well. There's me wages.'

'What wages?'

'I ain't been doin' all this bloody work for nothin'!' Michelle blurted angry suddenly.

At that moment there was a shout of 'yo!' from behind them. Penny was coming over the playground. The two girls turned to face him.

'Hiya,' he grinned.

Michelle and Jo remained mute.

Penny hopped on to the wall next to Jo and grabbed the railings.

'I've been lookin' for you two.'

Michelle almost spoke. But didn't.

'I sacked Tony,' he announced. 'Dick 'ead.'

There was no response.

'Don't need 'im any'ow. Not with all that gear.'

'You've not played anything for weeks,' observed Jo.

'Yeah, well I will now,' asserted Penny, doubtfully. 'I can afford to go it alone.'

Michelle jumped down. 'I'm gunna check something out at the office.'

'I'll come with you,' offered Jo.

'No, stay,' said Michelle. 'Keep 'im company.' She nodded at Penny.

Jo and Penny exchanged a look.

'That'll make a change, won't it,' observed Penny.

Michelle was on her way. 'See you later,' she called over her shoulder to neither of them in particular. 'And you keep your 'ands to yourself!' she said to Penny and was gone without so much as another backward glance.

Then, feeling some vague comradeship in rejection, the abandoned couple turned round to try and lose themselves in the view. Until, after a couple of melancholy minutes, Penny suggested a walk and they shuffled off across the playing field toward the moors.

They were sprawled on a hillside when it started to get dark.

Jo asked: 'Where you lookin' for a flat, then?'

When Penny told her, she said 'Oo-oo', as if to say 'very nice.'

Penny blushed. 'You comin' with us?'

'Na, I'm goin' into town.'

'Theresa doin' somethin'?'

'No. I'm gunna open a bank account.'

Penny grinned. 'You've been talkin' to Michelle.'

Jo said nothing.

They lay back and let the dusk engulf them.

Ten minutes later their legs were entwined and Penny's hands were welcome everywhere.

Nature was taking its course.

'I'm sorry Nicola, I really can't read another word.'

Father Vernon had been reading for nearly two hours and his eyelids were stinging.

'That's alright, Dad,' said Nicola. 'Here ... you lie down I'll finish the chapter.'

The tired priest did as he was told. Nicola began reading.

Great Expectations was nearing its climax and the young woman was enraptured. So was Father Vernon.

As he lay there vaguely following the familiar narrative, he had time to ponder his peculiar new circumstances. Here he was lying in bed with a girl who had just turned sixteen.

Which was a sin. Possibly a mortal one.

Yet, as Nicola herself had told him, she had been in less trouble over these last few weeks than at any time for years. And she and Betty were the best workers. Certainly the most popular among the elderly parishioners. Nicola was calmer and more settled.

Surely he had been good for the girl.

He gazed at her through tired eyes and she must have seen him, as she brushed his fringe to one side, smiled and murmured 'You alright, Dad?'

They were like a bizarre married couple, he thought, as he drifted into his prayers.

And what of the parish? Surely it was the best parish around, right now. He hadn't submitted figures for examination by the diocese, but there was no other church with such a fine record of attendance, especially not among the young.

Working-class youths crowded the aisles of the

church and co-operated with each other to provide meals for elderly people in the area. This was an unheard of, unprecedented achievement. Yet in order to keep it up, Father Vernon had lied to the diocese about the nature of the funding.

Which wasn't only a sin. It was illegal.

Could it be that there was virtue in sin? Or sin in true virtue? Had the world been turned on its head? His own life had. What was God's will for him?

Father Vernon had been down on his knees, of late, pondering these questions. Praying almost aloud for guidance. Begging God to enlighten him. But there had been no reply. Only a series of mad dreams. And possibly a touch of real madness. He therefore had to judge the matter for himself. And his conscience was clear.

Well, mostly.

He hadn't been to confession for weeks. And he did feel guilty about that.

He was afraid to confess his new sins to a fellow member of the church. So, to balance his spiritual accounts, he called to mind the scenes at Mass. The happy smiling faces. And those of the elderly people on the estate as they received meals from young people with whom they had previously been in conflict.

And that was all the absolution he needed.

Let God strike him down if he was wrong.

Father Vernon was just thinking how heavenly Earth could be given the proper circumstances, when he realised Nicola was no longer reading. And he was about to open his eyes and say goodnight, when he realised she was not about to leave the room.

Indeed she had settled down next to him and turned off the light. Presumably she thought he'd fallen asleep.

Something in him decided to play along.

Neither of them moved a muscle.

And Father Vernon almost forgot to breathe.

And then Nicola let out a kind of sigh and turned over. Possibly in her sleep. And possibly not. And definitely closer to him.

And gradually. Over the course of the next ten minutes she moved nearer and nearer until she was snuggled right up behind him and they were like two spoons in a drawer.

He felt like a spoon of honey.

Nicola was sound asleep within minutes. He heard her gently snoring. But he wasn't. He was electrified. Filled to the very brim with joy. He lay awake for hours, savouring the experience. With her beautiful arms around him and her warm legs curled against his, he felt as if he had been transported to to another time.

He felt chosen. He had been chosen.

Then, in a terrible moment, he became depressed. And was mortified.

He suddenly felt desolate and hopeless. He wanted to cry and felt doubly alone in the world. Utterly abandoned. In a flash he had realised the truth. And at the same moment accepted it. That nothing would ever – could ever pass between them. Except this. This very moment. This . . .

This what? What was it?

He didn't know. But he knew it was fantastic beyond words.

He was hurt and deeply moved at the same time.

And, at last, he was able to give praise.

He thanked God for sending him a beautiful daughter and fell into a profound sleep, without dreams.

They were still there, wrapped up together, when morning broke.

Father Vernon's arm had gone dead but he couldn't bring himself to move. He wanted to savour the never-to-be-repeated experience. Then he felt Nicola stir and decided to continue to play dead, giving her the chance to move away from him without embarrassment.

But instead she made herself more comfortable, moving up closer still and tightening her grip around his stomach, giving him a friendly squeeze. For a terrible moment the young priest thought she was about to make an assault on his manhood and was moved to defend himself by changing his position slightly. Still feigning sleep.

But he needn't have worried.

She shuffled harmlessly, giving him room to move and then pressed herself gently back against him.

'Morning, Dad,' she croaked, sleepily.

Father Vernon was just considering his response when there came a knocking on the bedroom door. He felt a sudden stab of anxiety and hurriedly sat up. But his dead arm let him down and he fell back on to Nicola, who giggled.

'Er ... just a minute,' he called, looking at his clock. He was surprised to see it was nine o'clock.

But it was too late. The door was already opening.

'Father, I'm ho ...'

It is difficult to say who was the more shocked by what they saw.

Father Vernon, or Mary, his former housekeeper, whose face, framed in the doorway, did little to express her true feelings, despite its contortion.

Community Care.

'Are you sure?'

Father Vernon was whispering into the telephone.

'I've got the order right in front of me. It's signed by the senior consultant,' insisted the voice on the other end of the line.

'Well, if you're sure . . . It seems a little soon, that's all.' The priest was seriously concerned. 'She was very ill indeed, not so long ago.'

'It did seem a little odd to me,' said the voice, 'I mean, it was a free-for-all after you left the other day. She can't even have recovered from the sedatives we gave her.'

'We'll just have to do the best we can,' said Father Vernon resignedly.

'They're a law unto themselves, these consultants.'

'Thanks for your help.'

Father Vernon rang off.

Nicola was sitting on the stairs, next to the phone. 'She's flipped, Dad.'

'Shhh. Where is she?' he asked, plaintively.

'She's helping Betty cook the dishes and wash the lunch,' replied Nicola with a grin.

'Apparently she was discharged first thing this morning.'

'They're as mad as she is.'

Father Vernon was too distracted to notice Nicola's humorous remarks. Just as well, probably.

'She's drugged up. And I should know.'

'It's quite possible,' said Father Vernon. 'As far as I know it's part of the *Care in the Community* programme.'

'Betty said she was asleep before, with her head in the shepherd's pie.'

The worried priest sighed, heavily. 'She's really not well.'

'She's jealous, Dad.'

'What?'

'Come on, don't play daft.'

He wasn't.

'Everyone knows – she's madly in love with you.

It's all round the parish.'

Father Vernon stood there, blinking. 'I hardly think . . .'

'Dad . . . She phoned slimy bastard. Broadcast it live on radio. Half of Lancashire knows about you two.'

The priest half laughed. Nervously.

'Now she's jealous as fuck because she saw us this morning. As far as she knows you were knobbing me.'

Father Vernon put his head in his hands. Partly to hide his embarrassment at Nicola's remark.

'And as far as everyone else knows, you were knobbing her.'

'Jesus,' he said and sat on the stairs.

Nicola came down a couple of steps behind him and began to massage his shoulders. He was about to put a stop to this by standing up, when Mary appeared at the kitchen door. Father Vernon got up all the quicker and ended up looking terribly guilty.

Mary sort of swept past them with her nose in the air and went out of the front door without a word.

Father Vernon looked at Nicola who just shrugged.

A couple of minutes later Eve rang the door bell.

She was wearing her bright red bandanna over her nose and half dived through the front door. She came running into the kitchen, where Father Vernon and Nicola were helping Betty clear up the mess Mary had made helping them out.

Theresa was drinking tea.

'D'you know the police are watching the place?' Eve asked.

Nobody did.

'There's a guy sitting in an unmarked car. I just saw him.'

'Doesn't bother me,' remarked Nicola.

'We ain't doin' nothin' illegal,' said Theresa, doubt-fully.

'Are you sure it's ... the police?' asked Father Vernon, nervously.

'E's got a guilty conscience, 'aven't you, Dad?' laughed Nicola.

'Friend of my Dad's,' said Eve, gravely. 'He's stuck a moustache on and thinks he's in disguise ... If he hadn't been swigging from a bottle of pop when I came round the corner he'd have sussed me out!'

'It's that fat bastard, isn't it?' said Nicola. 'Ser-geant ... what's 'is name? Shall I go and let his tyres down?' she offered.

'Offer him some soup,' said Betty. 'Mary dropped some of her pills in there before.'

They all laughed. Except Father Vernon.

'Did you say "Mary"?' asked Eve. 'Is she your old housekeeper?'

Father Vernon nodded.

'Does she look like Dame Edna Everage, only thin-ner and a bit mad?'

They all laughed at Eve's description.

'I thought so,' she said. 'She's out there in the car, talking to Sergeant Jones. I saw her get in when I was coming up the road.'

News and Views.

'How's the counter-revolution?'

'Come on, this is restricted parking ...'

Bill Carson could see that Inspector Swann's sense of humour was intact. He jumped in the car and the old copper drove off.

'Seriously, how was it?'

The Inspector kept his eyes on the road ahead. 'Satisfactory.'

The two men hadn't met in person since Swann's return.

'You did well while I was away,' said Swann.

'That's what allies are for.'

'How did you get her out of the hospital?'

Bill Carson grinned. 'Well, it's not what you know ... ' he finished the old saying with his shoulders. 'And I know more *whos* than most.'

'She's been very useful,' said Swann.

'Hell hath no fury like a housekeeper scorned.' Bill saw they were heading towards Manchester. He didn't question it.

Swann continued: 'She seems to have taken a shine to our Sergeant Jones. He's keeping an eye on the Presbytery and she insists on sitting in the car with him all day. Giving the game away.' Swann shrugged. 'Doesn't do any harm, though. If they know we're watching them, it might put the fear of God into them.'

Bill laughed. But it was hollow. He was on edge because he'd been summoned, by telephone and more or less ordered to make himself available that afternoon. He suspected it was a return favour for sorting out his court business. Or bad news about Nicola.

He wasn't wrong.

'Apparently she's an old drunk.' Bill was making conversation.

'She sings like one,' observed Swann. 'Telling us all sorts, she is.'

Bill sighed. 'What's all this about?' he asked finally, bracing himself. 'You said it was important.'

There was an unpleasant pause. As if the Inspector were choosing his words carefully.

He was, but it wasn't a very good selection. 'Your daughter's having an affair with the Catholic priest,' he announced.

Bill was silent. He didn't move. Or feel anything.

Swann looked across at him to try and gauge the reaction.

But Bill Carson was a rock. 'Drive on,' he said.

'The evidence is overwhelming. But the problem is, no crime has been committed.'

Bill Carson was flabbergasted. 'The man's a child molester! He was in bed with my daughter!'

'It's perfectly legal.' Swann kept his eyes on the road ahead. 'Unless I'm mistaken, Nicola is sixteen years old.'

'She was sixteen three months ago.'

'So it's been legal for three months.'

The two men fell silent.

The old copper was determined to win his ally over to his new way of thinking. After letting Bill boil for a while Swann said: 'I'm afraid the law is against us.'

'Fuck the law!' spat Bill.

'Spoken like a true believer!' laughed the Inspector and immediately wished he hadn't.

'Do me a favour,' said Bill. 'Try not to sound like you're enjoying this.'

Swann reddened slightly and gripped the steering wheel a little harder.

The silence continued, only now a little awkwardly.

'What exactly have we got?' asked Bill, when he'd recovered his composure.

The copper was business-like. 'Some kind of religious cult. They use those hosts you found in Nicola's bedroom, which we initially suspected to contain drugs. But the tests proved negative ...'

Bill could hear wind whistling in the old copper's nostrils.

'The priest surrounds himself with young girls ...
and a few lads. They do charity work around the
estate.' Swann's eyes narrowed. 'Trying to win the
population over to their side, no doubt.'

The evangelist thought how the Inspector looked
like a rat sometimes.

'It's the same lot doing all these ... ' Swann hesitated. He didn't like the word.

'Miracles?' said Bill.

Swann snorted. 'It's a con. Taking advantage of
vulnerable people.'

'They use my programme to publicise themselves.'

'There's people climbing out of bloody wheel-
chairs!'

'People really believe that shit.' Bill Carson stared
out of the window. They were speeding down the
motorway now. 'I thought this sort of thing only
happened in America.'

'You'd be surprised,' said Swann. 'They're setting
up roadblocks on the estate and screening people as
they come and go.'

Bill raised his eyebrows at this. 'Sounds like bloody
Belfast!'

'Precisely,' bristled the Inspector. He was getting
through.

'Papists and youths,' muttered Bill, darkly. 'Where
are we going?'

'I've made a few new friends,' answered the old
copper. 'One of them's going to help us out.' He
paused for effect. 'And then, so are you.'

Plotting.

Inspector Swann's Sierra 1.8LX swung into the compound and ground to an abrupt halt.

They were somewhere in Stretford.

'Wait here,' instructed the old copper, opening his door.

'What is this place?' asked the radio evangelist.

'A warehouse. It's full of confiscated contraband.'

'Huh?'

'Drugs,' said Swann and walked off.

Bill was depressed.

For the first time in a long time he was filled with self doubt. It was one thing for your daughter to run around town with lads from the estate – she was using condoms and it was to be expected these days at age fifteen.

Sixteen.

But it was quite another thing to sleep with an older man. Nearly his own age. Or at least in his thirties. And a bloody Catholic priest. That Catholic priest. Maybe it was some kind of revenge on him.

He had to admit that he had failed as a father.

That was it. He had let her down. Now she was avenging herself. She was cheating on him. And the more he thought about it, the more he realised it.

He felt jilted.

And what's worse, he was jealous.

Could it possibly be?

He gazed out of the window. Did he love the girl after all? What sort of relationship did they have? He pictured her. He had to struggle to find a picture of her face that wasn't scowling at him. And he saw her standing there in her underwear, in front of that dreadful lad, who hardly batted an eyelid.

Was it too late to start all over again? Could he make it up to her in some way? It was no good buying her anything – she even seemed to hate her pony. What could possibly be done now? Before it was too late?

And so it went on, until Inspector Swann appeared carrying a small package and they began the journey back to Bolton.

On the way back, the Inspector rattled on about the things he had learned on his training refresher, but Bill thought it sounded terribly paranoid. Especially in the context of Bolton. 'The IRA's one thing,' he thought. 'Child molesters are another.'

Shortly before they arrived in Bolton, Swann stopped his car in a quiet industrial car park. (There are a few of them left)

He killed the engine and took hold of the package, producing a small medicine bottle and a syringe.

'What ever's that?' asked Bill, astonished by the sight.

'Concentrated LSD,' replied the old copper. And before Bill had time to ask stupid questions, Swann said, 'There's an envelope in the glove compartment, get it out.'

Bill did as he was told.

'Open it.'

Inside there were two sacramental hosts.

If there had been music to accompany the scene it might have gone: 'Dun dun deerr! . . .'

'Where did you get those?'

'Sergeant Jones was at one of their little celebrations.'

Bill looked at Swann who was inserting the syringe into the little bottle and sucking up some liquid.

'You have to be very careful with this. One drop, even on your skin and you'll be hallucinating for six months,' explained the copper, casually. 'Normally

242

one or two drops dilute in a pint of water, which is then absorbed onto blotting paper. A hell of a lot of it.'

'Isn't this . . . illegal?' Bill's question sounded lame.

'Fuck the law,' replied Swann flatly. 'Put one on the dashboard.'

His hand trembling, Bill again did as he was told. The Inspector let a drop fall from the syringe onto the centre of the host, with a steady hand. 'And one for luck,' he quipped releasing another drip.

'Is this necessary?' asked Bill. 'I thought there was some stolen equipment?'

'All in good time,' answered Swann. 'We need as much against them as possible. Something their public won't like.' He held the contaminated host up, as if to bless it. 'We're going to find this in the Presbytery.' Swann turned to face his accomplice. 'Now the other . . .'

Bill hesitated, holding back the second host. 'What happens if someone eats one of them?' he asked nervously.

'They won't.'

'They might. Nicola might.'

'We'll raid the place straight away. Keep her away.'

Bill almost laughed at this. How could he keep his daughter away? She hadn't been home in weeks. 'They're only kids,' he said. 'She's my daughter.'

'Trust me,' said Swann. 'These people are a danger to everyone's daughters.'

Bill stared at his old friend, still withholding the second host.

The copper's face was set. 'When you give them to . . . what's her name? . . . the housekeeper . . .'

The penny dropped. 'You want me to give them to Mary!' Bill was truly shocked.

'It can't come from the police, now can it?'

'It's too dangerous,' Bill insisted.

Ignoring his remark, Swann went on. 'You can explain things to her. Make sure she understands that they're poisonous. Put them somewhere safe.'

'What if she refuses?'

'I'm quite sure she doesn't want to end her days in a hospital for the mentally ill,' pointed out the Inspector.

'It's where she belongs,' thought Bill. 'And she's not the only one!'

'She owes you a favour,' said Swann.

Bill was quiet.

'And you owe me one,' he added. To make sure.

Bill was defeated. 'Just do the one, then.'

The Inspector sighed and put his equipment away. Compromise.

Good Night and God Forbid.

Mary was in a new state of delirium.

She was still off the drink. Yet she had a vast supply of prescribed drugs at her disposal. She was able to mix lethal cocktails of trance-inducing barbituates and slide through the days in a dream.

After the initial shock of discovering Father Vernon in bed with Nicola and as the intensity of her jealousy subsided slightly, with the realisation that Nicola had been ejected from her beloved priest's room at night, the real madness began.

For now the poor woman became convinced that her wishes were to be granted. That her dream was to become reality.

Only more so.

Whereas before she had looked on Father Vernon as a saint, or an icon – holy and untouchable, immaculate and serene – she now saw him as he was, a man in the flesh. Troubled and earthly.

And whereas previously her visions of love had been heavenly – abstract and divine, reverential even – so now they were transformed into explicit sexual fantasies and her nights were filled with carnal desire.

Her unholy prayers had been answered. For if he could make love to one woman, then given the appropriate circumstances and sufficient encouragement, he could make love to any woman.

For two or three nights, as she lay in bed, drifting in and out of a trance-like state, she pictured the two of them coupling frantically. The young priest gasping and sweating in her arms, thrashing passionately and calling out her name.

Then the delirium got the better of her and with her heart pounding in her throat, her legs wobbling beneath her, she left the warmth of her bed and padded to Father Vernon's door, luxuriating in the feel of the cool night air drifting through her nylon night-dress.

But first she peeped in at Nicola, who was now housed on a mattress in the upstairs study, to make sure she was there. Then let herself into the priest's room, took off her nightie and slipped into bed behind him.

A few moments later the sleeping priest awoke from a very pleasant dream to feel a cold hand on his manhood. All the stricken man felt was a figure pressed against him and an arm reaching round, gently holding him in trance.

It was his first adult sexual experience and even though it was only a split second before his conscience seized him and he was forced to break free, the memory of that moment would chill his heart on many a lonely night.

He pretended to wriggle in his sleep, dislodged the offending hand and was about to send Nicola back to her own bed, when he heard Mary's voice say: 'Make love to me' Father . . .'

He was so shocked that he gasped.

Mary instantly misjudged the ejaculation and dived on him, kissing his protesting mouth, lunging once again for his manhood.

'Mary! No! . . .'

'Kiss me, Father . . . I won't tell!'

'Please I . . . wuuuh.' The priest's words were smothered in kisses.

Father Vernon bitterly regretted not wearing his pyjamas that night and swore that he would never again sleep naked.

Then there was a desperate struggle that poor Mary mistook for passion. Which made matters worse. More frantic.

'Mary, I think there's been . . . aauuh . . . a terrible . . . mmmmistake.'

The struggle was making him pant and gasp which really didn't help at all. Mary was sitting astride him now and moaning with desire, so that she hardly noticed his protestations.

All he could do was wrestle his housekeeper into submission, which in the end was quite easy. As soon as she realised he was trying to get on top of her she rolled over and helped him with a generous heave.

Poor Father Vernon ended up holding her wrists and pinning her to the bed. Mary was in a state of ecstasy.

'Yes . . . ' she gasped. 'Please . . . ' she begged.

It was a few moments before she realised that Father Vernon was talking to her. She opened her eyes and looked at him.

'Mary I . . .'

246

It was rather difficult to know what to say.

Mary lay still, hardly breathing now.

'It's difficult ... I can't ... It's not ... ' He wanted to be clear. There could be no more room for doubt. It was for the best. 'Mary, I don't want you. I don't love you in that way.'

Mary blinked.

'I love God. I'm already accounted for.'

She only heard the second of these last two sentences.

At that moment the door opened.

'Dad? Are you alright? ... I heard moaning ... ' Nicola saw the scene on the bed and froze. She was amazed and fascinated.

'Let me go,' said Mary, her voice as cold as death.

'Er ... yes of course.'

Nicola stood and stared as Father Vernon climbed off Mary and the poor woman wafted out of the room, her face set and her eyes staring.

They heard her bedroom door close.

'Go to bed, Nicola,' said Father Vernon before she could compose a sentence.

When he was alone again, Father Vernon put on his pyjamas and got down on his knees to pray.

But it was too late. The damage was already done.

Inside Dreams.

That night Father Vernon's mind reeled.

For some reason the youth club of his dreams was deserted.

All the walls were covered in tacky clumps of damp green moss, which stuck to the finger on con-

247

tact. On closer inspection the poor tormented man discovered that they were rotten vaginas.

'Don't smell as sweet, do they?' said a voice.

The Archangel was there.

'Where is everyone?'

'They've shut the place down. They've all gone.'

'Where to?'

'From whence they came.'

'Where's Nicola?'

'She'll be gone, soon, too.'

Father Vernon was saddened. 'Will she be the same?'

'Never again.'

The poor priest had a pit in his stomach.

They were no longer in the youth club, but standing outside a large Victorian building.

It was a prison.

They were admitted by an old copper who resembled Inspector Swann.

Inside it was like a holiday camp, except for a small alcove near the end, where, behind a glass screen, sat God.

'Is there no direct contact?' asked Father Vernon.

Again the Archangel shook his head.

'You have to guess what He's thinking now.'

'He looks angry.'

'Oh, He always looks like that.'

'How did He get here?'

'He claims He's innocent.'

God shook His head.

Gabriel sighed and corrected himself. 'Well, He maintains that it was the inevitable outcome of the life He was forced to lead.'

God looked satisfied with this explanation.

'What does that mean?'

'I think it actually means shop-lifting.'

God hung His head, apparently in shame.

'It wasn't really His fault. He got in with a bad crowd and they were all arrested. He didn't want to leave His friends to face the music alone.'

Next thing God seemed to shout something. Then He stood up, hurled His chair through the window and made a run for it.

An alarm went off and the three men were running along a street that Father Vernon didn't recognise.

God was up ahead. 'It was all stacked against me,' He called back over his shoulder. 'I didn't stand a chance!'

'It's a hard lesson to learn,' panted the old man.

Then they gave up the chase. The old man was utterly breathless. 'Dear boy, it doesn't look good at all.'

'What does it all mean?' asked Father Vernon. He was puzzled and anxious.

'I think it means disaster. He's abandoned the rules. I think He's going to abandon humanity.'

'Where will that leave us?'

The Archangel didn't have a clue so Father Vernon went looking for Nicola.

That night Theresa, too, had a nightmare.

She saw herself in a prison cell.

A fantastically beautiful man she recognised from her dreams was talking to her. Stroking her hair. Comforting her.

For some reason he was crying.

Then she was trying to comfort him, but he had to leave.

He seemed very apologetic.

And sad.

And she herself was crying.

And then he was gone.

She felt terribly alone, suddenly. She wanted to wake up. But she couldn't.

Then the cell door opened and two men were standing there. Looking very ugly.

'That's the one,' said a voice.

The two men came forward and took hold of her hands and her arms in such a way that it was impossible to resist.

'We've done this before,' one of them said.

'We're very good at it,' assured the other.

Then, very quickly, using strips of her blanket, they hung her from the cell window, telling her gently that there was nothing she could do to save herself.

The next day it was reported in the press that she'd committed suicide.

Theresa woke up and sat up, feeling alone and scared.

The room was as it always was.

All her friends were there.

She shuddered and closed her eyes, as if making a wish. Then she woke Betty.

'What?' groaned Betty.

Theresa whispered. 'Betty – my powers have gone!'

There was a pause.

'Are you sure?'

Theresa nodded.

'You don't use them, anyhow.'

Theresa stared into the darkness, then hissed: 'No. But they made me feel safe.'

'Welcome back,' said Betty and rolled over.

Driven to it.

Mary wasn't seen all the next day.

Betty said she'd received a phone call first thing and had rushed straight out.

Just after she returned, at about tea time, there came a knock on the Presbytery door. Nicola answered it. Bill Carson was standing there.

'Dad!' she said, despite herself.

Bill held up a hand, showing his palm. 'Truce.' He smiled as best he could. Submissive, almost.

Nicola was almost disarmed.

'What do you want?' she asked, avoiding inviting him in.

'To talk.' He shrugged. 'Come for a drive.'

She hesitated. She was suspicious. What the fuck could he want? 'I'll get my jacket.'

'You don't need it. It's a lovely evening.'

She resigned herself to his company and left her jacket hanging on the banister.

Mary watched them drive off through the kitchen window.

'Your mother sends her love,' said Bill, weakly.

'You have had a conversation, then?' Nicola was ill at at ease.

Bill took the unusual step of laughing at her quip. He looked at his daughter as she sat there glacier-like. She might have a viper's tongue, but she was quick witted with it.

'It's not easy being your father,' he said. 'You're too damn sharp.'

She knew he was complimenting her. And it made her all the more suspicious.

'Where are we going?' she asked.

'Nowhere fast,' he replied.

She almost smiled.

'Come on, what's up?' She didn't want to play coy games with him. 'Spit it out. Are you cutting me out of your will? Or just checking up on me.'

'It's nice to know you're still alive,' he conceded. 'And kicking.'

251

She ignored him.

He searched for a way into dialogue. 'It's you, isn't it?' he tried. 'It's your voice.'

'What do you mean?' She was playing daft. He was obviously referring to the interruptions on his show.

'Come on. I'm not cross,' he sighed. 'As a matter of fact I admire your audacity. And as it happens our ratings have gone up. Everyone wants to know where you lot are going to be next.'

'Is that what this is about?' she asked him. 'Are you going to offer me some kind of deal?'

'No. It's a mutually beneficial arrangement as it is.' He wasn't going to treat her like a kid any more.

Nicola picked up on this and thawed a little. She looked out of the window.

'They're on to you, Nicola,' he said at last, in a serious tone. Adult to adult.

She stared at him. He kept his eyes on the road.

'They're not going to let you get away with it.'

'Yeah? We'll see,' she said.

'There are some very dangerous people around,' he persisted.

'Yeah, like you.'

He snorted, smarting at the irony. 'Far more dangerous than me,' he replied.

Her intelligence took over. 'Who? How do you know?'

'I know a lot of people.'

'The police? We know they're watching us.'

'Yeah, and they know you know.'

'So?'

'The police are the tip of the iceberg,' he said. He was getting into deep water. He didn't want to incriminate himself. Yet he had to warn her. 'Someone might get hurt.'

'Like who?'

'Well, like you for one.'

252

'What, you mean I might be arrested? For helping people out?'

'Maybe.'

She almost spat. 'Well, let them come and get me!'

He was getting frustrated. 'I'm trying to help you . . .'

'Why?'

'I'm trying to stop my daughter getting into trouble, that's all.'

In a flash Nicola sussed him out. 'Stop the car!'

'What?' He was shocked. What had he said?

'Stop the car, I said!'

He did as he was told. She made to get out.

'What's the matter?'

She eyeballed him. 'You're a bastard!' It was the first time she'd ever sworn at him.

He was determined to take it in his stride. 'What?' He was wide-eyed.

She could hardly speak for her rage. 'What you're really worried about is your fucking self! If I get arrested you're worried it'll look bad on you and people won't listen to your fucking show anymore!'

She slammed the car door and stormed off.

Bill was left with his meditations.

She was wrong. But she was right. She was wrong that these were his intentions now. But as a description of his usual conduct, she'd got it right. That's what he'd done over the years. Thought only of himself. And he knew it. And now he was in the shit. Or she was.

He'd better act fast. She was quite a way from the Presbytery now so if the raid took place immediately it might be over by the time she got back.

And no one would accidentally eat the damn thing.

Bill stopped at a phone box and dialled the police station.

He got straight through.

'Swann . . . ' said Swann.

'I saw Mary,' said Bill. 'Act quickly. Immediately.'

There was a silence. 'Trust me.'

There was another one.

'Yes . . . yes.' Bill put the phone down and got back into his Rover 216/SLi.

'Words just aren't enough,' he lamented.

Inspector Swann replaced the receiver, sat back in his chair and stared into space.

'Now then,' he thought. 'Just sit back and wait.'

He was satisfied with himself and fell into a kid of a gleeful trance. He thought over what Sergeant Jones had told him about the housekeeper and her raging jealousy. And the likely outcome.

Then there was a moment of anxiety. Remorse, even. He wondered if he should order an immediate raid, after all. But no. People had to face up to the consequences of their actions.

Just then the old copper noticed something strange on the corner of his desk.

There was a large green insect perched there, with its hind legs twitching slightly. It seemed to be staring at him with its beady little eye.

What the hell was a grasshopper doing on his desk? Then he realised it wasn't a grasshopper. It was a locust. Was it? He took a closer look. No, just a grasshopper, surely.

He rolled up a newspaper and swatted it, hard.

But the damn thing wasn't dead. It hauled itself along the edge of his desk, it's body broken and its legs ruined.

So he took off his shoe and crushed it with his heel.

Then he picked up the phone and dialled a number. 'Can I speak to the newsdesk?' He waited for a moment. 'I have some information regarding the so-called miracle girls. I know who they are and where they're based . . .'

A couple of minutes later he bade Mrs Plunkett goodnight and headed home.

Surprise, Surprise.

When Nicola got back to the Presbytery, Eve was in the kitchen. The policeman's daughter was in tears and Mary was comforting her.

When she saw Nicola, Mary gave her a broad smile. 'Hello dear,' she said and Nicola wondered what could have happened to cheer the woman up so much.

'She's off 'er 'ead,' she thought. 'What's the matter?' she asked Eve.

'Her boyfriend . . . ' Mary grimaced. She didn't have the appropriate words.

'Tony sack you?' asked Nicola.

Eve nodded.

'Bastard,' said Nicola, supportively.

Eve smiled bravely at her through her tears. 'I'm supposed to be at home now. Dad'll kill me.'

'Fuck that!' declared Nicola. 'C'mon, let's go for a walk.'

Eve said 'okay' and Nicola went to get her jacket.

Where the fuck is it?' she called from the hall way. 'It was on the banister.'

'It's here,' called Mary.

Nicola returned to the kitchen. Mary was holding out her jacket. Smiling like a Cheshire cat.

'C'mon,' she nodded to Eve, taking the jacket, 'let's get out of this mad'ouse.'

Mary watched them walk off from the kitchen window, then went into the church to pray.

'Evey?'

She wasn't at home.

'That's odd,' thought the off-duty Inspector.

He was standing in the living room, gazing at the blank space on the living room wall.

'Eve . . . ' He called up the stairs. Perhaps she was playing a record.

The old copper went up with a vague feeling of unease.

He pushed open her bedroom door. 'Eve?' he said, gently.

Empty.

He surveyed the scene.

There was nothing unusual. Not at first glance, anyhow.

He decided to investigate, further.

The bed was rumpled slightly. She'd been sitting on it. Then he saw a note on the floor by the bed and pounced on it.

'Dear Eve,

I like you a lot but I don't want to get involved in a relationship. Sorry and all that. I won't forget you.

Luv Tony.'

Inspector Swann looked up and his brow twitched. Tony?

He folded up the note and put in in his pocket.

He could see he was going to have to have words with someone.

His curiosity was aroused now. And without hesitation he began to search her room. Poking round in her drawers and opening her cupboards. Leaving no stone unturned.

His first shock came when he found *The Joy of*

Sex, buried in her underwear drawer. And then he took a closer look at the garments themselves and received another jolt. There was some very adult lingerie indeed.

And then . . . no. It was impossible.

In her wardrobe he found a packet of condoms.

What was going on?

Tony? The name rang a bell.

He began palpitating. The search became somewhat frantic. He practically ransacked the room.

Then, under her bed he found a small box.

He opened it up and froze at the sight.

Holding it up between his forefinger and thumb, he pulled out a bright red spotted headscarf. Exactly like the bitch's. He stared at it and his blood turned to ice. Then he tore into the box almost retching with horror at his next discovery.

Hosts. Several of them.

And a strip of photographs from a photo-booth. Eve, Nicola and Tony. Their comically contorted faces mocking him.

In the next second and a half a thousand possibilities ran through his mind.

And then he arrived at the most terrible one.

Moments later he was screaming instructions down the phone to an astonished Mrs Plunkett.

Then he was in his car racing against time.

On the way to the station he cut through Sunnymeadow, squealing down the tiny little roads in a desperate rush.

As he turned into a street near the church, he saw his way was blocked by masked youths who were standing in the road, waving at him.

He gnashed his teeth, put his foot down and narrowly avoided killing two of them as he tore past.

The youths dived clear.

And with a screech of tyres the car was gone.

'Fuck was that?' spat one of the astounded youths.

'Dangerous twat!' replied the other.

''E's gunna kill someone.'

The other lad stood with his hands on his hips. 'What y'need's a fucking big machine gun to stop bastards like that.'

They laughed.

I Spy.

While Inspector Swann flew across the Estate, Betty gave Lisa her tea and cleared up the kitchen.

The little mite was in her high chair waving her arms and smearing food all over her head, when Theresa rushed into the kitchen, came up behind Betty and took her hand.

Betty looked at her friend's face. 'What's up?' she asked.

'They're coming for us.'

Betty stopped what she was doing and went over to her child.

Theresa continued. 'Something bad's gunna happen.'

''Ow can you tell?'

'I've got special powers.'

Betty frowned. 'I thought you said ...'

'Look,' said Theresa pointing at some goose bumps on her arm.

Betty grinned but took her seriously. She could see her friend was scared.

Little Lisa allowed herself to be picked up and chose a very serious expression.

'Better clean you up,' said her mother.

The little girl seemed to nod.

Theresa sat at the kitchen table. Her head in her hands.

'Bollocks to 'em,' said Betty, perhaps unwisely. 'Who gives a shit.'

Then there was a knock on the door.

They answered it together.

'It's your friendly community policeman,' saluted the fat Sergeant who had been sat outside in his car for days. 'Jones is the name ...'

'And spying's the game,' injected Betty, who was always quick off the mark when it came to the police.

'The same ... ' grinned the Sergeant who was in fine fettle. He tipped his hat and said 'Mind if I come in?'

Sitting outside the Presbytery, oblivious to his superior officer's race against time, with one eye on promotion, Sergeant Jones had decided to attempt some eleventh hour diplomacy.

He was shown into the front room and found himself checking for stolen property.

'Well, it's nice and cosy in here,' he said trying not to sound like he was nudging someone.

They ignored his observation.

'Quite a lot of you living here, really, aren't there?' It was no good. He really couldn't chat without sounding like he was making allegations.

'You tell us,' replied Betty.

'Well, there are five we know about. Youths, that is – oh ... ' he looked at little Lisa, 'five-and-a-half ...'

The tiny tot growled most offensively at the policeman.

'Takes after her mother, I see.'

Despite herself, Betty grinned.

'Let me see,' the fat man went on. 'Five we know

about, one we don't ... very mysterious that one, probably some kind of ring-leader. One housekeeper – very drunk. And one cleric – very peculiar.'

'Is that how you got so fat, sitting round all day watching people?' asked Betty when he was done.

'No, that's the cream cakes and beer,' sneered the Sergeant. 'I can afford a lot of both.'

Betty was summoning a further retort when Theresa interjected.

'What do you want?'

The Sergeant sighed. 'I was just getting warmed up there.'

'You look a bit sweaty,' said Betty.

'Touché! ... ' mugged the Sergeant, clearly enjoying himself.

After a moment or two the officer adjusted his trousers and sat back luxuriously displaying his vast crotch. 'You do know you're about to be swatted like flies?'

No visible response.

'Crushed like beetles.'

Theresa looked at Betty.

'It was my job to check the serial numbers on that stolen equipment.' He breathed sharply through his nose.'Quite a little haul you've got there.'

They remained unmoved.

'But you know, at the last minute I'm going to offer you a way out. Nothing's guaranteed, of course. but I can make certain recommendations.'

Six eyes watched him. And two hearts beat out of time.

He continued with an expansive gesture. 'We don't mind the business. Illegal though it may be. We don't even mind the congested motorways, or the illegal assemblies, so long as you keep it religious or commercial. And what's a bit of stolen merchandise among friends, eh? We'll even turn a blind eye to drugs.'

He paused for dramatic effect. 'But what we can't stand. What we cannot allow in any way, shape or form. What is absolutely forbidden is: we won't have you running the estate. Policing the streets. Interfering in local affairs. Sticking your oar in. ' He smiled, sternly. And left it at that. 'That's all. Quite simple really. Not at all difficult to understand.'

They all fell silent.

Then little Lisa broke free of her mother's grip and ran over to the policeman, slapping his knee repeatedly.

The two teenagers exchanged a glance.

Theresa heaved a sigh. 'Show him out Betty.'

Betty smiled. 'My pleasure.'

Sergeant Jones said, 'No, the pleasure will be mine.'

When he was gone Betty came back into the living room and she and Theresa fell into one another's arms.

Little Lisa let them get on with it for a moment and then cheekily broke them up.

There was another knock on the door.

This time they looked out of the window.

There was a large van outside with Granada Television painted on the side.

Sergeant Jones watched the press gathering with relish before returning to his vehicle for some light refreshment. Whereupon he received an urgent message to return to the station.

To the Top.

Eve and Nicola were sprawled on the side of a hill overlooking Sunnymeadow. Dark clouds were gathering but the two girls were oblivious.

'What does he mean, "don't want to get involved in a relationship"?' asked poor, suffering Eve.

'It means he just wants a shag,' explained Nicola.

Eve took this in. Nicola was the expert.

'Why won't he just shag me, then?'

'It doesn't work like that. People get keen. And they get annoyed when you don't phone. I always sack 'em first. Before it starts.'

It sounded like Nicola was sympathising with Tony.

'I never did any of that,' Eve protested.

Nicola just shrugged. 'Fuck knows.'

'I really liked him.'

'He was probably scared.'

'He said he really liked me.'

'He was definitely scared!'

It sounded to Eve like she couldn't win.

'They're all dick 'ead's,' pointed out Nicola.

Eve sighed miserably and they sat in silence for a while.

'The only guy I've ever met who's alright, is Father Vernon,' said Nicola.

'Yeah,' agreed Eve, 'he's lovely. But you wouldn't . . . ' she wrinkled her nose.

Nicola hesitated, then confessed. 'I slept with him the other night.'

'You didn't!'

'We never done anything.' She stared straight ahead. 'He wouldn't.'

Eve looked at her friend through wide eyes.

Nicola grinned. 'I would've if he'd wanted to.'

Eve was shocked. 'With Father Vernon?'

'I want him to love me. I don't care.'

'He does love you. You can tell.'

Nicola was proud. 'I know 'e does.'

They sat in silence for a few minutes, lost in the view. Eve took in these latest insights into human nature.

Then Nicola said, 'Eve? Has your dad mentioned anything about us, lately?'

'Like what?'

'I dunno. Slimy Bastard reckons they're gunna arrest us all. He came round this afternoon to warn me. I ain't bothered or anything ...'

Eve shrugged. 'No, nothing.'

They fell silent again.

Then, Eve shuffled uncomfortably and said, 'I feel a bit ... sorry for him, you know.'

'Who?'

She was embarrassed. 'My dad.'

'After what he did to Tony?'

Eve pulled a face. 'He was a bit cheeky.'

'Who, your dad?'

'No, Tony ...'

Nicola grinned, nervously. 'You've changed your tune!'

'I do. I feel sorry for him. He has a hard time. I've been horrible to him lately.'

Nicola felt betrayed. Eve was her first proper girl-friend for years and father-hatred was the main thing they shared in common. 'What would he say if he found out?' she asked.

'About me and Tony?'

'About you and us.'

Eve shrugged. 'He'd be shocked. But I'm sure he'd understand. He's very sensitive, underneath.'

Nicola wanted to say "bollocks", but she was afraid of damaging their friendship. So for once she held her wicked tongue. 'It's nice up here,' she said. 'I like it.'

'You know he cried when I broke his mum's mirror?'

'C'mon,' said Nicola who'd heard enough. 'Let's go.'

The two girls stood up and Eve, sensing her remarks had hurt Nicola in some way, linked arms to demonstrate her continued desire for friendship.

Nicola put her hand in her jacket pocket to make a secure loop for Eve to hang onto. Whereupon she found a couple of hosts she must have forgotten about.

'Look what I've found,' she said, stopping and holding them out with a grin. 'Fancy one?'

Eve shrugged. 'Why not.'

'One each?'

'Yeah.'

'Let's climb to the top,' laughed Nicola. 'Get the full effect.'

Had it Coming.

When Father Vernon arrived at the Presbytery he was dismayed to see that the place was besieged by journalists and was struck by the peculiar feeling that something dreadful was about to happen. Something final. He had a familiar pit in his stomach.

By the time he got to the front door he was sure of it.

And, as he ran the gauntlet of reporters, he realised that it had not been unexpected. He almost recognised the situation. As if he had seen it coming. The feeling too, was familiar, like it had been there all along. From the moment . . . from which moment? When had this feeling begun?

'Are you the parish priest? . . .'

'Father Vernon? . . .'

'Excuse me sir, are you involved in . . . ?'

'Miracle girls . . .'

'Your church ...'

He struggled with his key in the lock, blocking out the bombardment. He had to shut the door with his shoulder to prevent an invasion.

When he turned around, his back to the door, Betty, Theresa and little Lisa appeared, wide-eyed. The little girl in her mother's arms.

The priest stood for a moment, looking at each of them in turn. They all knew there was little or nothing they could do. The game was up. Father Vernon smiled gently at them to let them know he still loved them, as he always had.

Unconditionally.

They smiled back at him and he went upstairs without a word, sat down at his old bureau and lifted up his heart.

What was this feeling? Was it a sense of doom? Of abandonment? He felt an overwhelming sadness. He was going to be alone again. It had all come to an end.

That was the feeling. The familiar feeling that he had identified as if for the first time. The one that had always been there. Yes. And that was when it had started. When he started. This feeling was him. He was this loneliness. This overwhelming sadness.

The latest happiness had been to remind him of the sadness that was always present in him. He breathed a long sigh. The Lord giveth and the Lord taketh away.

He heard a siren. In the distance.

Then he suffered a fresh revelation. Something else he had known all along in his heart, but now realised in fact: that he was to be parted from more than just his bizarre family. He would be parted from his flock. And his home. And his church. And, it was just possible, his religion, too.

He was going to be thrown out.

Publicly reviled.

Humiliated.

Left to his own devices.

Out there. On his own. Without his collar. And his responsibilities.

He bit his lip and sat staring at this little, unavoidable grain of truth.

They would throw the book at him and he would be forced to resign. Be alone. Without the church to house him.

He would face the Bishop. He would confess everything. Bare his soul. Rid himself of secrecy. Come clean. Hold up his hands. Be done with it. Hand in his notice. Be himself. Alone.

The sirens had grown louder and had obviously stopped outside the church. 'Have I really done anything illegal?' he wondered suddenly. Prison wasn't something he had anticipated.

'It doesn't matter,' he thought. 'Whatever happens, I will still be myself. I'll survive it.'

At that moment there was a gentle tap on the open door of his study. Betty was standing there, looking shy.

'What is it, Betty?'

'Father . . . ' She flushed slightly. 'I want to know . . . '

As she struggled with her words, Father Vernon was touched by how young and vulnerable she could appear sometimes, even though she was a care-laden mother and the oldest of all his troublesome daughters.

'Well, it's just that if . . . something happens . . . if you can't stay here any more . . . '

The young priest smiled at her.

She smiled back. 'You could stay at my flat till you get sorted. If you need to.'

Father Vernon was touched. And he was about to

266

say something like 'That's very nice of you but it really won't be necessary', when there was a violent knocking on the front door.

Reasonable Suspicion.

'Where is she?'

Inspector Swann had to stop himself yelling, so as not to arouse suspicion. It was a tremendous effort of will.

Father Vernon, Theresa, Betty and little Lisa looked blank. Over the policeman's shoulder they could see cameras filming and taking photographs. Police were holding back the gathering crowd which now included several people in wheelchairs and some on crutches.

'Erm ... who are you looking for?' asked Father Vernon.

'My d ... A girl named Eve Swann.'

The old copper saw Betty and Theresa exchange a glance.

'Right, in you go, lads,' he ordered and several policemen entered, pushed past the small assembly and began poking around the Presbytery in all directions.

'Eve Swann,' repeated Father Vernon. He turned to Betty and Theresa. 'Is that .. ?'

The two girls nodded. And so did Lisa.

Father Vernon turned back to the Inspector. 'She's not here I'm afraid.'

The copper took this in, cautiously and seemed to calm down slightly.

Father Vernon vaguely indicated the intruding officers. 'Are you ... looking for her?'

'We're searching the premises,' snapped the policeman. 'Is there a housekeeper in residence?'

Again he caught an exchange of glances between the two girls.

'There's no one in except us,' reported Father Vernon. 'Is something . . . ? . . . Er . . . is this necessary?'

'We have reasonable suspicion that there are controlled drugs on the premises.'

Father Vernon looked at Betty and Theresa who shrugged.

'Well, if you . . . ' Father Vernon waved his hand helplessly. He had to admit it was a possibility. 'Carry on . . .'

'We intend to,' said Swann in a very unfriendly tone.

'Would you like a cup of tea while you're waiting?' asked Father Vernon.

Inspector Swann ignored the remark.

Forty minutes later, from the kitchen where he was sitting with his feelings, Father Vernon saw the fat Sergeant approach Inspector Swann in the hallway and mumble something to him.

He heard the copper say 'Are you sure?' and assumed the worst.

Swann came into the kitchen.

'Well.' He seemed angry. 'It seems we've made a mistake.'

Father Vernon quizzed him with his eyebrows.

'We didn't find anything.'

'That's good news, isn't it?' said the priest.

'Erm . . . yes, of course.'

'There are some young people staying here and I really didn't think . . . Well, they're very sound.'

The old copper grunted disconsolately.

'By the way, Inspector, I spoke to the . . . girls you met before and they tell me Eve . . . the girl you mentioned before . . .'

The policeman flinched rather than nodded.

'Apparently she was here. This evening. Earlier on.'

Swann's mouth moved, but no words came out for a moment. 'She . . . er this . . . ?'

'Eve . . .'

'Yes, yes. When? When was she here?'

'Oh, a couple of hours ago I think.'

The blood drained from the old copper's face. 'And the housekeeper? . . . Was she here, too?'

'Mary? Yes, I believe so.'

Father Vernon watched as the Inspector made several unnecessary movements, in several directions. He didn't seem to know which way to go.

'Is something the matter, Inspector?'

The man left the room without a word and stood in the hallway as if in a trance. When the phone rang a few moments later the poor man nearly jumped out of his skin.

Father Vernon answered and the Inspector listened. Apparently with baited breath.

'Nicola . . . Yes . . . You're where? . . . Sorry? . . . Calm down, I can't hear you . . . Eve collapsed! . . . Which hospital? . . . Bolton Royal Infirmary . . . Oh dear . . .'

At that moment there was a bang as the front door slammed shut.

Father Vernon finished and rang off.

He looked round for the Inspector, but he was gone.

Betty and Theresa were standing there.

Father Vernon was about to explain what had happened when he noticed something strange by the front door.

There was a pool of vomit on the floor.

They sat around the kitchen table for over a week.

Waiting.

Father Vernon was in and out, dividing his time between the kitchen and his upstairs study. But mostly his upstairs study.

Only Mary came and went freely from the Presbytery.

The poor woman had returned with a vengeance to her old demon, the drink. On top of her tranquillisers the brew was potent indeed and she became, by turns, a monstrous, raging animal – growling, incoherent, obscene – and a snivelling helpless child, pathetic and equally incomprehensible.

Occasionally she appeared in the kitchen doorway to berate the girls, her arms flailing, her face bloated, her eyes sunken. But no one could understand her and no one took any notice.

And when she was finished in the kitchen, she would take her gargantuan rage outside, to the press. But even the reporters, who had laid siege to the building since the story broke, avoided her.

Three times she had confessed her story to them. How she had been indecently assaulted; how the fiendish Catholic priest lured young girls to his bed; how he had a house full of them; how a strange man had given her poison which she had considered using on herself and then on the priest; how in the end she used it with murderous intent but poisoned the wrong girl; how she would burn in hell and suffer eternal damnation. It was a truly sensational story.

But nobody loves a drunk. Nobody believes them. And Mary was in such a state that no one would even go near her. So she slept and staggered around and drank and raged and everyone ignored her. As best they could.

For a couple of days Nicola tried to persuade her friends that Mary had poisoned Eve. She didn't want to explain the whole of her reasoning for the sake of Father Vernon's feelings, not to mention her own but the others just dismissed the idea. Mary was crazy. But she wasn't evil. And she certainly didn't have access to large quantities of LSD.

And then Nicola stopped believing it herself. Mary was such a helpless figure that even if she had poisoned Eve she was an unsuitable object for any serious loathing. Too pathetic a target for revenge. No, Nicola knew, on a gut level, that something more sinister was required for that.

Nicola, Betty, Theresa, Michelle, Jo and of course the little toddler kept as close as possible. Hardly venturing from the room. They sat in silence mostly. Each understanding the predicament and each of them powerless to change it. And so they stayed. As prisoners. Waiting. And in a curious way, they had never been closer.

They were in a state of shock.

Eve was in hospital and was going to stay there. Acute psychosis. Probable brain damage. They knew it wasn't an accident. The press had no idea about it. There was nothing they could do. They couldn't even visit her for fear of her father's wrath.

One evening as they sat, smoking endless cigarettes, Michelle said. 'They'll take us out, one by one.'

'Don't be fuckin' daft!' snapped Betty. 'We know who they're after.'

Theresa just sat there. She too had started smoking again.

Nicola said, 'My old man knows who did it. We should find out and get them first.'

Michelle was sarcasm personified, 'Yeah, maybe

we could start an army and blow the whole lot of 'em away!'

They relapsed into silence.

It was the best expression of the communal sentiment.

No one noticed it, but Jo didn't open her mouth once. She didn't utter a single word during the whole week and a half. She just sat there huddled up close to Michelle, who did everyone's moaning for them. And at night she held Michelle in her arms until, eventually, they passed out and slept in fits and starts.

Only Betty braved the storm and went out to buy the papers. So they could keep abreast of their own story.

Every morning she valiantly pushed Lisa to the shops in her little buggy. She was followed by hacks and onlookers, but Mrs Kershaw and other sympathetic elderly people came to their rescue, forming a cordon to escort them, indignantly pointing out the child to any jostlers.

None of them said a word to the press.

Indeed Mrs Kershaw and the others began a spontaneous programme of disinformation, contradicting all the rumours, patiently dissuading the coachloads of disabled who turned up hoping for a cure. All comers were told that there had been a mistake.

They said there was no one at the Presbytery who could perform miracles.

And it was true.

Father Vernon had expected a visit from the Bishop. Or a call. But there was a deafening silence from the diocese.

He lay awake at night, composing the story. He didn't want to lie to the Bishop. But it was difficult to know exactly what the real story was. Difficult to know how to put it accurately into words.

272

And then one night, exhausted by his meditations, he dropped off to sleep and suffered the last of his blasphemous dreams.

It was remarkably short and sharp.

Sunnymeadow was entirely gone. Only dust remained, over which Father Vernon found himself searching for Nicola.

And then, in the distance he espied God and the Archangel Gabriel. God was restored to his former glory and smiling serenely.

'Are you abandoning us?' asked Father Vernon.

'He's already done that, dear boy. Can't you tell?'

God held out a hand. Father Vernon shook it.

'Are you going back?'

'Far from it,' commented the Archangel. 'He's had a lucky break. Some talent scout spotted Him. He's going to work as a model. Travelling the world.' The old man raised his eyebrows. 'Bit of a coincidence, don't you think?'

God winked at Father Vernon.

'What about us?' he asked.

'You can look after yourselves,' boomed the great man. 'I'm having nothing to do with it.'

'He wants to make the most of His body, while He's got it,' explained the Archangel. 'Not to mention His considerable powers - which, I believe He intends to use for His personal advancement.' The old man shrugged his ancient shoulders. 'It's only natural, I suppose.'

'They don't seem to do you any good,' said the Lord of Creation, perhaps a little guiltily. 'So I'm leaving you to it.'

Father Vernon noticed the Archangel had tears in his eyes.

'Dear boy, I'm afraid we won't meet again.'

'What will you do?'

There was a deep, sad sigh. 'I'll just tag along for the ride. Like I always did.'

273

Father Vernon looked at his friend, and wanted to say something, but he was gone.

And so was the dream.

The story raged in the press for a week and the estate was thrown into chaos. Father Vernon had to fight his way to the church to say Mass, but the pews were devoid of true believers. Only cameras, tourists and anxious groups of hopeful disabled occupied the dreary aisles.

Mrs Kershaw and the others came to pray, of course, but their devout presence was lost amid the clamour and the lenses.

The miracle of the Mass was dead.

And then, after a little over a week, the story itself died and gradually the crowds dispersed. Only one or two people remained, watching the Presbytery from parked cars.

And then the phone rang and Father Vernon was summoned by the Bishop. He must have been waiting for the fuss to die down.

He wasn't the only one.

One morning, on returning from the shops, Betty came rushing into the kitchen where her friends were engulfed in a fog of cigarette smoke.

'Tony's been arrested!' she declared.

The Genuine Subversive Element.

Inspector Swann returned to work after only a week.

It all happened very quickly after that.

The heart-broken copper took the precaution of

asking Sergeant Jones to be with him at all times, to prevent him committing a murder.

They held Tony for two days, during which time he never even smelt a pizza. Let alone a solicitor. And the police learned something.

'Twenty five grand's worth of musical equipment ... you could get ten years for that, couldn't you Sergeant?' was all the Inspector needed to say.

Tony held up his hands and told them it belonged to Penny. Which was the truth after all. The poor lad thought he would be murdered in his cell after what had happened to Eve.

And he may well have worried.

Inspector Swann entertained vivid fantasies of slowly choking the life out of the lad. Of holding him under water and pulling him out, only to endlessly re-immerse him, until he coughed himself to death. Of throwing him on to a bed of embers and watching him squirm. Of crushing him like an insect. He wanted to hear the crunch. If only the lad were that damn grasshopper, he'd pluck his hind legs and let him bleed to death. Or squeeze him until his belly burst and leave him to rot.

But he had a job to do.

And discipline was required.

He was a professional after all.

So Tony was released and Penny was arrested.

And the police learned some more. Penny was most helpful.

'They're a spineless bunch of bastards,' Swann observed, after Penny blamed it all on Michelle. 'They won't even protect their own.'

'They're just kids,' replied the fat Sergeant.

'Get enough of them acting together and they're a danger to society,' growled Swann.

Sergeant Jones nodded. 'Like locusts,' he said.

The Inspector looked at him sharply. 'Yes. Yes, exactly.'

And so Penny was released and Michelle was arrested. At the Presbytery.

And the police learned the whole story.

Michelle even made a few things up to cover herself.

She must have been very scared because she even told them where she kept the money. Which she bitterly regretted later, as they would never have found it otherwise. But it's easy to say that now.

Sergeant Jones was impressed. 'Jesus. That's a lot of money!'

'I told you there was more to this than meets the eye,' purred Swann. 'Next we'd have had an armed siege on our hands. Like Waco!'

Sergeant Jones knew what the Inspector meant. 'What shall we do with her?'

'This one?' said Swann, casually. 'Let her go.'

The Sergeant looked surprised.

'We want the ring leader. The genuine subversive element.'

'Sounds like they were all involved, to me.'

The Inspector smiled, dimly. 'We'll make an example of her . . . that no one'll want to follow.'

Father Vernon saw the Bishop the day Michelle was released and Theresa was picked up.

The good priest decided against a full confession. He was going and that was that. The details of the whole affair would only cause unnecessary pain and damage the future work of the church in the area. He would simply resign from his position and leave it at that.

He expected to be admonished for bringing the faith into disrepute.

However the Bishop was nothing but concerned for the young priest. The old man knew the young priest's reputation among the young people of Sun-

276

nymeadow and was greatly saddened by his decision to leave the church.

'My son, you have done good work. Your style has been unconventional, controversial even. But your work has been valued by many of your brothers. Myself included.'

Father Vernon was taken aback and felt tears welling up.

'Are you sure, in your heart, that you're doing the right thing?'

The young man nodded. Suddenly his whole decision to leave the church was thrown into doubt. For a moment it felt reckless and hurried. Should he reconsider? The young priest thought of the lies, the fraud and the deceit of recent months.

'There are options open to you,' continued the Bishop. 'You could stay at a monastery for a time.'

'No, Father,' he managed, at last. 'My mind is made up. I cannot be true to God and remain in the church. My place is out in the world. Among the young. And the ordinary people.'

The Bishop nodded. 'The most Godly among us always leave,' he thought to himself. Father Vernon was a brave man. Foolish at times perhaps. But worldly. That was for sure. 'God bless you,' said the Bishop, smiling. 'And have a damn good life.'

Theresa was charged with the theft of twenty five thousand pounds worth of musical equipment from *Johnny Roadhouse* in Manchester and remanded in custody by Bolton magistrates.

She was taken to Risley women's prison and two days later she was found hung in her cell.

The suicide was was reported in the press.

It was only one of several suicides at the prison that year.

The morning after Theresa died, Bill Carson found a letter on his doormat.

He opened it to find a court summons. His heart stopped. And his first thought was: 'Jesus ... I could've opened that in front of my wife!'

His second thought was a feeling. Several feelings. Hatred. Shame. Fear.

'The bastard!' he thought. 'The double crossing ... bastard!'

He stood staring into the future for a moment then poked his head round the kitchen door and spoke to his wife. He had to get out and read the letter properly. 'I'm just off out. I'll be back later.'

His wife didn't look up from her breakfast. 'Yes, I'll have a lovely time today, thanks. I'm so glad you remembered about my day out with Pauline. I'll give her your regards, she always asks after you ...'

The front door slammed shut. Bill drove a little way down the road, stopped the car and opened his letter. It was what he had expected.

The worst.

He scanned the thing in panic. 'Summonsed to appear ... Manchester Magistrates Court ... Sexual Offences Act ... blah blah ... soliciting ... from vehicle reg no ... in such a way ... likely to cause a nuisance to the girl or passers by ... ' Oh my God.

Then he noticed the attached sheet. 'Postal plea form'. He read avidly. 'If you do not want to appear and wish to plead guilty by post ... ' his heart sang for a second. Maybe he could get away with it after all? If he didn't have to appear in person.

But then he realised that there was a thick rubber-stamp notice across the form: 'Not applicable.'

Fuck. He would have to appear in court.

He would be ruined.

'Maybe the press won't find out,' he hoped.

Mary was nowhere to be found.

Only Father Vernon noticed she'd disappeared. Only he cared.

He and Nicola were alone in the Presbytery now. Betty was back at her flat and Father Vernon had a few weeks to go before he had to vacate the premises.

Theresa's death was the final blow.

They all avoided one another.

Even Father Vernon and Nicola hadn't seen each other and they had hardly been out of the Presbytery.

The funeral was a dismal affair. A tragedy in itself.

Nobody came.

Only Nicola, Betty and Lisa, Theresa's mother, who was drunk and Father Vernon, who said the Mass, turned up. Jo and Michelle had returned to their respective burrows and were too scared or callous to show their faces.

And only Father Vernon and little Lisa cried.

Betty was still too shocked and Nicola too proud.

Afterwards Betty went straight home and stayed indoors for three whole days, refusing to see anyone.

Within no time at all on Sunnymeadow, policing returned to normal.

There was an almost reassuring crime wave and the number of burglaries rose to its former level. Petty criminals on the estate went back to their usual occupation of delinquency, keeping police busy answering calls from distressed people. And filling in reports of unsolved crimes.

But at least young people weren't standing round on street corners flagging down cars and interfering in the due process of the law.

For the space of a couple of months there was a disturbing increase in reported incidences of stone throwing at police vehicles.

Indeed for a while it became something of a sport.

But then, this too passed away without trace. Well, almost without trace. The Council did build two New blocks of flats in the area but denied any connection between their decision and the disturbances.

Even the religious revival slowed down.

There were no more angels sighted. No more ascensions into heaven. No more miracles of any kind. Except Bolton Wanderers won the F.A. Cup.

A little man on Sunnymeadow did try and persuade a gathering of elderly people at the local shops that a divine airship had landed in his garden on three consecutive nights.

And even though he showed them the holes in his lawn where the giant feet had settled, they all scoffed at him and had a jolly good laugh at his expense.

'I tell you no word of a lie . . . and this is the God's honest truth . . .'

Back to earth with a bump.

The End.

On the forth morning after Theresa's funeral there came a loud knocking on the Presbytery door.

Both Nicola and Father Vernon felt their hearts contract. They had both come to dislike the sound of callers at the door.

Father Vernon answered and Nicola hovered on the stairs.

'Father Vernon, look ... ' It was Betty and Lisa and ...

Father Vernon gazed in wonder. And blinked to make sure.

'Theresa! ...'

There was a scream of joy from the stairs and Nicola dived on her.

Sure enough. It was Theresa. Standing there in the flesh.

When she'd spun Theresa round a couple of times and got her breath back Nicola said: 'What the fuck have you done to your hair!' generously ruffling it with her her palm.

'Got it permed,' said Theresa.

'Suits you,' laughed Nicola.

And it did. Corkscrew perm.

'And new jeans! And ... new everything!'

She was a sight for sore eyes. Not only was she alive, but she was as vivid as she ever was. Eye liner, lip gloss. The works.

'Don't she look good!' said Betty.

'Top,' agreed Nicola.

'Eeeh!' shouted Lisa and everyone made a fuss of the little mite.

'And you look beautiful too, Tiny! ...'

'Ain't she cute ...'

The little child bounced in her mother's arms and Betty flushed with joy.

'You comin' out tonight?' inquired Theresa.

Nicola said 'you bet,' by puffing her cheeks and raising her eyebrows.

'Have you been to see your mother?' asked the ever-sensitive (ex-)priest of Theresa.

Betty pulled a face. 'Course she bloody has!''

'I'm not sure she even missed me!' laughed Theresa.

She looked at Father Vernon and gave him a warm smile, causing him to blush. Then she hopped forward and threw her arms round his neck, swinging him round happily.

The poor man could hardly splutter, 'It's really good to see you.' He thought how lame it sounded under the circumstances.

'Oi! That's my Dad!' said Nicola.

'What about Michelle and Jo?' asked Betty. 'They'll come out tonight, won't they?'

'I'll phone Michelle now,' said Nicola and darted indoors.

Father Vernon was just thinking that he hadn't even invited the new arrivals in, when he espied something across the road that made him gasp out loud.

Betty and Theresa turned round to see.

There was an old man standing over the road in a track suit.

'Looks like one of your shell-suits,' teased Theresa nudging Betty.

Betty ignored her. 'Who is it?' she asked.

Father Vernon stared at the old man who waved a friendly wave and then made off down the road. His own hand sort of fluttered a hesitant wave and he half smiled. But the old man was walking away.

'Who is it?' Betty persisted.

'Oh ... An old friend of mine,' replied Father Vernon. 'I think.'

'Michelle?'

'Yeah? Who is it?'

'It's Nicola.'

'Oh.'

'Theresa's back.'

'What?'

'Theresa's back. She's here now.'

Silence.

'She wants to know if you want to come out and celebrate tonight?'

282

'I ain't 'avin' nothin' to do with it anymore! What the fuck's going on?'

'We're going out for a drink.'

Silence.

'Will you see Jo?'

'She's 'ere now.'

'Tell 'er. See if she wants to go out tonight?'

Silence. Muffled conversation at Michelle's end.

'She says "no".'

'Alright.'

Silence.

Michelle's tone softened slightly. 'Tell Theresa I said Hiya.'

'Alright.'

'Tra.'

'Tra.'

Jo said: 'How the fuck d'she ...?'

Michelle shrugged.

They sat in silence for a few minutes. They were watching the television in Michelle's old bedroom.

Jo suddenly perked up. 'I forgot to tell you!'

'Wha'?'

'I saw Mary today.'

Michelle wasn't interested.

'No ... in town. She was with all these tramps.'

Michelle was a bit more interested.

'And guess what?'

Michelle tutted. She hated 'guess what's. 'What?'

Jo wrinkled up her nose in disgust. 'She was snoggin' one of 'em!'

Michelle opened her mouth, and pointed to the back of her throat with two fingers and carried on looking at the television. After a while she tutted and spoke without taking her eyes off the screen. 'I wish I 'adn't told them about all that fuckin' money!'

Jo looked serious. 'How much was it?'

'Fuckin' loads.'

Jo nodded gravely. 'What would you 'ave done with it?'

Michelle shrugged again.

'Would you have got a flat with Penny?'

'Would I 'eck!' It was Michelle's nose that wrinkled now. 'Dick 'ead.'

'Reckon it was 'im dropped you in it?'

'Course it fuckin' was!' Michelle was angry. Jo watched her simmer for a while. Then she pursed her lips. 'Would you get a flat with me?'

''Ow could I!' snapped Michelle. She thought Jo was rubbing her nose in it.

Jo stood up and went over to her wardrobe. 'Guess what?'

'Fuckin' 'ell . . . What!'

Jo took a small book from the inside pocket of her jacket and threw it into Michelle's lap.

'What's that?'

'I opened a building society account.'

'When?' Michelle asked.

'A while ago.' Jo nodded at the book. 'Open it.'

Michelle did as she was told and got the shock of her life. 'What? . . . Where the fuck d'you get all that? . . . ' she stopped short and grinned at her friend. 'You crafty bitch!'

Jo's ears were burning red. With pleasure.

Nicola was getting ready to go out.

Before she was fully dressed, she hopped into Father Vernon's study and plonked herself in his lap. 'Will you marry me now you're free, dad?' she asked with a wicked grin.

The ex-parish priest looked at her and she had no idea of the depth of his sigh. 'If God had intended it, Nicola, believe me, I would.'

'How d'you know he didn't?' She sounded indignant.

Father Vernon smiled. 'If He had intended it, He would have made you older. Or, preferably, me younger.'

She looked into his eyes, kissed his cheek and went back to her ablutions.

Epilogue.

The press did turn up to court.

Someone must have tipped them off.

And Bill Carson's career was ruined.

He lost his job, his friends (such as they were), his wife and his house.

He'd already lost his daughter.

But, somehow, he managed to keep hold of his Rover 216/SLi, which was a shame really because, some months later, while he was driving home from a country pub, accompanied by a young woman, the brakes mysteriously failed. The car span off the road and burst into flames.

He was identified by his dental plates and no one attended the funeral.

Later the police said that they thought someone may have tampered with the brake cables, but nothing was ever proved.

Eve was let out of hospital, eventually.

But her condition remained the same.

Hopeless.

Inspector Swann looked after her as best he could for a few years and then began to neglect her. She was no longer the apple of his eye and perhaps some deep feeling of guilt caused him to turn against her. Maybe she knew the truth and found some secret way to torment him.

Later he broke his hip falling from a roof whilst pursuing villains and was forced to retire early. He was awarded a gold watch and granted a measly inflation-proof pension.

And Sergeant Jones was promoted in his place

Swann grew old and bitter in the company of a vegetable that was his daughter.

Mary cleaned up her act and won back her post as housekeeper at the Presbytery.

The new parish priest, Father Adrian, was old and crotchety so Mary's sensitive heart was safe. Unfortunately the newcomer was a heavy drinker and within days Mary was back to her old ways.

Only this time it was worse.

Her binges were longer and the quantities consumed greater. And when the drink ran out she melted down boot polish, to extract the solvents. Until one day, after a bender that lasted months, her oesophagus burst and she died of internal bleeding on the Presbytery floor.

Mrs Kershaw said that God had a special place for Mary in heaven.

Nicola moved to a dingy flat in Manchester and got in with a bad crowd.

She kept up contact with Father Vernon for a while, but not for long. She was too caught up in her new life for that and felt ashamed of some of the things she was doing.

He suspected she was using drugs.

A couple of years later, he bumped into her in Manchester city centre and she completely ignored him. The saddened man was just walking away, reflecting on how quickly young people change, when he felt an arm tug at his from behind.

Nicola was standing there. Her hair was matted and her skin was a greyish colour. They both smiled awkwardly and Father Vernon asked what she was doing with herself. She muttered a few things and gave the impression she wasn't doing very much at all.

Then she said: 'There's something I wanted to confess . . . ' but obviously couldn't bring herself to do so. 'I'm a bit late. She just mumbled something and then said: Got to dash. Good to see you anyway, Dad.'

As she ran off they were both struck by how foolish their old term of endearment sounded, now.

They never saw each other again.

Michelle and Jo got a flat together.

But it didn't last long. And they soon spent their money.

Then Jo got bored with Bolton but Michelle didn't fancy moving away.

In the end Michelle got engaged and Jo found a good job in Manchester. Jo commuted for a while but eventually made the move. And in the end she went to London.

They still write to each other fairly regularly and Jo comes to stay sometimes. Michelle's husband gets jealous, but they don't let that interfere. Michelle's planning a trip to London soon, but it is difficult.

Jo feels a bit sorry for her now she's tied down with the children.

Tony joined a Manchester band that got to number four in the charts but proved to be a one hit wonder and then disappeared without trace.

Penny lives on Sunnymeadow and had two children

with a nice girl. He still plays in a band, but they're totally disorganised.

They do expect to make it soon, though. There's some talk of a record deal.

Betty and Tereasa stayed together.

Despite the talk.

And they bought up little Lisa between them as *single sex parents*.

Lisa's at school now and learning to read. And at the last count she had fifteen boyfriends. 'I did have sixteen, but one of them doesn't love me anymore,' she explained to Michelle one day, when they saw her at the shops.

Tereasa got a job in the town hall and ended up a NALGO shop steward. Betty does part time cleaning work, but she kept up her soup round at the parish church and Father Adrian helps out when he can.

And now Mrs Kershaw can't get about as much, Betty goes and sits with her three afternoons a week.

Father Vernon applied for Bill Carson's job and got it.

Bolton's second radio evangelist.

Although he did make changes. The phone-in time was cut right down and guests of all kinds were invited to chat about their lives and anything that interested them specially.

A surprising number of visiting celebrities wanted to appear and used the programme to promote themselves as caring human beings. There was also a popular slot that the ex-priest handed over to young people, so they could make their own programmes and express their views on contemporary issues.

During the day the ex-priest became involved in various youth projects and with the help of Tereasa, who obtained support form the council, he started a youth theatre group on Sunnymeadow itself.

All in all he kept himself busy.

The strange thing was though, despite his freedom and his good looks, he never took a lover.

But he did have his dreams.

And on some nights he would go to bed early, to be on his own with a good book and a Horlicks.